The Edge of Forever

Jeff S. Chimenti

authorHOUSE®

AuthorHouse™
1663 Liberty Drive, Suite 200
Bloomington, IN 47403
www.authorhouse.com
Phone: 1-800-839-8640

First published by AuthorHouse   4/6/2009

ISBN: 978-1-4389-5657-2 (sc)
ISBN: 978-1-4389-5658-9 (hc)

Printed in the United States of America
Bloomington, Indiana

This book is printed on acid-free paper.

To my youngest son, Mark,
who shares the vision with me
and is my constant companion
in the creative realm

Preface

From the time that we're young, we hear about theories that become accepted as doctrine in our lives. We see these theories illustrated in picture books and later in textbooks. The reality is that many of these theories are nothing more than an educated guess—an attempt to explain what we do not completely understand because we have not and cannot experience these things first hand.

The human mind has a strong need to understand as many aspects of life as possible. We are innately inquisitive, but because of our curiosity and strong need to understand the world around us, we also tend to accept theory as fact in a rather naïve manner. There is no better illustration of this than dinosaur extinction theory. Although there has been a longstanding debate among scientists, the general public has accepted the doctrine that a six- or seven-mile wide asteroid resulted in this extinction.

The story in this book may come as quite a shock to those who have accepted the asteroid theory as fact, because it presents a very different scenario that is in many ways much scarier than an asteroid. Most of us are unaware of the unbelievably powerful forces beneath our feet—forces that may not have our best interests in mind, but we continue to live in ignorant bliss because our experience has taught us that we are relatively safe.

Unfortunately, the human experience involves such a tiny blip of geological time that our "experience" is nothing more than an illusion of safety. The dinosaurs faced this realization sixty-five million years ago, and if the human race survives long enough, we will eventually realize that our time has come, as well.

Some of us still look to the sky in fear of giant rocks destroying our civilization, but maybe we should be looking at the Earth that we stand on instead, and maybe we should realize that there are things brewing that make huge asteroids seem benign by comparison. Maybe there are things that mankind was not meant to survive.

Contents

Acknowledgments

I would like to thank my three sons, Michael, Stephen, and Mark, for inspiring the creation of a story that revolves around three remarkable brothers and the courage that each possesses. I love all of you deeply, and I look forward to seeing what you will become as you advance into adulthood.

I would like to thank Chris for helping me raise our challenging, but amazing sons. She has a great heart and has passed this on to our boys. I'd also like to thank her for advising me to involve a dog in my story. I named it after a horse she rode on our first trip to Paradise Ranch in Wyoming.

I would like to thank Tommy G. Warren for his friendship, tremendous insight, and gentle guidance with my story. In many ways, it was Tommy's encouragement that led to the publication of this book by giving me confidence to believe in my work.

I would like to thank Susan Giffin for her excellent editing and literary gift that has enabled me to produce an even better novel.

Author's Notes

First and foremost, the following story is about people, not about an event or a catastrophe. I chose to involve my characters in a catastrophic situation, because when people are confronted with adversity, their true character frequently shines through the brightest; we get a closer look at the soul of men—some are good, some are not.

The disaster in this book is truly a worst case scenario, and although most of the science involved is factual or at least based on theory that evolved from scientific evidence, I will admit that it may be far-fetched, or maybe not.

At the end of December 2008, the Yellowstone Volcano Observatory announced that they had recorded a "notable swarm of earthquakes beneath Yellowstone Lake." The geologists noted that this earthquake sequence was the most intense in this area for some time and that they could not identify any causative factor without further analysis.

Certainly there are quite a number of tremors that occur in Yellowstone National Park each year (about 1,000 to 2,000), but the end of 2008 was remarkable, because 400 tremors occurred in only *one week*. It is also a known fact that the Yellowstone Caldera, the enormous magma chamber that fuels all of the hydrothermal activity at the park, has been rising as much as three inches each year.

What does all of this mean? Maybe nothing, but we won't really know the answer to this question until the event is already upon us.

Part 1

The Impending Inferno

———◆———

When all was said and done, no one could have ever predicted how dramatically the world would change in the blink of an eye—how horrific and terrifying those days would become and how close to the edge the human species would be pushed. The death and destruction was incomprehensible. The loss of life was unsurpassed in all known human history. Most suffered enough anguish, fear, grief and trauma to last a lifetime—and that was all within the first few days.

The real horror would surface after a week had passed and, as terrifying as this was, there were worse things to come—much, much worse. But let's start from the beginning…

Chapter 1

Pain and Rumblings

Reno, Nevada: June 18, 12:15 p.m.

This was the first time that Michael Hanson had ventured out of his hometown of Sonoma, California in over a year. He had randomly decided to drive to Reno, Nevada, although he honestly hadn't made any plans to do anything there. Just leaving Sonoma was difficult enough for him to do.

Upon arriving at a convenience store at the outskirts of Reno, he stopped to get a Coke and obtain information about accommodations in the city. When he first stepped out of his car, he felt a brief, unsteady, unsettling sensation that was very subtle, but one that caused him to take a balancing step to his right side. He dismissed this as unimportant and headed to the front of the store.

A young woman kneeling down on the sidewalk instantly caught his attention because she appeared to be upset. He could see that she was retrieving items that had spilled out of her purse so he stopped to assist her.

"Excuse me, do you need any help?"

She kept her head down. "No, thank you. I just tripped and fell. I'll be okay."

He could see that a few of the items were scattered out of her immediate reach, so he bent over and picked them up. When he handed them to her, she looked up. He was startled to see that her eyes were extremely bloodshot as if she had been crying for hours. He could also see that she was beautiful, but she quickly looked away before he could get a better look at her face. She hurriedly stuffed the items into her purse.

"Thank you, but I can get the rest."

Michael sensed that she was embarrassed and wanted him to leave, so he didn't push the issue. He watched her pick up the remaining items for a few seconds and then turned to leave. As he was walking away, he couldn't resist the temptation to glance back at her. She was now standing up and when their eyes met he could feel something looming at the periphery of his consciousness—something mysterious and strange that he could not explain. Something somehow connected with the past, but also linked to the near and distant future. He shook off the sensation, turned around, and stepped inside the store.

Turner, Nevada: September 13, 6:22 p.m. (3 months later)

Purple-black ominous storm clouds pushed aside the golden hues of a Nevada sundown and quickly consumed the darkening sky. Michael pulled the restaurant door open against the strong wind and intense downpour and slipped inside the truck stop quaintly named Mama's Place. It was the first eatery or, for that matter, the first building that Michael had seen in over thirty miles, and he was famished. At this point, any greasy spoon would hit the spot for him.

The interior décor was a Fifties diner-style and, although it wasn't gourmet dining, the odors wafting out of the kitchen smelled delicious and home cooked. He quickly made his way to a corner booth, sat down, and started reading the menu. He heard the waitress approaching his booth but finished reading the entrees before he looked up.

When he did look up, he was startled at first. It was one of the saddest, loveliest faces that he could ever remember seeing. The face was familiar—hauntingly familiar—that he could not yet identify. The young woman was in her late twenties, with long brown hair, sensuous lips, and huge baby blue eyes. The expression on her face was a thin mask trying to hide something painful, albeit unsuccessfully.

He knew this type of pain all too well, because it had become his daily companion over the past two-and-a-half years. He had seen this same expression in the mirror almost daily until recently when he decided to pull himself back into the land of the living.

The waitress looked down at him and attempted to smile, but this made her look even more beaten down. Michael started to feel something stir inside of him; something deep, and dark, and painful, which he quickly pushed away before it affected him and brought back memories that he had shielded from his conscious mind for years.

There was an awkward silence as he stared at her. To break it, he cleared his throat and looked back down at the menu. "So, what do you recommend? Something sure smells good coming from that kitchen."

He looked up again and smiled at her, hoping to chase away a little of the pain on her face. She gave him a shy smile, not as sad as before.

"Most people really like the meatloaf and chicken fried steak. I'm weird; I've never tried either of them, so I can't tell you which I like best."

Her voice, although sad, also had a musical quality—soft and sweet like a cool summer breeze.

"I don't think that's weird, but I think I'd like to try the meatloaf. So how about the meatloaf and a vanilla shake?"

"Oh, the shakes are wonderful here," she said.

"So, you drink shakes. Maybe you're not that weird, after all."

She smiled again, and this pleased Michael because that was his objective. She jotted his order on a ticket and turned to take it to the kitchen. As she walked away, he watched her petite, lovely figure as it disappeared behind the swinging door. He muttered to himself under his breath, *get a grip on yourself, buddy—you're pathetic.*

He recognized that, in his horrible loneliness, his heart was seeking something that he had consciously denied himself since the death of his wife and daughter. *You don't need this in your life—not now—not ever. Put it out of your head right now,* he said to himself.

He had been fighting the battle against depression, guilt, and grief for several years, had been suicidal on multiple occasions, and had spent almost an entire year in such intense misery that he had been unable to function in society. With the help of his two brothers and their families, he had finally begun to pull himself out of that stinking, black cesspool of pain. Now, he was becoming more interested by the minute in this complete stranger, partly because of her beauty, but perhaps more because of a strong aura of pain he could sense around her.

He waited for approximately fifteen minutes for his food, and when she brought it to the table, although it looked delicious, he was more interested in her than his appetite and decided to see if he could strike up a conversation with her.

"Okay, so what's your name? You're not wearing a nametag."

"Cassie."

"Hi, Cassie, my name is Michael. You worked here very long?"

"About two years."

"Do you live around here? I haven't seen any signs for towns for twenty or thirty miles."

"There's a small town five miles off the Interstate called Turner. We have only 270 people."

"So, what do most of the people…"

He noticed tears forming in her eyes. She became aware that he was staring at her cheek where a tear was settling and abruptly turned away while he was in mid-sentence with another question. He shrugged his shoulders and decided to eat his meal before it grew cold.

For the next twenty minutes, he purposely avoided looking in her direction and concentrated on his meal, which as it turned out was quite excellent. She initially avoided looking in his direction, but then chose to go directly to his table and speak before he had a chance to say anything.

"I'm really sorry about that. I know it was rude to leave when you were still talking to me. I've just had a tough day. I'm usually not like this. You forgive me?"

She smiled genuinely this time, which made her face even more beautiful than before.

"No, I won't forgive you…"

She looked at him with a confused expression on her face.

"…unless you bring me some apple pie. Then I'll consider it."

His eyes met hers, and he felt as though he could lose himself within them. Something stirred inside of him again, and he felt the need to reach out and touch her face. He pulled himself away from her gaze, feeling foolish for having such a strong attraction to someone that he had just met.

In fact, after the death of his wife, he had promised himself that he would never again get close to another woman. The potential for loss was too great, and the hole that he was crawling out of was too deep to survive a second time. Yet somehow this beautiful, sad woman was casting a spell on him that he did not understand. And strangely enough, he was unable to completely resist its pull.

"I'll go get the pie—it's on me," she said as she turned away.

When she returned, she again blessed him with her smile, but said nothing. He wanted to talk to her some more but was at a loss for words, and so he just smiled back. After he finished eating, he left money for the dinner, pie, and a hundred-dollar bill for a tip.

Before she could return to the table, he walked to the door and slipped outside into the blustery, cold, wet evening. He hurried to his Pontiac sedan, buckled his seat belt, and stared into the restaurant. He caught a brief glimpse of her bewildered face as she stared at the tip and the message he had written on a napkin: "Hope your day gets better. I forgive you. Michael."

He sighed and turned the key in the ignition. He shook his head, sighed again, and slowly left the small parking lot heading east on the Interstate. The steady rain slapped against the windshield, and even with the wipers on, all he could see in the pitch black night were occasional bright streaks of lightning that briefly illuminated the desert landscape.

When he had gone maybe two miles, he noticed flashing emergency lights on the left shoulder. He slowed down and caught a glimpse of a stranded sedan with a woman sitting inside. He stopped his car, pulled alongside the sedan, and lowered his window to talk to her. She was shivering from exposure to the chilly night air.

He waved at her to get her attention. "You need any help?"

"Don't know what's wrong. Heard a screech and a rattle and then it just died. Engine was smoking for a few minutes, but that stopped. I can't turn it over now."

"I'm no mechanic, but I can drive you into town if you want."

She graciously accepted, and he opened the passenger door for her. When she was inside, she introduced herself. "My name is Mona— Mona Thomas. Thank you so much for stopping. I would have been there all night, freezing; so few people stop to help others anymore."

She was a plump, but attractive sixty-something woman who appeared to be the good-hearted, grandmother type with a gentle, relaxing manner about her and a smile that could warm your heart. He turned the heat up and asked for directions to the town and to her house. While they were driving into town, a curious thought popped into his head.

"Mona, do you know anything about Cassie, the waitress at Mama's Place? She seemed so sad when she waited on me this evening."

Mona looked at Michael, shook her head, and acted as though she were reluctant to say another word.

"Please tell me if you know something. I just sense that she's in a lot of pain, and I'd like to know why."

Mona took a deep breath and finally said, "That poor girl. She's the sweetest, most charming young woman I've ever met. She's very bright, you know. And I'm sure you noticed how pretty she is. How she ever ended up married to that son-of-a-bitch I'll never understand. He has most of the people in this town afraid of their own shadow."

She stopped and again seemed hesitant to say anything further. Michael encouraged her to go on. "Are you trying to tell me she's being abused?"

She frowned and took another deep breath. "I shouldn't be telling you this—I don't know you. I don't know why you're asking these questions."

Michael pulled over on the side of the road. He looked at her with a haunted expression on his face. "Mona, I lost the two people that I loved most in this world several years ago, so I know something about pain and loss. I can't really explain to you why I felt a connection with Cassie because I only talked to her for a few minutes, but I did. I know this sounds foolish, but I feel that maybe there's something I can do to help her."

"There's nothing anyone can do."

"I know that's probably true, but..."

"Okay, okay. I'll probably regret this." She sighed deeply and stared at the rain streaming down the windshield. "She was a vibrant young woman before he came into her life four years ago. I'm sure he was charming at first; he is very charismatic. I guess I do understand how a young woman would be drawn to him. But when he's been drinking, he becomes a violent animal. They say she miscarried two months ago because he came home in a drunken rage and brutally hit her in the stomach. He always makes sure when he beats her, it's in areas that won't show in public—her chest, abdomen, and back usually. Everyone hates him, but they're too scared to do anything about it."

"Why doesn't she just leave him?"

She looked back at him with a deeply troubled look on her face and said, "I think because she's a broken person. I know she's still grieving for that baby. When he took that away from her, she had nothing else to live for. It's the saddest thing I've ever seen."

"Why didn't she go to the police?"

"Because she can't; he is the police—our wonderful sheriff, Kyle McMurphy."

Michael dropped Mona off at her house, declined an invitation to go inside for some cookies, and immediately drove back to the restaurant. He sat in the parking lot wondering what in the hell he was going to do. *What a great plan*, he thought to himself. *You're going to confront*

a violent law enforcement officer concerning the physical abuse of his own wife. Boy, this one is guaranteed to be a barrel of fun!

Although he knew this might be one of the worst decisions in his life, he just couldn't convince himself to walk away. He did feel some connection with Cassie McMurphy. Yes, she was beautiful, but it was something more than that. Something at a deeper level that he couldn't grasp in his conscious mind. Something that involved his inner turmoil and anguish as much as hers; something he was presently unwilling to face but would eventually be forced to deal with.

While he was sitting there thinking about her, the strangest thing happened. He had an eerie sensation of movement and felt a chill slither up his spine. Then, suddenly, without any further warning, his parked car jumped several feet into the air and landed with a thud. There was no further movement. No shaking or jerking. No unsteadiness. Only silence and stillness. He noted that some of the other cars in the parking lot had also shifted and moved.

That must have been an earthquake tremor, he thought. But it seemed unlike any account of tremors that he had ever heard of. "What a weird night this was turning out to be," he said aloud. What he didn't realize was that this night would change his life forever. He also did not realize that he was experiencing some of the very first manifestations of an event that would change the course of human history.

Michael entered the restaurant and sat down in the same booth he previously occupied. Cassie instantly saw him and approached the booth with her right hand outstretched. "I'm so glad you returned. You accidentally left a hundred-dollar bill. Here it is." She laid it on the table.

"That wasn't an accident. It was a tip for you."

"But your dinner was only twelve dollars."

"Haven't you ever gotten a good tip before?"

"Nothing like this. Never."

"Well, that's a damn shame. Consider this a first."

"I really did feel bad about how rude I was."

"Why? You were obviously upset about something—there's nothing wrong with that. Besides, I was asking you a bunch of stupid questions just to get you to talk with me."

"Why did you want to talk with me?"

"Honestly, I'm not really sure. But I did like seeing you smile."

She smiled again and then started to blush. Her embarrassment caused her to quickly look away from Michael, and it was this simple reaction that allowed him to make the connection that he had missed earlier. This was the same woman that he had encountered in Reno, the same sad eyes, the same lovely face, the same reaction to embarrassment. And that was when he made another more bizarre connection—a connection between this woman, the peculiar unsteady sensation when he exited his car in Reno, her spilled purse, and the inexplicable tremor that occurred outside less than ten minutes ago. He didn't know why they were connected; he could just sense they were.

"Hey, can I ask you a weird question?"

Cassie looked at him warily. "I guess so."

"Do you remember a man who stopped to help you when you dropped your purse in Reno several months ago?"

Cassie's eyes widened as she made the connection. "Oh, my God, you're the nice man who stopped to help me."

"What a coincidence, huh? I just made the connection a minute ago. Hey, about five minutes ago did you feel some strange movement, almost like the ground just suddenly jumped?"

"That was the weirdest thing. Several people fell down, glasses shifted, and tables suddenly moved, but there was nothing else after that. Do you think it was an earthquake?"

"I really don't know," Michael replied. "It seemed kind of brief for an earthquake. Structurally, the building seems unaffected—no cracks in the plaster, no broken windows. It was almost as if the entire state of Nevada suddenly jumped two feet in the air. Look, I know you have other people to wait on. The reason I came back was to ask you if you knew of any places to stay in town. I'm too tired to drive any further and really need to hit the sack."

"There's a bed and breakfast in town run by a really nice lady named Mona Thomas." (Michael already knew this but needed an excuse to continue his conversation with Cassie.) "So, where are you heading?"

"I'm going to see my brother Stephen and his family in Colorado. After that, I'm going to visit my other brother in New York. This is a cross-country journey that's long overdue."

"I can draw you a map to Mona's house or if you wait twenty minutes, my shift is over and you can follow me to her house."

"I can wait if that's okay with you." He gave her his best smile, and she smiled back and nodded her head.

Turner, Nevada: September 13, 8:10 p.m.

Michael followed Cassie's small Ford sedan back into the sleepy little town. Downtown Turner consisted of one street with about fifteen different stores, including a locally owned grocery store named Bucky's and a community center with a courthouse and police headquarters. The streets were lined with sodium vapor street lamps that gave an eerie bluish hue to the dark, wet, dreary surroundings. There were no townsfolk to be seen at that hour, and most of the shops appeared closed for the night. Cassie seemed to be taking him the long way to Mona's house, and the thought occurred to him that she might be trying to avoid some confrontation, perhaps on her own street.

13

Michael was following Cassie cruising at thirty miles per hour, when he had the strange sensation that something was about to happen. He immediately gripped the steering wheel tightly to brace himself, and the next thing he realized was that he had hit his head on the ceiling, and that the car had jumped halfway into the next lane. He barely missed colliding with a street lamp and slammed on his brakes, sliding to a halt on the slick street.

Despite his initial shock and disorientation, he quickly realized that Cassie had not been so lucky and had careened off of the curb, causing her car to spin out of control and into the side of a parked car. He jumped out of his car, and ran to the driver side of the Ford, and frantically pulled on the handle, to no avail—the door was locked.

Cassie was leaning forward over the steering wheel, with her hands covering her face, sobbing. He knocked on the window, but she ignored him. After a few minutes, she unlocked the door, and slowly got out. She was no longer sobbing, but her eyes were bloodshot and tears continued to pour down her cheeks. He gently put his hand on the side of her head. "Are you alright?"

She nodded, but her crying did not cease.

He softly stroked her hair and said, "It's just a car. It can be fixed. I think it's going to need only body work."

She looked up at him, continued to cry, and said, "You don't understand."

"Then tell me, so I will understand."

She shook her head, wiped her tears, and sat back down in her car. "I'll be okay."

As he walked back to his car he thought, *what in the hell just happened—that's two strange "jumps" in the last thirty minutes.*

14

The Edge of Forever

When they arrived at Mona's house, Michael pulled into the drive and watched Cassie's battered car continue down the street. When she was almost out of sight, he pulled back out of the drive and followed her from a distance, staying far enough back so that she could not identify him. After following her for a few minutes, he finally arrived on a small cul-de-sac street and noted that she was pulling into the driveway of a one-story brick home at the end. That was when he noticed the large man standing at the front porch.

Shit! Michael exclaimed to himself, certain that the man would notice his car turning onto the street. He quickly turned off the lights and the ignition and watched from the shadows in his car.

The man approached Cassie's car, seemingly unaware that another car was further down the street. Michael could see the man walking around the front of her car obviously taking inventory of the damage. When she opened the car door, he came back around to the driver side and reached into the car with his huge hand and literally dragged her out, ripping the sleeve of her shirt in the process. Then Michael watched in horror as he threw her down onto the concrete drive and kicked her viciously in the back. The monster then grabbed her hand, yanked her to her feet, and pulled her inside the house, slamming the door shut.

Michael sat in stunned silence, at first not knowing what to do. Then, without a second thought, he jumped out his car and ran to the front door of the house. It was now locked, so he made his way quickly to the back door adjacent to the garage. His heart was racing at a dangerous pace as the adrenaline pulsed through his veins. He could sense that time was running out for Cassie, and although he knew he could be racing toward his own destruction, it was too late to turn back now.

Inside the house, Cassie was sobbing and pleading with Kyle to let her explain the damage to her car, but instead he looked at her with a vicious reptilian look in his eyes. "You're gonna pay for this one, bitch! How much did you earn tonight at that slop hole?"

As he spoke, spittle sprayed from the corners of his mouth and the smell of his sour breath and cheap whiskey filled the room. He pulled the purse out of her hands and dumped the contents onto the floor. He saw the hundred-dollar bill and quickly grabbed it.

"What is this?" he said, shaking the bill in her face. "You tellin' me that someone gave you this as a tip tonight? What did you do for it, you fuckin' bitch?"

"Please, Kyle, stop this," she begged.

"WHERE DID YOU GET THIS?" he screamed.

"A nice man at Mama's..."

"SHUT UP, YOU STUPID WHORE!"

With that, he grabbed her by the neck with his large hand, lifting her off of the ground and throwing her violently into the wall. Cassie lay crumpled on the floor as the beast approached her and lifted his leg to stomp her in the chest. But before he could bring his large boot down on top of her, Michael slammed into him from the side, and the two men went crashing into a coffee table. Glass shattered and wood splintered under their weight. Michael was 5 feet, 11 inches tall and a muscular 185 pounds, but he was dwarfed by Kyle's 6-foot-5 frame with huge, powerful shoulders and arms.

Michael rolled over and quickly scrambled to his feet. As the drunken hulk rose to his feet slowly, he shook glass out of his hair and stared at Michael with his dark, brooding, bloodshot eyes. Michael was kneeling beside Cassie, trying to encourage her to get up, and he said to Kyle, "This is over. Just let us leave."

Kyle snarled back at him, "You're right. It's over, because you're trespassing in my house. That makes you a dead man."

When Michael looked back over at Kyle, he could see the handgun that Kyle was pointing directly at him. Kyle calmly walked over to Michael and pressed the gun against his forehead. "Say goodbye to your boyfriend, bitch. I'm gonna splatter his brains all over you!"

Black Diamond Military Base, Nevada
September 13, 10:35 a.m.

The Land Rover approached the front gate of the facility. Spencer Montgomery was surprised to find that there was only one guard on duty. He had been briefed on the nature of the facility by General Frank Donner while en route and had expected to find a substantial military presence. Instead, the Rover stopped in front of a small guard outpost at the edge of a large expanse of flat Nevada desert, maybe 500 acres, surrounded by an eight-foot razor wire fence with large, reinforced metal support posts every twenty feet.

General Donner looked at Spencer and smiled when he recognized his bewilderment. Donner waved at the guard, who immediately opened the electronic gate, admitting the Land Rover into the facility. Donner turned to Spencer. "So, are you surprised by our level of security?"

"Well, to be honest, when you described the purpose of this facility, I expected to be greeted by an entire army battalion."

"I assure you that this is the most secure military installation in the country, and probably in the world."

"I guess I'll just have to reserve my opinion for later, when I've seen a little more of the base."

"Oh, I don't think you'll be disappointed." With that Donner chuckled and drove through the gate.

They traveled approximately half a mile until they came to several large boulders and rock outcroppings protruding from the desert floor.

"We need to get out of the car now," Donner said, as he motioned to Spencer.

The sun was bright with very little cloud cover, and a cool desert breeze washed sand and debris across the barren landscape. As far as Spencer could see, there were no buildings and certainly no military fortification. The land revealed very little vegetation, with only a few patches of scrub brush and an occasional cactus, mixed in with the sand and rock.

Donner walked up beside Spencer, tilted his head to the sky, and said, "Now all you have to do is to smile and say cheese."

They waited at that spot for several minutes, and then Donner said, "We should be able to get back into the car by now."

When they were again seated, they waited another five minutes in silence. Donner was content to let the suspense build, until finally Spencer could sense some movement, as if monstrous gears were grinding together in the sandy floor beneath them. While he stared out of the front windshield, he started noticing that a huge area of sand and a few massive boulders began moving away from them. Then, to his astonishment, a gigantic cleft in the ground began forming in front of the car.

When the cleft was almost a hundred feet across, the movement ceased, and Donner drove the Land Rover directly into the cleft and down a huge ramp that led into the underground facility.

"We use satellite imaging with detailed computer analysis of facial features for every person who attempts entry into the facility," Donner explained. "There is no possibility of fooling the computer—not even with extensive plastic surgery. The gate we are now entering is twenty-five feet thick and made of solid steel with a titanium covering, and this is just the first of seven gates leading to the core of the facility that is over a mile below the surface.

"When we enter the first chamber, do only what I instruct you to do, and keep in mind that there are ten anti-tank guns target-locked onto our vehicle at all times. We'll pass through another gate before we exit the Rover, and then will need to undergo extensive security checks (including fingerprint analysis, corneal scanning, and rapid DNA analysis) before passing to the next level. Security clearance alone will last about three hours, and we'll be down at the core in about four hours. Any questions?"

Spencer shook his head no, and they began their descent into the facility.

Black Diamond Military Base, Nevada
September 13, 2:52 p.m.

Spencer and Donner sat across from each other at the table in the conference room. The security procedures had been tedious, but Spencer now had a new appreciation for the U.S. military, and the exhaustive technology that they had used to protect this facility from intruders. Donner had explained that exiting the facility was even more tedious in order to prevent possible contamination of the outside world.

Six other men sat around the conference table—three in military uniforms and three in white lab coats. Finally, one of the men in a lab coat stood up and identified himself as Thomas Pierce, PhD, director of research for the Black Diamond facility. He was a tall man, with a bony, cadaver-like facial structure, jet black hair, wire-rimmed glasses, and piercing black eyes. He made a gesture in Spencer's direction, focused his steely eyes on him, and said, "Dr. Montgomery, exactly what do you understand about the nature of this research facility?"

Spencer shifted in his chair, stared back at the scientist, and cleared his throat. "I was briefed by General Donner. I understand that this facility is involved in research concerning mostly biological warfare. Apparently, there's some scary, advanced stuff here that has the Department of Defense very nervous. I understand that the facility is having certain structural problems, and that's why I've been called in to evaluate and make some recommendations. Sounds like a very straightforward situation to me."

"I'm not sure you completely understand the gravity of the situation that we're facing here. We have over 150 labs on the core level of the facility, each staffed by top scientists in the field. Our containment procedures are exhaustive, because we are housing and storing every known biological agent that exists and are constantly in the process of developing new ones."

"Wait a second," Spencer interrupted. "I know that there are labs that contain dangerous biological agents, but I thought that it was illegal to stockpile them."

Pierce shook his head and looked exasperated. "Dr. Montgomery, it's obvious to me that I need to give you some background on the history of this subject and this base. Biological warfare, in one form or another, has actually been around for centuries and has been used to inflict devastation on humanity throughout history. One example would be in the Middle Ages when bubonic plague victims were used in attacks flinging their corpses and feces over castle walls using catapults. In 1941, the United States, along with England and Canada, initiated the Biological Warfare Development Program in response to suspected development in Japan and Germany. Initially the center for research was located in Maryland and Utah, but it has now been transferred entirely to our facility since 1994 (as have all of the biological agents)."

Pierce cleared his throat and continued. "We do maintain "dummy" facilities in multiple other states. In 1972, over a hundred countries, including the U.S., signed the Biological and Toxic Weapons Convention, which banned—and I quote—'development, production and stockpiling of microbes or their toxic products except in amounts necessary for protective and peaceful research.' During the Cold War era, most of the research was performed by the U.S. and the Soviet Union. Although the Cold War is over, there will always be countries and terrorist groups developing biological weapons, and we must remain at the forefront of all research if we are to maintain any advantage over these groups. What we are involved in here is defensive research—and you must understand that this research is crucial. All of the people who work here have families, and we have no intention of ever using biological weapons under any circumstances."

Up to this point, Pierce had been stern and matter-of-fact in his presentation. Spencer could now detect a distinct change in his demeanor. He no longer fixed Spencer with his intense stare, shifted his feet, and lowered his head briefly.

When he looked up at Spencer again, his expression had changed to that of concern and weariness. "Because of our ongoing research, we now have a new generation of biological agents that have been created in our laboratories using genetic manipulation. By comparison, they make agents such as anthrax, plague, smallpox, cholera, and Ebola seem harmless. These are true doomsday organisms that have been created. Some kill rapidly, but the worst of these agents kill slowly but inevitably, so that dissemination is widespread. Even more disturbing are the agents that produce genetic alteration in the host that will then become the vector for further spread of the organism. Much of the host genetic alteration that we've witnessed in the labs is random and utterly unpredictable."

"So you're talking about mutagenic viruses?" Spencer asked.

"Not in the way that most scientists think of them. Mutagenic viruses cause alterations in individual cells, causing these cells to reproduce autonomously and rapidly, resulting in cancer and death of the host. Some viral strains that have been created here, specifically one that we call DM-19, will cause genetic alteration in *all* cells of the host, resulting in random and sometimes horrifying changes. Often the changes are lethal, but occasionally the genetic changes are viable, resulting in an organism with an entirely new genetic sequence. What this creates is a new species that could continue to spread the virus and possibly even reproduce, depending on the extent and nature of their genetic changes. It is conceivably possible for one of these viruses, if it escaped containment in our facility, to wipe out or genetically alter the entire human population in two to five years."

"Where does the name DM-19 come from?"

"Initially, it started out as a bad joke. DM stood for doomsday, and the number represented the estimation in months for the virus to wipe out or alter all human life on the planet. We based estimates on the known rate of viral transmission and mathematical models of potential human spread. Later, we decided to keep the naming system, because it gave us a way of grading the speed of devastation for each new generation biological agent."

"So, why don't you just destroy these agents?" Spencer asked.

"Well, obviously DM-19 refers to a worst case scenario. The mathematical predictions may be much too severe and spread may be self limiting. There are many contingencies that we just don't know about and therefore aren't involved in the model."

"My God, just listen to yourself!" Spencer exclaimed. "A virus that could *potentially* wipe out all humans in nineteen months; I don't care if that represents worst case scenario or not. Why take the chance?"

At this point, General Donner stood and addressed the question. "It's not that simple, Spencer. We have information that China is developing agents similar to DM-19, and therefore our research must continue for defensive purposes."

Spencer shook his head. "And what if the structural problems can't be resolved? What will you do then?"

"We would then be forced to transfer the agents to another facility," Donner explained, "but that would be very complicated and dangerous."

"And what if you didn't have enough time?"

"Then we would destroy the agents."

"And what if you didn't have enough time to do *that*?"

"The process to destroy the agents would be very quick, so I have no concern whatsoever about that possibility. But even if all scientists are incapacitated in some way, then it would proceed automatically. We'll show you how that works later."

Pierce again spoke up. "We obviously don't want to be put in that position. Hundreds of billions of dollars have been spent on our research here. We can't just simply flush it down the toilet. That's why we've asked you to come here and help us. We understand that you're excellent at solving complex structural engineering problems. The facility was built to withstand a direct nuclear hit and an earthquake that has a magnitude of 9.5 on the Richter scale."

"I guess I still don't understand why you chose me. There are many experts in the field of structural engineering with as much experience at solving complex problems as I have, if not more.

"We know that you have a PhD in geology as well as in structural engineering and are well thought of in both fields."

"Now you've got me really intrigued. Exactly what kind of structural problem are we dealing with here?"

"I think the easiest thing would be just to show you."

With that cue, all of the men started to exit. Spencer remained seated for a few minutes with a perplexed look on his face, until General Donner waved at him to follow the group. As they were leaving, Spencer looked over at the general and thought to himself, *Frank, what in the hell have you gotten me into here?*

Turner, Nevada: September 13, 8:55 p.m.

Cassie looked up at Kyle with terror in her beautiful blue eyes. "Please don't do this! I'll do anything you want; just please, please, don't do this."

The desperation in her voice and on her face was as real and unmistakable as the gun pressed against Michael's forehead. He could feel death holding him in its grasp through the cold barrel. In his mind's eye, he could see the explosion as the bullet shattered his skull like an eggshell, carrying chunks of soft gray matter with it as it tore through his brain and exploded again through the back of his head.

He closed his eyes and felt the sweat rolling down his temples. He could hear the ragged inhalation as he took one of the last few breaths of his life. He could feel his heart pounding furiously, even though it would soon cease to beat forever. Time seemed to slow down as he waited for the inevitable end. And then …*BLAAAAAMMMM!*

Cassie reacted to the explosive gunshot as if it were a nuclear detonation, her entire body bouncing away from the floor and becoming airborne for a few seconds. The noise was so loud that she instantly experienced tremendous bone-shattering pain radiating from her ears into her temples, followed by a loud, nauseating hum in both ears. She felt as if she might throw up, but then the brutal reality of the situation pulled her quickly out of her nausea and disorientation.

She looked up, expecting to see Kyle looming over her, but he was nowhere in sight. She turned on her side away from the wall and saw that Michael and Kyle were both sprawled out on the floor of the family room.

Much to her surprise, Michael was the first to stand. Although he looked a little shell-shocked and confused, he spotted the gun lying on the floor and kicked it across the room away from Kyle. As Kyle tried to push his body up into a crawling position, Michael turned to face him and saw that his cruel face was flushed with anger.

Michael decided to act quickly before he lost his advantage and fiercely kicked Kyle in the face. He heard a loud crunch as the nasal bones collapsed and blood spilled onto the floor.

Kyle groaned and fell forward into a pool of his own blood. Michael then bent down and held his hand out to Cassie. "Are you okay? Can you stand?"

Tears again rolled down her cheeks, but she wasn't sobbing or hysterical this time. "What just happened? I don't understand."

"I think we just experienced another "jump" or "tremor"—whatever you want to call it. It knocked Kyle off balance, so his shot missed my head, and both of us fell down."

"What keeps causing this to happen?" Cassie asked.

"I don't know, but I don't think it's just an earthquake. It's something stranger than that."

"I thought you were dead."

"I know. I thought I was, too. Listen, we've got to get out of here right now before he wakes up."

"You go ahead and leave," Cassie said. "I think I can calm him down if you're not here when he wakes up."

"Cassie, he would have beaten you to death if I hadn't showed up tonight."

"Really, I think it'll be okay."

"Do you really believe that? You really think that things will be okay? How much more can you take before he does beat you to death?"

"But I can't leave!"

"Why not?"

"Because he told me that if I ever left, he would track me down, and when he caught up with me, things would be much, much worse."

"Cassie, it can't get any worse! Your only hope is to come with me until we can find help for you. I have family in Denver. We can contact the police when we get there so that you'll be safe. We need to leave now!"

With that, she finally conceded and rose to her feet. She followed Michael out the front door and looked back once at Kyle who still lay on his chest in a drunken slumber with a pool of blood by his face.

When both of them were inside Michael's car, he headed out of town toward the Interstate. He unplugged his cell phone from the charger and considered calling Mona. Earlier that evening, he and Mona had had a long discussion about his plans to try and help Cassie. She had explained that Cassie became her surrogate daughter when she was twenty-one years old (eight years ago), after a chance meeting between the two of them at Bucky's.

Although she had been acquainted with Cassie since she was a little girl, they both had reached a lonely spot in their lives. Mona was living alone following her husband's death from prostate cancer the previous year. Cassie had been living by herself since the age of nineteen, when her father remarried Sandy, a woman who "hated small towns" and finally convinced him to move to Las Vegas.

Sandy was intensely jealous of Cassie, who previously had had a very close relationship with her father, and Sandy set out to make every interaction between the two of them as painful as possible. In the end, she accomplished her goal, because Cassie's father was unable to convince her to move with them to Vegas.

Cassie and Mona had grown very close over the years, but a rift between them occurred when Cassie started dating Kyle McMurphy four years ago. Mona recognized the abusive potential in the man and tried to direct Cassie away from him, but this backfired on her and drove a wedge between the two of them.

Because Mona still cared deeply for Cassie, Michael had promised to let her know what happened that evening. Michael reached across the seat and softly touched Cassie's shoulder to get her attention. "Do you really believe that Kyle will try to track you down?"

She looked at him, and nodded her head yes. Although he could barely see her face in the darkness, he could still sense how frightened she was. She stared out the passenger window while hugging herself and started trembling.

Almost in a whisper, she said, "He'll never stop until he finds me. You don't understand what he's like—what he's capable of. He'll use his position as sheriff to try and find me. He has to find me. I'm his possession."

Her voice was flat with no emotion—the voice of deep, hidden pain—the voice of hopelessness—the voice of defeat and submission— the voice of a broken person. Michael then knew that Mona had been right about Cassie.

He decided to wait and call Mona later, when he had a better idea of what he was up against. If Cassie was correct and Kyle was truly determined to track her down, he might have the resources to access telephone records, and Michael didn't want the connection made between him and Cassie (at least not until they had a chance to give a statement to the authorities in Denver).

Right now, Kyle didn't know who the man was that had stopped Cassie's beating that night and had no way of knowing where he might take her. In fact, the only person in Turner who knew Michael's name was Mona, and he hoped for the sake of them all that Kyle wouldn't be able to make that association.

Michael turned his car onto the Interstate and headed east toward Denver. The rain had finally stopped, but the road was still slick, so he slowly accelerated up to highway speed. There were no other cars on the road as he left Turner, giving him the eerie sensation that they were the only two people remaining on the planet, almost as if a giant comet or meteor had destroyed the remainder of the population. He would later remember this strange sensation and would be chilled at the thought of this revelation.

He knew he had done the right thing tonight, but he was now facing the reality of his current situation. He was on the run with an emotionally damaged woman from her abusive and dangerous husband, who had access to police computers and most certainly had many other law enforcement connections. Michael had chosen a path that he would have to continue to its completion—even though it might prove to be life threatening and extremely painful. But he knew that he could not abandon this woman now.

He was still grappling with guilt from the past and from the self-inflicted wounds concerning his failure to protect those that he loved the most. If he failed again, even though he barely knew this woman, the burden of guilt, which had crippled him for years, would be incapacitating.

As he started his journey down the lonely highway, he could see that Cassie's ordeal tonight had turned to exhaustion, and she was now slumped down in the passenger seat breathing the slow, rhythmic patterns of sleep.

Jackson Hole, Wyoming: September 13, 10:15 p.m.

Senator Clinton Wolfe sat quietly in his large leather chair and stared at the fireplace directly across from him in his study. He rubbed his deeply furrowed brow to try and ease the headache that had been burrowing into his brain like an insidious worm for the past thirty minutes, when he first received the call from U.S. Geological Survey (USGS) headquarters in San Francisco.

He mumbled to himself, *Fucking scientists, who do they think they are? They're trying to shit on my parade!*

He had planned on beginning his re-election campaign the following week after a brief retreat at his vacation home in Jackson Hole. After the phone call, he knew that his vacation and his re-election campaign would have to be put on hold.

First, he called his girlfriend to tell her to cancel her visit to his vacation home tonight. Next, he called his wife and told her that business was going to keep him away from home longer than usual. Finally, he called the private office of Governor John Stamper and, after waiting on hold for ten minutes, he was connected to a secure line.

He heard the governor's deep, gravelly voice say, "Clint, just what the hell is so urgent that I had to leave my dinner party?"

"John, we've got a big fucking problem!"

He described his conversation in detail with the scientists from the USGS. After he was finished, there was silence on the line for almost a minute before John Stamper responded. "Well, Clint, you're right—that is a big fucking problem. So what are we going to do about it?"

"I'll tell you what we're going to do. We're going to keep a fucking lid on it! Neither of us needs this interfering with our re-election campaigns."

"I don't see how this will cause problems with the campaigns."

"I'll tell you how: If any news of this gets out, the financial markets will crash, people will lose jobs, times will be hard, pessimism will dominate, and we'll be held accountable for the hard times."

"But, Clint, what if the worst case scenario predictions come to pass?"

"Then we're all screwed anyway."

"But couldn't we save millions of lives with an early warning?"

"This is all bullshit scientific speculation. These are just theories— not facts. Why should we put our political careers in jeopardy because of some speculation? If it doesn't come to pass, then our political careers aren't unnecessarily wasted."

"But what if it does?"

"Then that's just something that we'll all have to live with."

Black Diamond Military Base, Nevada
September 13, 4:01 p.m.

Spencer followed Donner, Pierce, and the other men as they proceeded through the bowels of the extensive military complex. After exiting the conference room, they had traversed a maze of hallways leading to a large complex of elevator shafts. They traveled down one of the elevators for what seemed to be twenty floors to the very bottom level, and after exiting the elevator, they started walking down a long hallway. The darkness seemed to be more pervasive and the heating systems less effective, the deeper they descended into the facility, as if they were wandering into increasingly remote catacombs.

At the end of the hallway, they keyed in a digital code to open a door resembling that of a bank vault. They entered a stairwell which descended over a hundred feet. As they finally entered their destination, Pierce motioned for Spencer to pass the other men and join him at the front of the group. The room they were standing in, although it was only two stories high, appeared to go on forever. Spencer could see rows of at least fifty columns, each ten feet in diameter, spreading out in all directions, but darkness obscured his vision beyond that point. This gave the illusion of being inside a vast subterranean cavern.

Pierce pointed his finger into the room and said, "You're looking at a buffer zone between the bottom of our facility and the exterior wall of the complex. This buffer zone, with its exterior wall, extends in all directions and completely surrounds the facility on each of its four sides and its floor—which is where we're standing right now. The exterior wall is forty feet thick and is composed of concrete and multiple layers of solid steel with relaxation joints to allow for ground shift and enough strength to withstand an earthquake over ten times stronger than the most intense quake ever recorded."

"I assume you're talking about the 1960 quake in Chile that was 9.0 in magnitude?"

"That's right."

"Okay, so let's get right to the point. Show me the areas where you've identified structural problems."

"You're looking right at them."

"What are you talking about?" Spencer glanced around the room and could see no obvious problems. There was no buckling of the floor, and the columns appeared to be intact. He could not see the side walls because of the darkness, but the remainder of the room seemed to be unremarkable.

Pierce glanced up at the ceiling and said, "The room you're standing in used to be four stories high. Now, as you can see, it stands only two stories."

"Then how are the columns still intact?" Spencer asked.

Another man in a lab coat identified himself as Ed Foster, Chief Facility Inspector and Engineer. He explained that the facility had a full-time crew of thirty people responsible for not only maintenance, but also continual inspection to rapidly identify any and all problems on an ongoing basis. He then responded to Spencer's question. "The columns were built to function as huge shock absorbers and have the ability to stroke or telescope without damage if enough force is generated against the exterior walls."

"How much force is necessary to cause movement of an individual column?"

"In our structural simulations, we tried to reproduce a worst case scenario with forces equivalent to those that would be generated during a catastrophic earthquake—multiple times greater than 9.0 on the Richter scale. I can give you the exact figures later."

"So how much movement did you see with the simulations?"

"Approximately two feet with a quake that was 9.3 on the Richter scale. There was no collapse below that degree of intensity."

"And exactly how much collapse are we looking at right here?"

"About twenty-five feet."

"Over what time period did this occur?"

"It started two weeks ago."

Spencer looked at him incredulously. "Are you sure that the simulations were correct? How long ago was it that they were performed?"

"Over ten years ago, and I wasn't involved, but we repeated the simulations last week, and they seem correct."

"If what you're telling me is accurate, then this makes no sense at all. The forces that you're talking about would be astronomical. We know of nothing in nature that can generate as much intensity as the massive tectonic forces that move the Earth's plates and result in earthquakes."

"It didn't make sense to any of us, either. That's why we need your help."

"I need to examine one of the columns, and I need to look at the structural details of the exterior wall and columns. I'd also like to see all of the data from the simulations. Oh, I'll also need access to a computer, and I'll need to make a few calls to some colleagues."

"We can arrange all of that for you within an hour," Pierce said.

Spencer shook his head and started walking over to one of the columns. General Donner walked over to him and smiled sheepishly. "So are you going to be able to help us, Spencer?"

"I don't know, Frank. I sure hope so, because if I can't, then we're all screwed."

Interstate 80 en route to Salt Lake City, Utah
September 14, 1:22 a.m.

Michael looked over at Cassie and noticed that she was stirring, moving from side to side as if she was unable to find a comfortable position. Although he had been tired earlier, the evening's events had circulated enough adrenalin through his bloodstream to keep him up for hours. In addition, there was an extra excitement that all of this had stimulated in him. It was a feeling that he had not experienced for years and that he thought was lost forever—a sense of purpose. A feeling that someone he cared for needed him—a feeling that he was protecting someone by putting them under his wing.

As he thought about this, he reminded himself that he barely knew anything about Cassie. How could he have decided that he cared for her? He was being as flighty and impulsive as a teenager—a thirty-six-year-old teenager. This wasn't at all like him. He always took his time to make decisions. Things needed to make sense. All the pieces of the puzzle needed to fit. That was one of his problems and weaknesses, according to the therapist he had seen when he was working through his depression. The death of his wife and his daughter would never make sense to him—those pieces would never fit into the puzzle of his life.

So, now, he sat next to this woman that he didn't know but had some connection with and that he cared about for some inexplicable reason. And somehow, he was happier than he had been for a long, long time.

Life certainly is the great mystery that none of us would ever solve. We just need to realize that we are only along for the ride.

Cassie opened her eyes when the top of her head violently impacted the roof of the car and she was thrown forward against the dashboard. A hematoma instantly formed where her forehead hit the front windshield, and she could see that Michael was fighting to regain control of the car. When the car slowed to a stop, she realized that they had experienced another "jump", but fortunately Michael's driving had allowed their vehicle to remain on the highway.

When Cassie got out of the car, she could see that the highway behind them had broken in half by a five-foot step up that extended in a north and south direction as far as the eye could see. Four other cars had stopped haphazardly on the road, and a trailer-truck had jack-knifed and was now sitting on the shoulder.

Michael urged her to get back in the car, and when she did he accelerated quickly away from the area as if trying to escape demons that resided on that stretch of highway. But moments later, Cassie could see flashing lights in the distance with at least ten patrol cars forming a roadblock in front of them.

Now we're in a really tough position, she thought, *between a rock and a hard place. If we continue, we'll have to deal with the authorities,*

*but we can't turn back because the highway behind us is fractured with a
five-foot step up.*

She could feel the anxiety building in her chest as she turned to
Michael. "We're trapped, Michael. What can we do? They might already
have a description of me from Kyle. If he finds me…"

"Shut up and quit worrying," Michael snapped. "I'll deal with this!
I don't need this crap right now!"

Cassie was stunned by his response, but she didn't know what else
to say as they approached the roadblock. There were five other cars in
front of them that had stopped at the roadblock, and when Michael
pulled up behind the last car, Cassie could see that his knuckles were
white from gripping the steering wheel so tightly. She could also see
extreme anxiety on his face and sweat dripping from his brow. When
she tried getting his attention, he ignored her and stared straight ahead
at the flashing lights.

"Michael, this is a bad situation. We need to get out of here
before…"

"Shut the hell up!" he responded without looking at her.

She could hear the anger in his voice. Now she realized that she
was in a very dangerous spot, as the volatility of the situation increased.
Michael started pounding the steering wheel with his fist as they both
watched a police officer approach the car. At first, he walked toward
the driver's side, but when he was even with the front of the vehicle,
he abruptly turned toward the passenger side and was rapping at the
window seconds later.

Cassie looked behind to see that they were now trapped by another
car that had just pulled up. She nervously lowered the window and
waited for the officer's response. But she was not prepared for what
happened next.

The officer quickly reached inside the car, unlocked the door, pulled the door open, and yanked Cassie out of the vehicle by her shirt. She tried to scream, but the officer's hand was clamped on her throat seconds later. She knew without looking at the man's face what was transpiring, and she knew who the officer was before she even smelled his rancid breath.

He smiled at her with malignant intent. "Hi, sweetie, have you missed me?"

As Michael scrambled to get out of the car, Kyle pulled out his handgun. Seconds later, there was a loud blast from the gun, and Cassie could hear Michael screaming in pain. Kyle dragged Cassie around the front of the car so that she could see Michael kneeling on the ground with blood pouring from the right side of his chest. He looked up at Kyle and begged him to stop. "Please don't hurt me! Please!"

Without a word, Kyle shot him point blank in the abdomen, as Michael once again screamed out in pain.

Then Kyle chuckled with amusement. "Now we get to see his brains splatter everywhere, just like I told you earlier, bitch!"

Another blast and Michael's skull was shattered by the projectile. Before his body even hit the ground, Kyle was dragging Cassie over to his police cruiser. As he was violently stuffing her in the trunk of his car, he said, "Do you remember what I told you I'd do if you ever ran from me?"

The world went dark for her as he slammed the trunk door shut—just like a coffin…Cassie tried to scream but there was no sound—there was just darkness…

Michael could see that Cassie was having a bad dream, so he softly placed his hand on her shoulder. She suddenly opened her eyes with a look of alarm and confusion. Michael instantly withdrew his hand because he could see that she was staring at it uneasily.

Cassie shook her head a few times to clear the cobwebs and sat up straight. After a short while she said, "How long have I been asleep?"

Michael yawned and shifted in his seat. "You've been sleeping about five hours."

"You've been driving that entire time?"

"Sure have. We're almost at Salt Lake City. I'd planned on stopping there. I'm too tired to drive much longer."

Both of them remained quiet for the next few minutes, content to watch the car headlights penetrate the darkness of the Utah desert. Cassie reached up and touched her right hand on the passenger window. The cold glass and the sound of the frigid wind whistling past the car like a banshee transmitted a chill to her that spread its icy fingers up the back of her neck and along the base of her skull. She visibly started trembling, and Michael immediately turned up the heater and offered her his jacket. She accepted the jacket and stared at him for the next few minutes.

Although his features were partially obscured in the dark interior, she could still remember his intelligent, kind, hazel-colored eyes when he was seated in the booth in the restaurant. They were without question his most striking feature, but there were several other qualities and features about him that she found equally attractive. He was in good shape—lean and muscular, with a masculine brow and chin, strong chiseled facial bones, and silky dark brown hair. All of his mannerisms conveyed confidence without conceit, and when he talked, he had a smooth Southern accent with a relaxed, comforting tone.

Despite all of these features, there was something about him that she found unsettling, something hidden that she couldn't identify. But with what she had been going through with Kyle, perhaps it was just a general distrust of men. All things considered, this stranger had put his life on the line for her, but she knew from past experience that this meant nothing, and he could still turn on her like a rabid dog. She started to develop increasing anxiety when she focused on this point and on the fact that she was now hundreds of miles from home. Maybe she had simply jumped out of the boiling pot into the fire.

Michael reached across Cassie's lap, and she winced when she felt his hand touch her knee. He noticed her reaction and quickly pulled his hand back. "Hey, I'm sorry if I startled you. I was just trying to get a map out of the glove compartment. I'd like to see how much farther it is to Salt Lake City."

She blushed with embarrassment, but fortunately it was too dark for him to recognize. She decided that if she was to form an opinion about this man, she needed to know more information about him. Even still, she did not really trust her opinions, because some of them had been so horrendously off base, and she had paid dearly for these errors in judgment.

She turned to Michael. "I'm just still a little freaked out about what happened earlier. I'll get the map for you."

She opened the glove compartment, unfolded the map, and turned on the passenger reading light. They decided that they were approximately forty miles from the city, and she offered to drive, but he said that he could stay awake if they struck up a conversation. She didn't see any harm in that and agreed to try and keep him alert for the remainder of the drive.

"So, where do you live? Didn't you mention that you're traveling across the country to visit your brothers?"

"That's right. I'm going to visit both of them. My brother, Stephen, lives in Denver with his wife, Kate, and their two kids. My youngest brother, Mark, lives in New York City. I've been living in California for the past nine years, most recently Sonoma."

"Are you in the winery business?"

"Well, actually—I guess I was. But that was a few years ago."

"Did you own a winery?"

"I did—I mean, I guess I still do—a small one."

"So why did you quit?"

"Uh—that's a very long story."

Cassie could see a change in his posture and tensing of all visible muscles. She sensed that the questions about the recent past were bringing back some unwanted memories for Michael, so she decided to change the focus of her questions to earlier times. "Where did you grow up?"

"Mostly South Carolina, but my parents moved around a lot when I was a child."

"So what did you do before you moved to California?"

"I went straight into the military after high school. I'm not really even sure why. My family was shocked when I told them I had enlisted with the Marine Corps. I guess I was just another naïve eighteen year old with a strong sense of duty."

Cassie could see the lines of his face relax as he concentrated on conveying details of his life from the more remote past. Initially, she was surprised that he was willing to talk so openly about his life with a relative stranger. He anticipated her reaction to his openness and explained that this was a peculiar feature of his personality. With a few exceptions, his approach to life was to present himself as an open book with very few if any secrets or skeletons in the closet. This made life simpler for him, because he had no false pretenses. He could always just be himself. That way, if you liked him—great! But if you didn't, then that was okay, too. He called it his "No Bullshit Approach to Life."

He told Cassie to be honest if she found this too overwhelming, and he would shut his mouth. At first, she was nervous and little uncomfortable with his honesty, but she wanted to know more about him, so she encouraged him to continue. The longer he talked, the more enthralled she became with his story.

Michael told her that after joining the Marines, the military quickly became his only passion, and eventually his dedication and intelligence were noticed, which resulted in his rapid advancement in rank over the next eight to ten years. Because of certain skills that he possessed, he was selected to be part of an elite group of Marines—Force Recon. Many of their missions involved the rescue of American civilians kidnapped by hostile regimes or trapped in foreign countries in the midst of civil war or rebel uprisings. He spent the better part of seven years dodging bullets in Africa, the Middle East, and South America.

He touched on the specifics of several rescue missions, but Cassie had the distinct impression that he was probably downplaying his role, as well as the danger and courage that must have been involved with each of the harrowing situations that he described.

In one particular rescue mission in Somalia that succeeded in the release of all seventeen hostages, two Marines were seriously injured, and one was killed. The man who died—Darius Johnson—was the closest friend that Michael had while in the military. He talked extensively about the special bond between the two of them. They both had two brothers; both were dedicated to the Corps, and yet they had grown weary of cavorting all over the world with Force Recon. They each secretly wanted to settle down and have a family, and they considered each other a "true brother," despite the difference in their skin color.

Michael explained in detail how Darius died while trying to help the hostages, but Cassie noted that Michael was extremely vague when he mentioned the two injured Marines. She wanted to hear more about this mission, but when he wasn't forthcoming, she decided not to press him further.

Michael planned to make a career out of the military, but when he was twenty-seven years old and stationed in California at Camp Pendleton, his life took a dramatic turn. He met a young school teacher named Amy Dorman and, for the first time in his life, he considered a life outside of the Marines.

Within five months, they were married and ten months later, Amy gave birth to their daughter, Tabitha, whom he later nicknamed "Tabby." Michael knew that Amy loved him and would stay with him no matter what, but he also knew that she yearned to share a life with him as a civilian, where she didn't have to constantly live in fear of the next Force Recon mission. Therefore, at age twenty-nine, he made the difficult decision to leave the Marine Corps.

Amy had always talked about how she loved San Francisco, so they rented a small apartment in the city and started their civilian life together. Michael took a chance and used most of the money he had saved to start a small business, renting high-end furniture to individuals who couldn't otherwise afford such exquisite pieces in their homes. Eventually, he had in storage a huge collection of one-of-a-kind pieces that the ultra wealthy started buying from him in truckloads, providing him with substantial profits. Within a year, he had a multi-million dollar business. Amy, who had stayed home to be with Tabby, was both amazed and tremendously proud to see how successful her husband's business had become in such a short period of time.

A year later, when Tabby was almost three, Michael sold his business for $3.8 million. He and Amy decided that it would be better to raise their daughter in a smaller town, and they moved to Sonoma, where they bought a small winery. Their house was located on a hill surrounded by large oak trees, which overlooked the vineyard, and was graced with a cool, refreshing breeze the majority of the year.

Michael described how happy they were living in Sonoma over the next few years. The winery was moderately successful, but the lifestyle was phenomenal. He described the joy that he and Amy shared watching their daughter grow up in the lovely, little town. He spent summers horseback riding through the vineyards with Tabby sitting in his lap. He remembered her wonderful, innocent laughter when they galloped and she bounced in the saddle, with her long, brown hair flying wildly in the wind. She was the spitting image of her mother, and every time he looked at her, he was reminded of how dramatically his life had changed since first meeting Amy and how lucky he was that the two of them were a part of his life.

Once again, Cassie detected a change in Michael's demeanor, as he continued to talk about his life in Sonoma. His voice started to trail off, and he appeared to be increasingly lost in memories of his wife and daughter. She noticed the tension returning in both his voice and facial muscles, with deep creases forming on his forehead. Intuitively, she knew what was coming in the story that he was telling her, and she wasn't sure she was ready to hear it.

When Michael paused for a few seconds, Cassie chimed in. "Why don't you tell me the rest of this later. I know you must be exhausted, and we need to look for a place to stop."

Her voice seemed to break him out of the dark place that he had descended into in the past ten minutes. He looked over at her, let out a sigh of relief, and said, "Thanks."

"For what?" she asked.

"For knowing when I needed to take a break from my memories."

"You shouldn't have to talk about anything that you don't feel comfortable sharing with me."

"Cassie, this is something I'll probably never feel comfortable talking about with anyone, but I told you there are no secrets with me, so you might as well hear about it now, rather than find out about it later.

"My wife and daughter both died in an automobile accident two and a half years ago. I was the one responsible for their deaths."

Chapter 2

The Pilgrimage

Salt Lake City, Utah: September 14, 3:47 a.m.

After his revelation to Cassie, Michael sat in silence and concentrated on the road signs, searching for the first adequate lodging available. As they approached the outskirts of the city, he spotted the Desert Inn on a neon sign and decided to pull off the highway in order to give his weary eyes a rest.

As he entered the parking lot, he could sense that Cassie was staring at him, but he avoided looking at her, because he knew he had revealed too much and was unsure how she would respond to his inappropriate ramblings.

He stopped the car, opened his door, and without a word, walked to the office. Cassie remained in the car and began to consider her options. She could return to Turner on the next bus and simply tell Michael that she had made a significant mistake by leaving with him. Or she could part ways with Michael right now and begin a new life on her own away from Kyle and the abuse she had endured. Her final option was to continue the journey she had started with this strange, but intriguing man. She found his openness both awkward and somehow refreshing.

She wasn't sure what to make of his personal confession concerning the deaths of his wife and daughter, but even though he had only talked to her about them for a short while, she was certain that he deeply loved both of them, and that he must have suffered terribly with this loss and his subsequent guilt.

A part of her longed to reach out to Michael and try to ease the pain that he was still carrying with him, but she immediately pushed these thoughts away. Never again would she let a man control her physically and emotionally the way that Kyle had. After first seeming to love and care about her, he had systematically set out to destroy all of her dignity and hope. The only true protection from a similar situation in the future was to keep emotional distance between herself and others—especially men.

After considering all options, she decided to go with her gut feeling that right now she was safer with Michael, than without him. He appeared to be honest, kind, and humble. Although she was not willing to completely trust him, she did not sense that he was at all dangerous. She also sensed a strength in him that gave her the feeling of being protected. With his military training and background, she had no doubt that he could be a formidable adversary for anyone who crossed his path. She presently thought that this might be important in the near future, especially if Kyle or anyone else tried to forcibly impose their will. Of course, at that point, she could never have predicted how events would escalate in a horrifying fashion to create a virtual hell on Earth in less than a week.

Michael returned to the car and after sitting down, he turned to her. "I'm sorry about dumping my personal stuff on you like that. I guess I didn't get the hint that you needed a break from my story, so I just kept going on and on."

"Michael, I don't think…"

"No, that's okay. I understand. Look, why don't we both get some rest, and we can talk more about this tomorrow? We still have a long way to drive, but I promise I won't do that to you again."

Before she could respond, he handed her a key and said, "You're in bungalow No. 26, and I'm in No. 28. They don't connect, but they are right next door to each other. If you need anything, let me know. They do have a small gift shop inside the office, and there are vending machines around the corner. Let's try to leave at 10:30 a.m. which gives us about seven hours to rest. We'll stop somewhere in Salt Lake City to get a good breakfast before we hit the road again."

Cassie wanted to say something, but found that she was at a loss for words. There were many questions she needed to ask, and some important things she needed to set straight, but she did not know where to start, and so she remained quiet.

He parked the car in front of the two bungalows, and they walked to their respective rooms. She glanced over at him briefly and quickly looked away when he turned his head to make sure she was able to get in.

Black Diamond Military Base, Nevada
September 14, 9:25 a.m.

Spencer woke to the sound of music on the clock radio by his bed. He dragged himself over to the mirror and stared at his bedraggled face. Dark circles and deep creases surrounded his eyes, and his hair was contorted in a bizarre fashion, sticking out in different directions. His temples throbbed with dull pain that radiated down into his jaw on both sides. He grabbed four Advil from the bottle on the dresser and quickly swallowed them with a gulp of water.

He'd spent almost eight hours yesterday evening studying structural details and simulation data. He was certain that he would find some discrepancies in the information to explain what was happening at the facility, but by 1:30 a.m. this morning, he had found absolutely nothing to discredit the data or better elucidate what was occurring. As a matter of fact, the more he looked at the information, the more confused he became. It actually appeared that whatever the intermittent forces were that had been responsible for the columns moving, they seemed to have increased in frequency and intensity over the past few weeks and then they just stopped three days ago. There had been no reported earthquakes in the area, at least nothing out of the ordinary.

It appeared that he was coming up with absolutely nothing that was helpful, and his frustration became almost unbearable by 1:30 a.m., so he retired to his room and decided to make a few phone calls the next morning.

What had awakened him was a dreadful dream involving fire, destruction, turmoil, and terror. Although he could recall that the dream had involved all of these elements, he could not remember what caused these things to cascade out of control, but he was sure that they were doing just that. Most disturbing was the perception of thousands of voices, somehow in the background of all the turmoil, screaming in agony—screaming for deliverance to a different place.

Spencer was not one to put much credence in dream interpretation; however, this particular dream seemed to haunt him. He kept visualizing entire fields of people with their flesh burned off, blood oozing from their eyes, and their bodies horribly mangled and dismembered. These thoughts were so disturbing that he was in a state of constant anxiety until mercifully the dream memories began to fade.

Spencer sat down on the bed and tried to clear his head, so that he could focus on the difficult task that lay ahead of him. As he was sitting there, he heard a beep coming from the adjacent wall. A green flashing light on the wall caught his attention, and he then noticed the flat panel video screen. Somehow he had missed this earlier—probably his fatigue and frustration had distracted him when he first entered the room hours ago. He pushed the button immediately below the light, and the screen instantly lit up with the smiling face of Frank Donner. "Rise and shine, sleepyhead."

"I'm already up, Frank." Spencer presumed that this was a two-way video intercom system, and that Frank could see him as well.

"We have more information for you that the engineers dug up last night. I'll pop over to your room in ten minutes to take you to the lounge for breakfast. After that, Dr. Pierce will take you down to meet with the engineers. I'm actually leaving the facility after breakfast. I have my grandson's fifth birthday party to attend. Huge pain in the ass to leave the facility again, but I promised my daughter that I wouldn't miss another birthday party. I've missed the last two. You'll be ready in ten minutes?"

"Sure, Frank." With that the video screen went blank.

Ten minutes later, almost to the second, Frank met Spencer at his door, and they proceeded to the lounge. Everyone else had already eaten breakfast and left, so the two of them were able to eat and talk in private.

"So, what kind of headway have you been able to make with all of this?" asked Frank.

"I'll be honest; I don't know what in the hell is going on here. I've never seen anything like this before. All of the simulation data seems correct. The mechanical and structural details look like they're right on target."

"Don't you have any theories at all?"

"There are only two possibilities that I can think of. First, that the construction of the walls and the columns were somehow defective. The problem is that I don't know how to test for that without tearing out part of the wall and some of the columns. We could probably do that in a small area on the side of the facility, but we really need to do it on the floor where all of this is taking place. That would create a weak spot, so I don't think that would be advisable right now."

"Do you really think there could be a construction problem?"

"Nothing is for sure, but the construction companies that built Black Diamond were all top notch and because of the importance of this facility, I know that the Department of Defense had many oversight engineers breathing down the necks of the contractors in their typical anal-retentive fashion."

"I guess I'll take that as a compliment. So, what's the other possibility?"

"The other possibility is a little crazy and far-fetched." Spencer rubbed his chin and frowned, but said nothing else.

After a short while, Frank spoke up, "Hey, don't keep me in suspense here."

Spencer sighed and finally said, "Okay, Frank, let's suppose that the structural engineering and mechanical specs are accurate, the simulation is correct, and the actual engineering and construction was top notch. Unless there's something that I'm missing, then only one other explanation seems possible—that what we're seeing here doesn't represent a structural failure or mistake, but the effect of truly massive forces being generated below the facility."

"So, what could do that?"

"It would have to be a singular geological event."

"Singular? What do you mean by that?"

"Unprecedented. Something that we've never seen before, at least since man has been on Earth."

"So, give me an example," Frank said.

"I can't. That's why I told you this is far-fetched. Anything I came up with would only be theoretical, not fact. We know bits and pieces about the Earth's history millions of years ago, but there are so many things that we just don't know."

"Alright, let me go out on a limb here," Frank offered. "Are you talking about events like the extinction of the dinosaurs?"

"Yes and no. The dinosaur extinction sixty-five million years ago is thought to have been linked to the Chicxulub crater in the Yucatan Peninsula, which they think was created by the impact of a six-mile-wide asteroid. But, you see, that's just a theory. The reality is that there are several other theories involving geological events that could have been responsible for this extinction. Asteroid impact is just the most popular one right now."

"I know this is all just theoretical, but what type of geological event could we be dealing with?"

"That's what I'm telling you, Frank. I don't know of any that could do this."

The frustration was starting to show in Spencer's tone of voice, so Frank decided to back off. "Well, thanks for talking to me about it. If you get any more ideas, will you let me know?"

"Sure, Frank."

"I've got to take off if I'm going to be able to make this birthday party. I have to stop and get a present for him beforehand. He wants something that shoots very high in the air; you know how young boys are."

"Good luck with that."

"Thanks. I'll see you when I get back tomorrow." With that, Frank stood up, shook Spencer's hand and walked out of the lounge. He hesitated briefly at the door and said, "Dr. Pierce should be here in the next half hour so just relax."

When Frank Donner was gone, Spencer leaned back in his chair and closed his eyes. A thought was tickling his brain that seemed to be triggered by something Frank had said. It was right at the edge of his conscious mind, but he couldn't quite pull it into focus. He then realized that it was not the context of what Frank had said, but a few words he had said that stimulated his brain and pushed it into searching its memory banks.

What are the words? Maybe…extinction…dinosaurs. But there's one more…shoot? No, that's not quite right…shot! That's the word—shot. But what does that mean? He pondered this for a few minutes, repeating the words over and over, *Extinction, dinosaurs, shot—extinction, dinosaurs, shot—extinction, dinosaurs, shot…*

Finally, he made the connection between the words, and that's when he decided to spend the rest of the morning calling several colleagues and friends around the country. He first called Thomas Pierce using the video-intercom system and asked if he could have access to a phone line and delay meeting with the engineers until the afternoon.

A short while later, he went into a private office and received authorization codes to make unlimited phone calls. The first call was to the U.S. Geological Survey headquarters in San Francisco. Then he called the Yellowstone Volcano Observatory in Yellowstone National Park, Wyoming.

Yellowstone Volcano Observatory, Wyoming
September 14, 11:37 a.m.

Stephen Hanson sat at his desk inside the main building at the observatory, studying hundreds of pages of raw data, graphs, and diagrams. He had been at work since seven o'clock that morning. When he was away from home, as he had been for the last two weeks, he liked getting an early start. He missed his wife and children tremendously and spent most evenings talking to them for at least an hour. He had hoped that this particular consulting job would keep him away from home for only a few days, but the situation here appeared to be escalating daily, and now he was hoping to get home in a few more weeks.

A part of him wanted to stay close to the action for now, though, because his expertise was needed and because he wanted to know first hand the degree of danger that his family in Colorado might be in. He thought of himself as their "early warning system."

His assistant Marsha entered his office. "Dr. Hanson, you have a call on line two. He says he's an old friend and colleague of yours when you used to work for the U.S. Geological Survey. His name is Spencer Montgomery."

A big smile formed on Stephen's face, and he asked her to transfer the call to his office right away. When he answered, he instantly recognized the intelligent and friendly banter that characterized Spencer's speech. "Hey, buddy, what've you been up to?"

"Not much—just trying to save the planet. How about you?"

"Oh, I guess the same thing here. God, it's been a long time since I've talked to you. I thought you were still with the USGS, so I called them and they told me that you lived in Denver now but were doing some consulting work for the observatory. They said that you'd been talking to them on almost a daily basis for the past few weeks but wouldn't tell me what it was about. So, what's the big mystery?"

"Boy, you get right to the point, don't you?"

"Well, you know me—I'm a no bullshit kind of guy," said Spencer. "I might as well tell you what's on my mind."

"Yeah, you and my brother Michael do it better than anyone else I know."

"Well, I don't think I'm in the same class as your brother. So, how are your wife and kids?"

"They're doing great. Did you ever get married?" Stephen asked.

"No, I never did. I guess I'm married to my work."

"That doesn't make such a good bed partner."

"You're right about that, my friend. Okay, so back to the mystery. What's going on up there?"

"I've been given instructions, as of this morning, not to leak anything until we have a clearer idea of what's going on—not even to outside colleagues—sort of a gag order. I absolutely don't agree with it, but it's coming from the governor of Wyoming."

"Come on, Stephen. You know who you're talking to here. Nothing that you say goes past my lips. Plus you owe me one. I introduced you to your wife."

"I do owe you one, but I don't think I can do this."

Spencer pushed further, "Okay, you need to listen carefully to what I'm going to tell you. Right now, I'm at a secret military installation in Nevada, and there is some weird shit going on here that I think is geological. I'll tell you about it, but then I want to know what you're seeing there at the observatory. I think I already know what changes you've seen; I just need to confirm it. I have a theory about what's going on that I'll tell you after we've discussed this for a while."

As Stephen listened to Spencer describe what he had discovered at the military facility, he would never have suspected that his phone line was tapped.

Salt Lake City, Utah: September 14, 11:50 a.m.

Although Cassie had been up since seven-thirty, she and Michael had gotten a late start because he was so exhausted that he slept through his wake-up call, and Cassie did not want to disturb him. Instead, she walked down to the coffee shop and sipped some fresh brewed Columbian coffee and spent several hours reading a book she had bought in the gift shop.

When she finally made her way back to the bungalow, Michael was waiting for her outside. "Have you already eaten? I'm starved."

She told him that she had waited to eat with him. He smiled and told her that he'd be ready in just a few minutes.

After checking out of the Desert Inn, they continued east on I-80, passing through Salt Lake City. On the outskirts of the city, they stopped at a casual Italian restaurant, because it was too late for breakfast; besides, Michael said he was craving pizza.

As they were being seated, Cassie scanned the room for any sign of trouble and then felt foolish for having paranoid thoughts. She knew Kyle could not have tracked them this far so quickly. He didn't even know Michael's name, and he had no idea which direction they took. For all he knew, they could have headed west toward Reno and then on to California. But she couldn't forget how persistent and obsessed he became whenever he set out on a mission. Plus, he did have that badge that gave him access to information that most people would never be able to obtain.

Cassie and Michael both looked around at the drab interior of the restaurant, with its faded yellow walls and dirty linoleum floor, and wondered if they had made a poor choice. They did notice that the restaurant was fairly busy for lunch and took that as a good sign. It did have a large elevated plasma TV, which looked out of place with the remainder of the cheap décor.

A very rotund waitress, with her bright red hair pulled up in a bun, waddled over to the table and wrote their order down on a slip of paper smudged with grease.

Michael and Cassie looked at each other and shrugged as if to say, *do we leave or do we take our chances with the food?*

Before Michael could say anything, Cassie started the conversation that she had rehearsed many times that morning. "Michael, you didn't dump your personal stuff on me, and I didn't need a break from your life story. The only reason that I asked you if we could continue the rest of the story later was because I could see that it was becoming increasingly painful for you to talk about your wife and daughter. I was initially surprised and a little uncomfortable with your openness, but not because it's a bad thing. I admire people who are open and honest; I'm just not used to it. I also thought that what you did for me was very brave—a little stupid, but still very brave. I never thanked you for that, but I should have."

"You don't need to thank me. I just wanted you to be safe, and you're not ever going to be safe in that town."

"I know you're probably right."

"You don't have to talk to me about this if you don't want to, but I don't understand why you stayed there as long as you did."

Cassie hesitated to respond, at first. She had expected him to ask this question eventually, but she wasn't completely prepared to face some of the difficult issues concerning her life. Still, she felt compelled to open herself to him, probably because he had been so honest about his life.

She looked straight at him, swallowed hard, and with a tremor in her voice, she said, "This is not easy for me to explain, but I guess I was really frightened about leaving. Part of it had to do with Kyle's threats of what he would do to me if I ever left, and part of it was fear of the unknown. But another big thing was the fact that I didn't have any other place to go. My dad has had nothing to do with me since he remarried and moved to Vegas. I have no other family—no other relatives. I was very close to Mona Thomas, but Kyle made sure he destroyed that relationship by threatening to hurt her if I didn't stop meeting her and talking to her."

"I see. Well, now, something that Mona told me suddenly makes a lot more sense."

"When did you talk with Mona?" Cassie asked with obvious surprise.

Michael realized that he had failed to tell her about meeting Mona. "She was stranded on I-80 after her car broke down, so I drove her home. I came back to Mama's Place after she and I talked. She's very worried about you, and she thinks that you quit talking to her because she was meddling in your life concerning Kyle."

"I was afraid that she might feel that way. I couldn't tell her the truth, because I was afraid that she would try to stand up to him. She just doesn't understand how dangerous, cruel, and vindictive he can become, especially if someone defies him."

"I guess you must know this from personal experience."

"The bastard—excuse my language—Kyle, made it his goal to beat all of the defiance out of me, and I guess he succeeded."

Michael noticed that the tone of her voice had changed to one of anxiety and anger. "So how did you end up with that monster to start with?"

Cassie looked at Michael, as if he had just thrown a rock at her. Then she quickly looked away and became quiet for a few seconds. At first, Michael was confused, but then he realized that he had hit on a sensitive subject.

Just before he spoke up to apologize, she said, "I know what you're thinking. You think I'm one of those pathetic women who are attracted to angry, abusive men. I've had people point that finger at me over and over again."

"Cassie, I never meant to imply…"

"No, just hear me out," she interrupted. "Yes, I made some bad choices, and I was terribly naïve, but I never would have gotten involved with Kyle if I'd known what kind of man he really was…"

"Cassie, you don't need to tell me this; I already believe you."

She seemed to relax a little bit but still had a look of concern in her eyes. "Michael, please tell me the truth. What did Mona tell you about me?"

He relayed to her everything that Mona had said. As he talked, her look of concern seemed to fade.

When he had finished, she said, "Mona is a dear woman, but she's wrong about me. I'm not a broken person. I just couldn't see how to get out of the hole that I was in."

"Believe me, I understand about being in a hole," Michael said. "I've been trying to drag myself out of one for several years."

"I really need to know something else. Why did you really come back to the restaurant and ask about a place to stay in town?"

"Because I needed an excuse to talk to you."

"But why me?"

"I already told you. I like your smile."

She could see the grin forming on his face. "Michael, seriously, why me?"

He looked up at her and gave an exasperated sigh. "So, if I tell you, will you tell me more about your life? You have an advantage, because I've already spilled my guts to you."

She smiled. "Okay. I'll tell you my story later. So, why me?"

Now, Michael looked concerned. "You're going to think that this is either stupid or corny or weird or crazy—maybe all of them."

"I don't think so," she said calmly. "Try me."

"When I first met you, I thought that there was something special about you. I didn't know what it was exactly; it was just this feeling that I had. I could also tell that you were hurting, and your sadness struck a cord with me, because I've been living with pain and sadness for years. After I talked to Mona, I thought that you might need a hand to help pull you out of your hole, and I wanted to be there if you needed me."

Cassie sensed that there was something else—something vitally important—that he wasn't quite ready to tell her. She decided to back off and not press the issue right now, but she promised herself to find out what it was later.

They looked at each other with quizzical expressions, not really knowing what to say for the next few minutes, until the waitress shuffled back over to their table with the pizza. This broke the stalemate between them, as Michael commented on the delicious aroma and the hearty heaping of meat, cheese and tomato sauce on the deep dish crust.

He was pleasantly surprised when Cassie seemed to enjoy the pizza as much as he did, softly moaning with pleasure at each mouth-watering bite. He was also surprised when she consumed almost as much pizza as he did, despite her petite figure and the fact that he outweighed her by at least seventy pounds. It seemed that with every passing minute, he discovered something surprising and fascinating about this young woman.

While he sat there marveling at her, his eye caught a glimpse of the plasma TV and was instantly drawn to it because of something familiar. When he focused on the TV, he realized that he was looking at a picture of Cassie, while the news reporter commented on her brutal abduction while at home with her husband, Kyle McMurphy, a law enforcement officer in Nevada. According to the reporter, Cassie had been abducted after her husband was violently assaulted by a stranger at gunpoint. The man in question was a white male, five-eleven, weighing 190 pounds, with dark brown hair, brown eyes and a muscular physique. He was considered armed and dangerous.

Michael looked at Cassie and softly said, "Oh, shit!" He leaned forward and quietly told her not to turn around, so as not to draw attention to them. Then he told her to calmly excuse herself to go to the restroom, while he paid the bill. He would meet her back at the car.

Michael carefully looked around the room to see if anyone was paying attention to the TV or looking suspiciously at Cassie or him. Although the restaurant was bustling with customers, fortunately very few of them were paying attention to the TV. The few that were, did not seem at all interested in other customers.

Maybe they were safe, but Michael still felt beads of sweat break out on his forehead. He tried to remain calm and collected as he paid his bill in cash and slowly left the restaurant. He was intensely relieved when he saw Cassie standing beside the car, waiting for him.

As he drove out of the parking lot, Michael almost expected to find police cars forming a roadblock, preventing their exit. As they set out on I-80 again, he described what he had seen on the TV.

Cassie gasped with surprise, anxiety, and anger. "Damn him! I knew he would do something like this. I can't put you at risk like this any longer. I need to go to the authorities right now and tell them what really happened."

"That's exactly what he wants you to do. He'll use his law enforcement connections to get to you, claiming that you've been brainwashed by me and that I'm the leader of a violent cult or something like that. He'll try to make me conveniently disappear, and when he gets you alone, he'll beat you to death and blame it on me."

"So, what do we do?"

"I've been giving this a lot of thought, and I think we should avoid the police altogether. Let's go instead to a newspaper in Denver that will promise to keep your whereabouts a secret. Once we've established what's really going on here and have many people on our side, then we'll approach the police. We'll get this bastard. We just need to be cautious right now."

She looked at him with skepticism. "You know you're really putting yourself out on a limb here. They have you tagged as a dangerous criminal. What if they find us?"

"We're simply going to have to be more cautious. You can't be seen in public, so I'll be the one to get our food or anything else, for that matter. They don't know what I look like, just a poor description from a drunken man. We'll pass into Wyoming in another hour. The further we get from Nevada, the better our chances are of making it to Denver without being noticed."

She knew that there was no point in arguing with him, so she quietly watched the mountains and rugged terrain pass by and thought, *Why me? Why is he going through all of this for me?* As she pondered these questions, she noticed flashing lights in the rear-view mirror and realized that they were being tailed closely by a highway patrolman.

Jackson Hole, Wyoming: September 14, 12:30 p.m.

Clinton Wolfe's demeanor had significantly improved since yesterday. He was a man of action, not reaction. That's what he would constantly say to himself when he needed a morale boost. Politics was a never-ending roller coaster, but as long as he was in control—acting, not reacting—then he could prevail from any fall, no matter how steep.

After listening to the recording of the tapped phone conversation between Spencer Montgomery and Stephen Hanson, he was pleased with himself for deciding to tap phone lines at the Yellowstone Volcano

Observatory as of last night. If he had not had this foresight, then they would certainly be facing a leak of this "scientific catastrophic bullshit" to the press, which would likely endanger his political career.

He knew what his next move must be, and he used his secure line to call a number that he had used on only three other occasions, when he had identified certain individuals as threatening to his elected political office. He usually did not approve of violence, except maybe in the bedroom during recreational fun with his girlfriend, but these fucking scientists had been instructed to keep their mouths shut, and they just couldn't do it, so he would make sure that their mouths were shut permanently.

After he made the call, he felt a surge of power rush through his body, which gave him an instant erection. He was a man of action, and he was powerful, with the ability to snuff out another person's life with a simple phone call. No other individual would ever stand in his way, certainly not these short-sighted, pathetic assholes.

He became so stimulated by his power that he decided to call his girlfriend, Janelle, for some "afternoon delight." The use of his power was the strongest aphrodisiac that existed for him. It always stimulated his need to dominate someone in the bedroom. Today was going to be a much better day than yesterday.

Clinton heard Janelle's car driving up his circular driveway and instantly got another hard-on. He calmly waited for her on the couch, as she unlocked the front door.

When she entered the room, she was dressed in tight jeans, a short T-shirt revealing her taut stomach with a belly button ring, and a green bow in her long, blond hair to accent her large green eyes. She was twenty-four years old but dressed and talked more like a seventeen-year-old. She always seemed to have a look of need and deep hunger in her eyes.

For a man in his mid-fifties, she was quite an eyeful, but it was her innocent look, combined with her desire to be abused in the bedroom, that really turned him on.

As he rose from the couch, he said, "Come here, you stupid little bitch. What sick shit are you going to do for me today?"

Her eyes glimmered with desire as she approached him. "Anything you want."

Yellowstone National Park, Wyoming
September 14, 1:47 p.m.

Stephen had driven his Explorer to the Norris Basin area of the park. Now, he stood outside admiring the incredible beauty of this natural wonder. As he stared at the dramatic changes that had been quickly altering the landscape over the past few weeks, he was reminded that most people did not understand what this park represented. Most came to see the amazing hydrothermal features (geysers, hot springs, steam vents) or the wonderful wildlife. What the majority did not realize was that they were standing on top of a hidden volcano—one of the largest volcanoes in the world. In fact, if the public understood what was going on right now, they probably would want to get as far away from this area as possible.

His conversation with Spencer had been tremendously illuminating. He now had a handle on what was really happening here, and he was so frightened that he couldn't think clearly, so he had driven around in the park to try and clear his head. The impact of a super volcano eruption would be more devastating than anyone could imagine in their worst nightmare. But if Spencer was correct, what might truly occur would make a super volcano eruption seem trivial.

The longer he considered possible outcomes, the more he thought about his family, and the more frightened he became concerning their safety. He knew what he needed to do and what would be in their best interest; he just prayed that he had time to pull it off.

He picked up his cell phone and first tried calling his older brother, but there was no answer. He knew from what his wife had said that Michael was en route to his house in Denver and should be there later today. He would have to try calling another time, because he really wanted to talk with Michael privately before he reached Denver. Next, he called his younger brother, Mark, at his office in New York City and, after identifying himself, was transferred to a private line which was answered almost immediately.

"Stephen! God, it's great to hear from you. Kate tells me that you're in Yellowstone. How the hell are you doing?"

"Hey, little brother, how's the corporate world treating you?"

"Oh, you know how it is—same old crap day in and day out. I'll tell you, owning and running a company with hundreds of employees sounds great, but sometimes it's more like a glorified day care. If I have to listen to one more person whining about their co-workers, I think I'm going to pull my hair out."

"That's what managers are for. Why do you torture yourself with all of that?"

"You know me; that's how I've always run things. I think I just like to bitch about it."

Mark Hanson was by far the most financially successful of the three brothers. He was brilliant—a true prodigy—who had started developing computer software at the age of fourteen. By the time he was twenty-four, he had his own computer software company, which he eventually moved to New York City. By the time he was twenty-eight, his net worth exceeded 300 million and presently at the age of thirty, this had more than doubled. Even though he was undoubtedly one of the ultra-wealthy, Mark did not think of himself that way and continued to operate his business just as he did when he first dipped his toes into the business world.

"Mark, I have some very important things to tell you, and I'm not really sure where to start. I'll explain to you as best as I can what's going on, but I'll warn you that a lot of this is going to sound unbelievable."

Stephen outlined the facts for over an hour. Mark remained quiet throughout most of the talk, only speaking up a few times to ask questions about some confusing points. Despite his personal brilliance and phenomenal success, he had tremendous respect for both of his older brothers and listened carefully to everything that Stephen said.

When the discussion was over, Mark promised to leave for Denver the following morning after he wrapped up a few loose ends with his business.

Stephen paused for a moment and then with some emotion in his voice, he said, "I'm really bad at this, but I'm going to say it anyway. I'm so proud of you, little brother, and I hope you know I love you, even though I usually don't say it."

With tears in his eye, Mark said, "I love you too, big brother."

They both knew that they might never talk to one another again, but there was nothing left for them to say, other than goodbye.

Interstate 80 en route to Cheyenne, Wyoming
September 14, 2:25 p.m.

Michael looked in the rearview mirror, and his heart froze when he realized he was being tailed closely by a highway patrolman with lights flashing. He knew that it was suicide if he and Cassie were apprehended by the authorities right now, so he considered trying to outrun the patrolman. He thought about all options but was unable to come up with anything better than running from the authorities and hoping to make a lucky get-away. He was just about ready to floor the accelerator, when the patrolman changed lanes and went flying by him to pursue another motorist.

Michael let out a huge gasp of relief. "There's too damn many scary things that have happened in the last twenty-four hours—that TV in the restaurant, the gun to my head, you being thrown against the wall, the strange tremors that occurred three times, your car wreck, and now this. I didn't imagine that this bad luck streak would continue like this."

He would later reminisce about this statement and laugh at himself for not realizing how lucky they had been, and that the storm had not even begun. Both of them remained relatively quiet and content to listen to the radio for a while. Michael then noticed that the gas gauge showed less than a quarter tank, so he pulled into the first gas station they saw and started filling the tank.

Then he poked his head back in the car and said, "Hey, do you want anything from the convenience store? I'm getting a Coke."

"No, thank you," Cassie said, so he walked across the parking lot to the store. After he had paid for his purchase, he started to walk outside, but something made him freeze in his tracks.

Cassie was now standing outside of the vehicle on the far side of the car, and there were five men in black suits surrounding her. One of the men was holding her by the wrist, and Michael could see that each was armed with a handgun.

Without a word, he stepped back inside the store and grabbed a reel of high grade fishing line and a pocket knife from the shelf. With some urgency, he tied the end of the line to the knife and started toward the doorway, but two more men in dark suits stepped inside and looked at him ominously with handguns held at their sides. They motioned for him to come closer as they raised their guns in his direction, so Michael cautiously approached the two men with his right hand holding the knife behind his back.

"Get your fucking hand where we can see it right now!" growled one of the men.

Michael slowly pulled out the small pocket knife to show them, and the men both smiled when they saw the pathetic weapon. Michael shrugged his shoulders and walked toward them with his right arm at his side. When he was within five feet, he unexpectedly lurched forward and slammed the knife into the closest man's thigh and then switched directions, running down an aisle leading deeper into the store.

The second man pursued him, but didn't see Michael unreel the fishing line as he fled. The man's foot became entangled in the line as Michael turned the corner to avoid being shot. When he felt tension on the line, Michael yanked hard, which caused the first man to scream out in pain as the knife dug into his thigh. When the other man tripped and fell, Michael was on him almost immediately with a brutal kick to the face. Seconds later, both men were disarmed and lying unconscious without a single shot being fired.

A few minutes later, Cassie could see Michael walking toward the entourage that surrounded her on the far side of the car, and she was confused at his nonchalant manner. Without any hesitation, he walked around the front of the car so that he was within ten feet of the group. When he saw the gun pointed at Cassie's head, he raised his hands indicating surrender.

"I don't want any trouble. What do you want?"

"Are you Michael Hanson?" asked one of the men.

Instead of responding, Michael took a step closer to Cassie, looking intently into her eyes. When he did this, two of the men re-secured her arms, and all of them pointed their guns directly at Michael's head.

"What did your car do earlier that surprised you?" he asked.

At first, Cassie was thoroughly confused, but then she started to understand his cryptic meaning. Michael looked at the man who had asked him his name and said, "I think you have the wrong guy. Please let her go."

The men stared at him with intensity as he shrugged his shoulders and said, "Well, you can't say I didn't ask nicely."

Some of the intensity from the men was replaced with confusion as a truck on the other side of Michael's car started to pull out of the parking lot. Michael gave Cassie one more warning about what was going to transpire when he quickly glanced down at her feet. As he reached out to grab her hand, she took this cue and "jumped" just like her car had done yesterday.

The five men still looked confused when they were slammed face first to the ground by the high grade fishing line that Michael had managed to wrap around their feet while they were preoccupied with Cassie. They never expected him to subdue the men in the store without gunfire, and they certainly didn't expect him to climb under the truck and under his car to slide fishing line around their feet, and then secure the line to the trailer hitch of the truck.

A few of the men got off desperation shots from their guns, but none of them caused any damage. There was, however, significant screaming from the men over the damage that the concrete inflicted as the truck drove out of the parking lot.

When Michael and Cassie were both inside his car, he sped off as rapidly as he could. Cassie let out a big sigh of relief as she turned to him. "How could Kyle have found us so quickly?"

"I don't know, but I'm not so sure that greeting party was from Kyle. It reeks of some clandestine government agency. Plus, they asked for me not you—that's the part that really has my head spinning. Why would they want me, and how would they know my name?"

"Did you make any cell phone calls when I was asleep?"

"Only one; I tried calling my brother Stephen to ask him about these weird 'jumps' that we've been experiencing, but I had to leave a voice mail message."

Michael was quiet for a minute and then said, "I don't want to sound paranoid, but I was in the military for eleven years, and so I know that with current technology there are scary things they can do in just a few minutes. And depending on what authorities are involved, it would be simple for them to set up roadblocks to surround our location. Remember I'm a violent, armed kidnapper from what they're saying on the TV. This could become a huge manhunt very quickly. And whoever is after us, they apparently know that we're on I-80 heading east toward Cheyenne. To be safe, we need to take a detour that may take us an extra day to get to Denver, but it would ensure that we don't drive right into a trap."

Cassie nodded in agreement and immediately pulled out the map so that they could plot a course. Within a few minutes, they had decided to take a fairly long detour north toward Riverton and then east to Casper, Wyoming, where they would stay the night. The following morning, they would head south on I-25 to Cheyenne and then further south into Denver, arriving sometime Saturday afternoon.

Although neither of them understood exactly what or whom they were dealing with, it would soon prove to be every bit of the nightmare they had imagined. But for the present, they had the illusion of safety, so they each breathed a sigh of relief when they exited I-80 and started heading further north into Wyoming.

Michael decided to call his sister-in-law in Denver to let her know that he wouldn't be arriving until Saturday. When he called the number on his cell phone, someone answered after the second ring but remained quiet, and Michael could hear someone breathing softly into the phone.

He said, "Hello—Kate, is that you?"

No response.

"Hello—can you hear me? Do we have a bad connection?"

No response.

"Uh—I guess I'll hang up if you can't hear me." He then heard soft giggling and figured out what was going on.

"Sam, is that you?" More giggling.

Cassie looked confused. "I thought your brother's name was Stephen."

Michael held his hand over the phone and said, "I think it's my niece, Samantha. She's not saying anything—just giggling."

"Samantha—what a cute name."

"Oh, wait until you see her. She's adorable. She's only six, but as Kate says—quite a handful!"

Michael spoke into the phone. "Sam, this is your Uncle Michael. Can I talk with your mom or dad?" More giggling.

"Sweetie, this is very important. I need to talk to your mom or dad." Still more giggling.

Michael shrugged his shoulders, not knowing what to do.

"Here, let me try," said Cassie. Michael handed her the phone.

"Hi, Sam, my name is Cassie. I haven't met you yet, but I'm a friend of your Uncle Michael. We're coming to visit you, but we really need to talk to your mommy or daddy. Can you find them for us?"

With that, the giggling stopped. "Sure," said Samantha. "Wait a second."

Cassie beamed a big smile and handed the phone back to Michael, who looked perplexed, but said nothing.

After waiting for a minute, Kate answered the phone. "Hello? Is this Cassie?"

"Kate, this is Michael."

"Oh, Michael, sorry, I was confused. Sam told me this was someone named Cassie. This is a new thing. She really likes answering the phone, but about half of the time she just giggles and then hangs up."

"No problem. Listen, I've run into some complications with the trip, and I won't be there until Saturday afternoon. Also, just to warn you, I'm bringing a friend. Her name is Cassie—that's who Sam was talking to."

"That's great. We're looking so forward to seeing you, and I'd love to meet your friend."

"So, has Stephen returned from Yellowstone yet?"

"He was supposed to be back yesterday, but they keep extending his stay. I hope he's back this week. I know he really wants to see you. He also told me to have you call him, if I heard from you before he did. I'll give you the number for his direct line at the Volcano Observatory, in case you can't reach him on his cell phone."

"I actually have that number already. I tried calling him earlier but he didn't answer. I'll give him another call right after I hang up with you."

"One more thing, Michael, something weird is going on. I can sense it in his voice when he calls. I think it may have something to do with all of these strange ground uplifts that they're talking about on the news. I'm really worried about him."

"Kate, what ground uplifts have they been talking about?"

"According to the news, starting yesterday evening, there have been some huge areas of sudden ground uplifts in Nevada, Utah, Idaho, and Wyoming. Some of them have covered almost a thousand square miles."

"Holy shit—that's huge! That's what we must have experienced yesterday. Cassie wrecked her car because of it."

"Oh, they've been reporting thousands of minor accidents and a few hundred major ones with each of the uplifts."

"What do they think caused them, an earthquake?"

"That's the strange thing—they're not calling it an earthquake. They don't know what caused them, and they don't know if we'll have any more of them. If you're driving in one of those states, please be careful."

"I will. Don't worry about me—I'll be fine." He thanked her for the information, told her he was looking forward to seeing her and the kids, and said goodbye.

He and Cassie talked for a few minutes about the ground uplifts, and then he called Stephen's cell phone, but there was no answer. Next, he called the direct line at the Yellowstone Volcano Observatory, and a few seconds later Stephen answered the phone, "Hello?"

"Stephen, it's your big brother."

"Michael! I'm so glad you called."

"It's great to hear your voice, too."

"When are you getting into Denver?"

"Not until tomorrow—some things have come up, and I'm taking a detour to Casper, Wyoming this evening. That's not so far from where you are."

"If you're going to be in Casper, then I'll arrange a flight and meet you there this evening. I have to talk to you."

"Are you sure? Why don't you just talk to me in Denver?"

"I don't think I'll be able to make it. I can't explain everything right now, but I'll tell you this evening. Also, I really want—I need—to see you."

Michael could hear desperation in his voice and wanted to ask him what was wrong, but he decided to deal with that tonight. "Just want to let you know that I do have a friend with me, so you won't be surprised."

"A friend—do I know him?"

"No, you don't know *her.*"

"Are you serious—a girlfriend? What's her name?"

"Cassie—Cassie McMurphy."

"Well, tell Cassie that I'm looking forward to meeting her."

"I will." Michael told Stephen that he would meet him at the Natrona County International Airport just outside of Casper after they found a place to stay for the night, and he would keep his cell phone on so that they could coordinate when to meet.

After he said goodbye, Michael was very solemn and quiet, until he finally shared his concern with Cassie and talked to her about his family and his brothers. He had sensed more than just desperation in Stephen's voice. There was a distinct quality of fear, sadness, and hopelessness. The thing that bothered him the most was the fact that his brother was an eternal optimist—always positive and happy even when no one else was. It was one of the features that he loved and admired about his brother, and the darkness that he sensed in Stephen's mood had him extremely rattled.

Even after three hours of driving, Michael did not appear to have shaken off the dark cloud that engulfed his emotions. Stephen had been the most instrumental person in his recovery from depression over the past two years. If he had not been the eternal optimist and loving brother that he was, it's likely that Michael would still be lost in that vast wasteland of pain and despair. Michael would gladly give his life to help save his brother, but he was fearful that he would be powerless against whatever ominous forces had driven away Stephen's positive outlook.

Cassie was unsure how to break the spell that had descended over Michael. She knew that he was tremendously worried about his brother, and that in his entire life he had never met a more uplifting, wonderful person than Stephen. In an amazingly compassionate, unselfish, loving move, his brother had quit his job so that he could spend all of his time commuting to California and devoting his efforts toward pulling Michael out of his depression. Eventually, with Stephen's love and persistence, he began to slowly see some light remaining in the world.

Stephen's wife, Kate, and their two children, Christopher and Samantha, also had visited quite frequently on the weekends. The children were sympathetic with Michael's pain, but in their innocent way, they would ask him questions that the adults were afraid to voice, but would go straight to the heart of the problem. He adored his niece and nephew and never took offense at their probing questions. In fact, one of those questions triggered the beginning of his recovery. He remembered lying on the couch in the middle of a Saturday afternoon, when Stephen arrived at his house after picking Kate and the children up at the airport.

The front door opened, and Michael heard footsteps crossing the entryway into the family room. Most of the room stood in shadows, but a few slits of light slanted across the room from partially opened blinds from the adjoining kitchen window that overlooked the beautiful Sonoma scenery.

Samantha, who was only four at the time, was the first one to reach the couch, and she wrapped her little arms around Michael's neck, softly kissing the side of his head. She then put her mouth right next to his ear and whispered, "Uncle Michael, do you think that Aunt Amy and Tabby are watching you right now in heaven?"

It was a simple question, innocently posed, but it forced Michael to re-evaluate how he was handling his loss. What would Amy and Tabitha want him to be doing with his life right now? Certainly not what he had been doing for the past year.

Michael also had explained to Cassie that Stephen had given up an excellent, well paying job to spend time with his brother, which resulted in almost complete depletion of his bank accounts. But in typical fashion for his family, Mark, his youngest brother, set up a multi-million dollar trust for Stephen and his family.

Cassie had been very moved when she listened to Michael's account of his brothers' role in pulling him out of his depression, and tears glistened in her eyes when she thought about the devotion that they had for each other.

In an effort to lighten the mood, Cassie started commenting on the wonderful Wyoming scenery. There was dramatic geographic diversity and gorgeous countryside, with huge, soaring mountain ranges. There were vast, virtually untouched forests and rangelands, along with desolate deserts, plateaus, and pristine lakes. The state actually represented a great plateau broken by a number of major mountain ranges—the Absaroka, Owl Creek, Wind River, Wyoming, and Teton Ranges, as well as the Laramie, Medicine Bow, and Big Horn Mountains. It also boasted some of the most spectacular national parks in the U.S., including Grand Teton and Yellowstone, as well as Devil's Tower National Monument.

Despite Cassie's description of the landscape, Michael's disposition remained unchanged, so she hesitantly decided to bring up the one subject that she least wanted to talk about, but that might get him thinking about other things.

"Michael, I guess it's time for me to tell you my story." She let the impact of those words sink in, which resulted in the effect that she had hoped for.

Michael almost immediately looked over at her. "Are you sure you feel comfortable talking about it?"

She could see that the expression on his face had brightened considerably and the worry lines around his mouth and eyes had softened. "Honestly, it is very difficult for me to talk about some things in my life, but I do want to try—you've spilled your guts to me, and it's time for me to do the same."

"You know you don't have to. I don't want to lead you anywhere you don't want to go."

"I know that, but just let me do this while I still have the courage— or foolishness—to spit it out." She stopped talking briefly and finally took a deep breath, with a long, slow exhale, and started her account of the past thirty years.

Cassie was born in Reno, Nevada, twenty-nine years ago and when she was three, her parents moved to the small town of Turner, midway between the eastern and western borders of the state. Her father was a trucker, who was gone most of the time, and her mother was a beautiful, small town girl, who was swept off her feet when she was only eighteen by the rugged, good looks of her father. After living in Reno for a few years, her mother convinced her father to move to a small town, so they settled in Turner.

Cassie had a happy childhood, with a loving mother, although she did miss her father. She gained an appreciation for nature and art from her mother and began painting at the age of eight.

When Cassie was thirteen, her mother was diagnosed with ovarian cancer and died the next year. Her father was forced to change careers, so that he could stay home with his daughter. He began working as an all-purpose handyman in several surrounding towns. This allowed him to come home each evening, and he developed a close relationship with

Cassie. But that all changed when he remarried three years later, and his new wife cleverly dismantled their relationship.

When Cassie was nineteen, her father and stepmother moved to Las Vegas, and Cassie chose to stay in Turner, which disturbed her father, but not enough to make him stay. She worked multiple jobs, including babysitting, housekeeping, and waiting tables at several different restaurants, in an attempt to save money for college. All of her spare time was spent with her one love in life—painting.

She was twenty-one when she met Mona Thomas, a widower, and they rapidly developed a close relationship in just a few months. She eventually moved in with Mona, who became a loving mother figure for her, and they enjoyed relative happiness over the next few years. Mona wanted to send her to college, but Cassie had since decided that she would obtain a degree online to leave her more free time for her painting. She even had some art enthusiasts interested in her work but lacked the personal connections to get it into art galleries. She painted landscapes mostly, and all of her paintings had a distinctive melancholy quality to them.

Four years later, at the age of twenty-five, she met Kyle McMurphy at a chili cook-off in town. He was sheriff of Turner and, although he was known to have a stormy past, he was very charismatic and fun to be around. He also had a great fascination with her painting and, as time went by, he spent much of his time telling everyone he met how incredibly talented she was.

Kyle became her biggest advocate and, although she questioned the depth of her feelings for him, she appreciated his interest in her talent and felt that he was a close friend who had her best interests in mind. What she failed to see was that his interest in her paintings represented one of the many pathologic obsessions and addictions that ruled his life. He had grown up in an oppressive environment with an abusive father and a despondent, mousy mother, who ultimately committed suicide when he was fifteen.

A year after they met, Kyle convinced Cassie to marry him. Everything seemed fine for the first year of their marriage, but after a while, Kyle's obsession switched to alcohol and prescription narcotics, which he obtained from a doctor friend for his "lower back pain." At that time, Cassie tried to get help for him, but he became angry with her and threatened to burn all of her paintings if she didn't leave him alone.

It was one night in the August, two years ago, that the physical abuse began. Kyle came home late at night, barely able to walk after his latest drinking binge, and demanded sex from Cassie, which she refused.

"Don't you ever turn me down; I'm your husband, bitch!"

With that, he hit her in the face hard enough to blacken her left eye and cause a conjunctival hemorrhage, which filled her eye with blood. She spent the next three weeks telling everyone that she had slipped and hit her face on the counter, but Mona knew better.

Up to that point, Cassie had frequently visited Mona during the daytime, while Kyle was at work. But Kyle became convinced that Mona would try to break them up, so Cassie was forbidden to see her unless he was present. She resisted this at first, but one day when she came home, she saw that he had burned all of her paintings. He told her that he would burn Mona's house down with her in it, if Cassie ever visited her again. Following that day, the beatings became a regular occurrence, although he made sure that the bruises were in more concealed locations.

Cassie considered leaving on hundreds of occasions, but she had nowhere to go and was afraid that, if she left, he would do something horrible to Mona in retaliation. He had also sworn to track her down and slowly torture her to death when he found her. She saw no way out of her predicament and started feeling hopeless and lost. She had even given up painting, but then started working at Mama's Place to supplement their income, which was being drained by Kyle's drug, alcohol, and gambling addictions.

Until now, Michael listened to her story with fascination, but he started having some concern, because he could see tears welling up in her eyes and some pain forming on her lovely face. He decided to intervene at this point. "Cassie, I know something about facing pain from the past. Sometimes it's easier if you do it in small bites. Just like you told me yesterday, we can always talk about this later."

She immediately responded. "I've come this far, and I've got to get this all out now. It's been sitting on me like a 2,000-pound weight. And you deserve to know what kind of person you're sitting next to."

He could definitely hear more emotion in her voice now and was a little perplexed by her last statement. "I've known you for only a few days, but I think I know what kind of person you are."

"No, you don't!"

He pondered this for a few minutes, and then asked her to continue. Although tears were flowing at this point, she returned to her story. Kyle became increasingly hostile and violent over the past year, lashing out not only at Cassie, but at anyone else who crossed his path. In addition, she was scorned by other people in town for staying with such an abusive, drug-addicted, alcoholic husband. Many in town thought she was emotionally disturbed with a sick craving for abuse, was drug-addicted, or both. Eventually, she became ostracized by most people in town, giving her a greater sense of isolation and hopelessness.

Then, four months ago, Kyle returned home from his latest drug and alcohol binge and savagely raped Cassie while he was choking her, slapping her, and spitting on her at the same time. In his drunken state, he finished the attack by vomiting on her. Several weeks later, Cassie discovered that Kyle had impregnated her on that horrible evening, and she spent the next few weeks in her bedroom crying almost continuously.

Although Cassie knew she should love the baby, she was so horrified with the manner of its conception, that she couldn't bear the thought of being pregnant. The baby had not chosen to be conceived, but as hard as she tried, she couldn't disconnect her baby from the savagery of her rape.

Finally, two months ago, Kyle came home in another of his drug- and alcohol-induced rages. Instead of hiding from him, like she usually did, she confronted him with her disgust at the pathetic animal that he had become. Instantly, Kyle punched her ferociously in the abdomen. The following morning, she started bleeding and went to her obstetrician, who discovered that Cassie had miscarried.

At this point in her story, Cassie sobbed frequently, but she continued to push on with the painful tale. The anguish on her face became even more pronounced as she finally revealed her dark secret to Michael. "I knew he would probably attack me if I let him know how much he disgusted me, but I did it anyway."

By now, Cassie was so overwhelmed with pain that she had to stop every few words to catch her breath. "The baby died…because of me… It died because…I didn't love it…and I didn't want it…inside of me… and after it died…I was glad it was gone."

When she finished talking, she buried her face in her hands and sobbed miserably. Michael was so affected by Cassie bearing her soul to him, that he could literally feel her pain coursing through his body, as if someone had mercilessly pummeled him with a sledgehammer. He had never before experienced emotional transference, but this sensation was so real, so visceral, that he instantly knew that he was somehow getting a glimpse of the pain she was experiencing.

He could barely breathe or keep his hands on the steering wheel, so he quickly pulled the car onto the shoulder and parked the vehicle to let the intense sensation pass. When it dissipated, he sat there watching her sob uncontrollably, not knowing what to do.

Perhaps it was because he had experienced similar pain in the past or because of the bond that was forming between them or because he understood the kind of courage it took to reveal her story to him, but he chose that moment to do something completely unexpected. He leaned over and gently kissed Cassie on the side of her head and whispered, "I think I loved you when I first saw you, but now I love you more."

San Diego, California: September 14, 4:18 p.m.

Frank Donner sometimes wondered if he had made the correct choices in his life, especially in moments like this. His dedication to the military had frequently prevented him from taking part in family activities, especially after he had achieved the rank of general and had been put in charge of overseeing all weapons development. Despite his allegiance to the military, he still considered himself a good family man and felt truly saddened that he had missed so many family events.

His daughter was ecstatic when he arrived at his grandson's birthday party, probably because she expected him to cancel, as he had done so many times in the past. She walked up to him and threw her arms around him. "Dad, I'm so glad you came. Thank you for this—you've made my day!"

He even took part in the games, playing "hide-and-go-seek" and "pin the tail on the donkey" with the children. He ate way too much cake and ice cream, and by the time that the sun had set and the children had gone home to their own families, he was exhausted and retired to the family room of his daughter's house.

Frank had spent the remainder of the evening telling war stories to his grandson and talking with his daughter and son-in-law about current events. They had been talking for almost three hours, when Frank received a beep on his pager, which prompted him to check the mobile phone he had left in his car. He could see that he had missed fourteen calls from Black Diamond, all within the last thirty minutes. "Shit!" he muttered. "Can't they leave me alone for just one day?"

He called the facility and talked at length with several individuals. He then made six other phone calls. After he had finished, he walked back into his daughter's house and, with a troubled look on his face, told her that he was going to have to cut their visit short, because he needed to head back to the facility tonight.

His daughter thanked him again for coming to the party, although she was disappointed that he wasn't staying longer. He hugged her, kissed her on the forehead, and waved goodbye as he headed toward his car.

Frank was given the option of returning to the base via military helicopter, but he chose to drive back because Black Diamond was in the southern part of Nevada, so the drive from San Diego was only about five hours. He always enjoyed driving the Land Rover and, with the information he'd been given, he also needed time to think. He had never faced a situation like this before and, although he'd been given specific instructions on how this should be handled, he was unsure of what to do.

Despite his dogmatic military background, Frank was known to question higher authority and to struggle with moral dilemmas when certain decisions made by others conflicted with his own personal values. He had successfully kept his occasional dissention with authority a secret; otherwise, he would have jeopardized his military career many times. But he sensed that this time, things would be different in several ways. This was not merely a situation where he disagreed with decisions made by his superiors. If his hunch was correct, this could represent a major political cover-up. He was told that it involved a matter of national security, which he knew could be ridiculously exaggerated or even completely conjured up without any validity in order to hide something more ominous. In addition, it involved a friend that he cared about and respected highly—one of the best minds and finest men that he had ever known.

As Frank drove toward Nevada, a battle of epic proportions was being waged in his mind between his duty, allegiances, loyalty, and morals. He eventually let his mind wander into the past before his late wife succumbed to breast cancer, and he could hear her voice echoing familiar phrases. "Frank, you're a good man, and I know that you'll make the right decision. I believe in you—I always have."

God, how he wished he could talk to her right now! When she was alive, she had always been his moral barometer.

After contemplating all of this for the better part of an hour, he decided on a dangerous course of action that required him to first obtain more information. He made another call to Black Diamond and was eventually connected to one of the research labs, where he talked briefly with Spencer Montgomery and instructed him on the location and proper security codes to his personal office. He told Spencer to be there in fifteen minutes and then hung up.

When twenty minutes had passed, Frank called the secure phone located in his Black Diamond office, and Spencer answered, "What the hell is this all about, Frank?"

"Spencer, we've known each other for a long time. I consider you to be a close friend that I trust implicitly, and that is the only reason I'm making this call. I may live to regret this, but here it goes. Around noon today, you made a phone call to the Yellowstone Volcano Observatory and spoke with a geologist named Stephen Hanson."

The sudden surprise and guilt that quickly covered Spencer's face gave him the appearance of a child caught with his hand in the cookie jar. "That was a necessary phone call to a colleague," Spencer said defensively.

"I understand that you were talking to a colleague, but you gave him critical information about Black Diamond that you knew was classified."

"I had to share some information with him in order to try and figure out what in the devil is going on here, and I gave him very little information about this facility. You debriefed me thoroughly on what's classified, and I didn't violate that."

"I have a report indicating that you supplied detailed information concerning the location, security, construction, and purpose of the facility on that phone call."

"Frank, that's bullshit! You know me better than that. What a load of crap!"

"Calm down, Spencer. I believe you."

"What?"

"I said I believe you."

"Then why did you throw this shit at me?"

"I needed to see what you'd say; especially if I'm going to put my ass out on a limb here."

"What are you talking about?"

"Apparently, the phone line was tapped at the Yellowstone Volcano Observatory when you made the call to Hanson. They called me this evening to inform me that you had divulged classified information and were threatening national security. None of these people know that you're a personal friend of mine. They just think I consulted you because of your excellent reputation. I was given specific instructions from high levels in the government to personally eliminate the threat that you posed to national security."

"Eliminate the threat? Does that mean what I think it does?"

"Yes, I'm supposed to quietly make you disappear forever. Now, you understand the position I'm in here."

"Holy shit, Frank, why would they be doing this?"

"You must have said something that scared the crap out of some powerful people—something that they absolutely don't want to get out. Now, Spence, it's your turn to be honest and tell me what they're so scared about. I'm sure you know what it is."

"I was planning on talking to you when you returned to let you know what I had discovered."

"Well, you better go ahead and spill the beans to me now, because both of our lives are at stake here."

Over the phone, Spencer started softly chuckling, and Frank said, "What, in the name of God, could be funny about that?"

"Frank, our lives are not at stake here. What're at stake are the lives of the entire human population."

"The entire human population? Now, I really don't know what you're talking about."

"Do you remember when we were talking earlier about dinosaur extinction?"

"Sure—the huge asteroid that hit in the Yucatan sixty-five-million years ago."

"That was what we call an *extinction level event*—something that causes mass extinction of species. There have been many others that occurred throughout Earth's history; that was simply the last major extinction event. In fact, it wasn't even close to being the worst extinction in the past 500 million years."

"What was the worst one?"

"They call it the Great Dying. It occurred 251 million years ago at the boundary between the Permian and Triassic periods, and it resulted in the extinction of 96 percent of all marine species and seventy percent of land species, including plants, animals, and insects. The more recent extinction only killed fifty percent of all species, but did completely eliminate the dinosaurs. Most people don't realize it, but humans were pushed close to extinction 74,000 years ago, during a relatively minor extinction event, when a super volcano erupted in Indonesia."

"I'm still confused. Are you trying to tell me that you think another huge asteroid is about to hit?"

"No, Frank, I'm trying to tell you that I think something much, much worse is about to occur. For all of our sakes, let's hope I'm wrong."

Hwy 26 en route to Casper, Wyoming
September 14, 6:53 p.m.

After a few hours of riding, Cassie had completely recovered from the painful sojourn into her past. By revealing her inner pain and her deep secret, she was already feeling some positive effects from this catharsis. She felt that a mammoth weight had been lifted from her, almost giving her a sense of euphoria. Although she knew that more demons would have to be exorcised in the future, she thought that this might represent the beginning of her healing.

She was surprised at how her life seemed to have changed in the blink of an eye. Just yesterday afternoon, she was a depressed, beaten-down, abused woman who could see no way out of her prison-like hell hole. But today, her life had an entirely new direction and focus. She knew that she would never again let herself descend into the place that she had spent the last few years. She was the same woman, but with a completely different outlook on life.

Cassie was certain that Michael would have only contempt for her about her miscarriage. To say that she was surprised by his reaction to her story would have been the understatement of the century. After he affirmed her, she slowly stopped sobbing and crying and sat in stunned silence for the better part of an hour. At first, she was angry at him, because she thought that this must represent some type of manipulation. Then she realized that this didn't make any sense and wasn't consistent with anything that she had learned about him, and so she started searching for another solution to this mystery.

After contemplating this for almost two hours, she realized that she was going to have to ask some questions in order to unravel this enigma. But first, she needed some food to appease her growling stomach. She turned to Michael and spoke for the first time in several hours. "How far is it to Casper from here?"

Initially, he was surprised that she had finally spoken to him, and it took him a few seconds to clear his heavy thoughts. "I think it's about 45 miles, so we should be there in less than an hour."

"Can we stop at some place to grab a snack to eat before Casper?"

"Sure. I'll stop at the next place I see."

Michael was pleased that she had finally spoken but was still concerned about her reaction to his statement. He knew that he had spoken from the heart, but how could she ever accept this as truth? He'd known her for only one day—definitely a very intense twenty-four hours—but it had only been one day. Michael was certain that the feelings he revealed to her were real, but he was angry at himself for once again jumping the gun and overwhelming this woman with things that she didn't need to deal with right now. These were feelings that he knew she couldn't reciprocate, and so she would feel uncomfortable and under pressure if she did believe that his revelation was true. His intention was to let her know that he didn't despise her because of what had happened with her baby, but he had taken it too far and revealed too much.

They stopped at a small gas station/convenience store along the highway, and Michael bought some snacks. They decided to eat lightly, because they would be going to dinner in just a few hours with Stephen in Casper.

As they sat in the parking lot eating potato chips and chocolate chip cookies, Michael was thoroughly surprised when Cassie jumped directly into the fire with her questions. "I don't understand why you said that to me, earlier."

"I didn't think you would."

"So why did you say it?"

"Because there was a part of me that thought you needed to hear it at the time. You know by now that there's also an impulsive part of me that says things before I should. I almost ran my wife off after knowing her for only a week, when I told her things she wasn't ready to hear."

The look of confusion and puzzlement on Cassie's face increased as she wrinkled her brow and forehead. "Are you telling me that you really meant what you said?"

Michael looked away from her and remained silent for the next few minutes. He tried to think of a way out of this conundrum that he had created for himself but found no easy solution.

"Cassie, the story you told me was shocking and terribly sad. At the end, I could literally feel your pain as if it were mine. I've been living with the type of guilt that you described for a long time, and I know how horrible and oppressive it can become. It took me over two years to face my guilt the way that you faced yours today. I know you thought that I would look at you differently after hearing your story, and you're right—I do. Because of what I've been through, I know that it was tremendously courageous for you to share your story with me and face your pain and guilt. So now, I see you as not only a beautiful, kind, wonderful, young woman, but one that also possesses significant strength, courage, and fortitude."

"You see nothing wrong with what I did?"

"You were in a no-win situation. Both you and your unborn baby were victims. I don't think anyone would question the horror that you felt concerning the baby's conception. Maybe you would have eventually worked through that, but you didn't kill your baby—Kyle did. He didn't hit you in the stomach by accident. He's a sick, control freak, son-of-a-bitch who put that baby inside you and then took it away."

Now Cassie sat in silence, considering what he had just said. He actually thought that she was courageous and that she had strength. These were completely new concepts for her that she resisted at first, but then she started to consider the implications of what he was saying. He didn't see her as a damaged, pathetic loser that she had assumed most people thought she was. Instead, he saw something in her that was under the surface—something that she didn't even recognize about herself until now.

Then she began to consider what all of this meant concerning Michael. By listening to his stories, she knew he had a wonderful, caring family. She also knew that he was intelligent, very attractive, and had the heart of not only a good man, but also that of a loving husband, father, and protector. He was someone who would stand by friends and family to the very end. But maybe there was something even more amazing about him than all of these good qualities put together.

It was then that something they had talked about over lunch at the Italian restaurant started tickling her brain. When she had asked him, "Why me?" he had given her an answer, but she had known that he was leaving out something vitally important—something critical and meaningful for both of them—something that she suddenly had to know, because it might make some sense out of this entire perplexing situation.

She looked over at him with her large, beautiful, blue eyes and gave him such a beseeching and imploring stare that he could not have turned away from her even if he wanted to. He knew that this moment was a turning point for the two of them, and that this was a one-way ticket for better or worse.

"Michael, I need to know something. At lunch, I asked you a question and you answered me, but you didn't give me the complete answer. I'm going to ask again, but I need you to give me the full answer this time."

A preternatural silence descended over them in the car; everything in the background seemed to fade from view, but their faces became even more distinct and vivid. Cassie gave Michael another imploring look. "Why have you been doing all of this for me? Why are you subjecting yourself to all of this? With everything that we've been going through, the risks to you are huge. I know you're a good man, but you can't be doing all of this because of "love at first sight." There has to be something else."

He heard the pleading tone in her voice and knew that he was going to have to tell her everything or she wouldn't be satisfied with his answer. She sat expectantly while he summoned the courage to share his feelings and while he thought of how to explain everything to her. Finally, he looked directly into her lovely eyes and said, "What I told you at the restaurant was true. I did think there was something special about you the first time we met at Mama's Place. I honestly don't know if it was love at first sight or not. I just know that you stirred something inside of me that I thought had died when I lost my wife. I was also drawn to your pain and sadness because of my own experiences, and I wanted to help you even more after talking to Mona, but you're right—there's more that I didn't tell you."

Michael stopped and leaned back in his seat, but he didn't take his eyes off of Cassie, and then he continued with his answer. "I don't believe in mystics or fortune telling. I think we make our own fate by our personal decisions and the actions we choose to carry out. Despite my beliefs, I've had three premonitions in the past twenty-four hours, and two of the events occurred immediately after the premonition. Do you remember the strange tremor or jump that occurred at Mama's Place and also while we were driving to Mona's house?"

Cassie nodded.

"I sensed that each of these events was about to occur before they actually did. Now maybe it was just some physical phenomenon—like how animals can sense a storm before it occurs—but I still somehow sensed these things before they happened. I had a third premonition that was very different from the other two, and it hasn't yet come true. It was a much more intense and complex feeling—something that I could feel in a way that I can't explain, but that I know will come to pass as sure as I know the sun will rise tomorrow morning."

Cassie interrupted him at this point. "When did you feel this premonition?"

"I felt it when I went out to my car the first time I left Mama's Place and was looking back at you through the front window of the restaurant. It was a feeling that I just ignored at first, but then it became more intense, and I couldn't ignore it. I'm not sure I can explain this well enough, but I'll try."

Cassie could tell that this was uncomfortable for him, but she had to know what this premonition involved and so she remained quiet while he continued.

"It was a feeling that I'll need you in the near future, just like you needed me that night. It was a feeling that something is coming very soon that we were meant to go through together. Something that is so devastating and profound, that neither of us can make it through without each other."

With that, Michael shrugged his shoulders and sighed. "I know it sounds crazy—like someone who's lost their grip on reality. You can see why I didn't want to throw all of this at you before. But there's something else. I also had the strong sense with each of the jumps that occurred that they were also connected with this thing that is coming. I guess that's everything. I'm sure you must think I'm a lunatic."

Cassie smiled back at Michael, because she had finally discovered something that had put a few of the puzzle pieces together for her. She also had the sensation that Jack Frost had slithered inside of her spinal cord and was sending a chill down all of her nerve endings at once.

She looked directly into Michael's hazel eyes and said, "I don't think you're crazy. I had the exact same premonition about you, just after you left Mama's Place, as I was staring out the window at you sitting in your car."

Chapter 3

Catastrophism

Casper, Wyoming: September 14, 8:17 p.m.

Michael and Cassie eagerly awaited the arrival of Stephen Hanson at Natrona County International Airport, just outside of Casper. They sat in the upstairs lounge looking expectantly out the window and watching the passengers as they exited the plane one by one.

Michael finally spotted Stephen, and his excitement and fear increased dramatically, as Stephen approached the terminal. He loved his brother and wanted more than anything to spend time with him, but he was also frightened about seeing him, because he knew that the desperation and darkness he had detected during their previous phone call might still be present.

When Stephen entered the terminal, Michael approached him with his arms wide open, and the two brothers embraced. Cassie stood back to let the brothers share greetings and words of affection. Eventually, they turned to face Cassie, and Stephen walked right up to her and gave her a big hug. She could feel the warmth and kindness, which seemed to emanate from him and surround him with a distinctive aura. She could not detect any of the darkness that had rattled Michael when they were on the phone earlier.

They walked out to the parking lot and drove away in Michael's car. Within fifteen minutes, they had arrived at a small restaurant named Colby Jack's Steakhouse and Grill near historic downtown Casper and were seated in a comfortable dark leather booth in the corner. A young blond waitress with a plain face but an infectious, sweet smile took their drink order and left them to peruse the menu.

The lighting, dark mahogany paneling, and beautiful rustic oak floors gave the restaurant a sense of comfort and warmth. Several large chandeliers were adorned with hundreds of antlers that had been fused together in an interesting pattern. One had the feeling of being transported back to the turn of the century, when Casper was a relatively young town on the banks of the North Platte River and served as an outpost for all major westward trails, including the Oregon Trail and the Pony Express Trail. Somehow Colby Jack's had captured the feeling of excitement and adventure that characterized the old west. The long wooden bar was littered with historic memorabilia, and the wooden bar stools were all hand-carved with engravings of different Wyoming wildlife.

Stephen looked across the booth at Cassie and Michael. "Great place! How did you hear about it?"

"We checked into the hotel first—we're staying at the Casper Private Suites on the River," said Michael. "One of the front desk clerks recommended this place and told me that it wasn't terribly busy, so we would have plenty of privacy to talk. She also said that the steaks here are great, especially the buffalo rib-eye. I knew that you loved good steaks, so here we are."

"I can't tell you how good it is to see you, Michael. And what a pleasant surprise that you have such a lovely friend with you." Cassie smiled and started to blush upon hearing Stephen's compliment.

"So, how did you two meet?" Cassie and Michael looked at each other, and Stephen could sense some embarrassment from them, so he decided to change the subject.

"Oh, that's okay. We'll talk about it later if you want. I'm starving, and a good steak with a cold beer sounds heavenly."

Cassie noticed that Stephen had a charm about him that was also present in Michael, and she wondered if all of the Hanson brothers shared this very appealing trait. He was a few inches taller than Michael, with a well-trimmed goatee and a ruddy complexion consistent with an outdoor lifestyle. She could see how this man could brighten a room with his outgoing personality and his easygoing, positive manner.

The waitress brought draft beer in frosted mugs and took their food order. For the first few minutes, the brothers talked lightly about Kate and the children, but as time went on, Cassie could detect anxiety and a sense of urgency in things that Stephen said, as he commented several times on how long the food order was taking.

When their order arrived, he ate quickly with little enjoyment despite the buffalo rib-eye, and it was clear that some of the darkness that Michael had detected over the phone had now returned, and that Stephen was unable to focus on anything but what he needed to tell his brother.

Although he dreaded bringing it up, Michael also sensed Stephen's anxiety and knew it was time to find out why he was so desperate to meet with him this evening. Sometimes enlightenment is a painful process, especially when you must face something unpleasant. What Cassie and Michael would soon discover was that all previous enlightenment would pale in comparison to what they were about to learn. From that night forward, they would come to understand that all past bloody battles, wars, exterminations, persecutions, famines, plagues, natural disasters, and other horrific tribulations that humans had faced since they first appeared on Earth were collectively minor inconveniences compared to what they were about to face. They would come to think of everything in terms of whether it was before Casper (B.C.) or after Casper (A.C.), because nothing would ever be the same after their enlightenment.

Michael took a large swig of beer and reluctantly started the inevitable conversation. "Stephen, I think it's time that we talked about why you needed to see me so urgently—why you couldn't wait until we met in Denver."

An expression crossed Stephen's face, as if a dark, unholy eclipse had just descended upon him. Instead of addressing Michael's inquiry, he responded with something so unexpected that Michael and Cassie were both utterly stunned. He looked directly at Cassie with a glare in his eyes that conveyed extreme importance and gravity.

"I don't need to know how you two met, and I don't need to know how long you've known each other, but I need to know this, Cassie. Do you love Michael, and are you willing to lay your life down for him or his family, if necessary, because otherwise you shouldn't be here."

She was so shocked by his question that she let the beer mug slip from her hand and land with a thud on the table. Foam spilled over the edges of the mug, but no one at the table even noticed.

Michael was the first to respond. "Stephen, I don't think that this is the right time to discuss…"

"Oh, it's absolutely the right time. There has never been a time in the history of mankind that this question was more crucial than right now!"

Michael had rarely ever heard his brother raise his voice or purposely interrupt someone during a conversation before, but it was the intensity with which each word sprang from his mouth that let Michael know how serious he was about this seemingly inappropriate, bizarre question.

There was a definite sense at the table that a fight between the brothers was imminent, when Cassie reached over to Michael, took his hand gently in hers, and said to Stephen, "The answer to your question is "yes.""

This was the second time this evening that Cassie had shocked him with something she had said. Now, he stared at her with amazement and confusion that Stephen instantly recognized. He softened his expression and smiled knowingly at his brother and the fascinating woman holding his hand.

Stephen then told them that he would wait until they were back at the hotel room, before he started discussing the critical details of what was happening. He had some charts and maps to show them; and he didn't feel comfortable discussing certain issues in public.

Just before they were to leave, Cassie excused herself to the restroom, leaving the two brothers alone at the table.

"Hey, I'm really sorry for putting Cassie on the spot like that," Stephen said, "but you'll understand after I've explained everything to both of you. By the way, she's not only gorgeous, but she also seems to be one incredible woman."

"You're right—she's something special."

Once Cassie returned to the table, Michael paid for the bill, and they headed to the parking lot. Although it was just after nine o'clock, they could still see the outline of Casper Mountain rising 3,000 feet above the silhouette of lights in the city. It was a very short drive to the Casper Private Suites on the banks of the North Platte River. Michael had reserved a two-bedroom bungalow that had a view of the river from its back door.

Once they arrived at the room, Stephen started arranging his charts, maps, and graphs in order to assist him in his explanation. Cassie started brewing some coffee, because they expected it to be a very long night. The beer had caused her to have some minor drowsiness, so she took a short walk down by the river, and the brisk wind quickly restored her alertness.

By the time she had finished her walk, the two men were sitting on the couch in the living area with the maps and charts on the coffee table in front of them. She sat down between the two brothers, and Stephen began to explain what he had come to tell them.

Interstate 15 en route to Black Diamond Military Base, Nevada
September 14, 9:34 p.m.

Frank knew that he would need to act quickly and use his authority in every way possible if he was to have a prayer in hell of saving Spencer's life. After what Spencer had shared with him about upcoming events, he wasn't sure that it made sense to try and save anyone's life anymore; but, when truly faced with the dark finality of oblivion, the only things that really mattered were friends and family. So, Frank would do everything within his power to help his friend, even if it meant betraying military command and putting himself at significant risk.

First, he called Black Diamond and gave instructions to take Spencer Montgomery into custody immediately and begin procedures to have him taken to the surface and ultimately out of the facility. He explained to several military officers that he would meet them at the surface in three hours and, because of the national security issues involved, he would personally escort Spencer to a detention facility for further interrogation.

He detected substantial resistance from the officers despite his superior rank, which could only mean that they had alternative orders from an even higher authority. He tried to convince them of the importance of getting Spencer out of the facility before any more damage to national security and military intelligence occurred. He promised them that he would take full responsibility for the decision to relocate Spencer, but he could still tell that they were skeptical.

Nevertheless, he told them to start the long process of moving Spencer to the surface, and he would meet them in the main loading dock of Level 1. There, they would get confirmation of the relocation plan for Spencer from a higher authority in the Department of Defense. He assured them that there would be no objections to this plan, but that he would make some phone calls right now to further facilitate this by the time he reached the base.

When he had concluded his phone call, he tried to increase his speed, because he realized the importance of arriving at Level 1, prior to Spencer's ascent with military personnel. Frank had the distinct impression that he was driving directly into a hornet's nest, but he knew that he had no choice—the stage was set, and Act One was about to start with or without him.

Two hours and twenty-five minutes later, Frank arrived at the facility and within ten minutes, he was sitting in his Range Rover in the Level 1 loading dock, nervously tapping his fingers on the dashboard of the car. He wasn't sure how all of this would go down, but he knew it wouldn't be a cakewalk. Somehow Frank had to convince the personnel escorting Spencer to release him into his custody, despite alternate directives given by some powerful people who were still unknown to him.

If they suspected his true motives, both he and Spencer would be seen as traitors and might both be executed on the spot. He was not afraid to die—he had faced death many times before, and a part of him was even looking forward to being reunited with his departed wife. But he had a strong feeling that Spencer would be needed elsewhere and wasn't meant to die here.

As he sat there waiting for the inevitable confrontation, words from his conversation with Spencer several hours earlier started flickering through his mind: *Extinction level event ... massive geological upheaval... super volcano eruption...nuclear winter ... domino theory ... catastrophic climate change ... unprecedented death and destruction...domino theory... mega tsunami ... global geo-physical disaster ... domino theory...domino theory...*

The term "domino theory" seemed to push everything else out of his mind, until it was the only thing that he could focus on. He wasn't sure he really understood what this referred to, because his conversation with Spencer was cut short due to poor cell phone reception. However, he knew that Spencer became very excited and agitated when he mentioned the term.

Then, without warning, several images popped into his head with such clarity that he lost track of his surroundings and was completely immersed in the images imprinted in his brain. In the most pervasive image, he could see a massive field of human bodies, perhaps millions, with much of their flesh charred and black, and the remainder covered with yellow pustules surrounded by reddish-brown, oozing, rotting tissue. He could see men, women, and children with their bodies mangled and their limbs sticking out in impossible directions, with their underlying skeletal structure reduced to Silly Putty by unimaginably destructive forces. The image was so vivid and disturbing that he was able to smell the vile, putrid stench, as if he were standing in the midst of the decaying corpses.

As the horrifying image was mercifully fading from his mind's eye, he noticed a group of six men, five dressed in military attire, walking across the large loading dock toward his car. To his dismay, he noticed that the leader was Colonel Dax Colquitt, who happened to be one of the biggest hard-ass, pain-in-the-butt military men that Frank had ever met—and there were a lot of hard-asses in the military.

Shit! Frank muttered to himself, as he opened his car door. Frank had hoped that Hernandez or Bishop, whom he had spoken to on the phone earlier, would be the commanding officer meeting him. Dax was frequently referred to as "Pulpit" Colquitt, because of the ranting, raving fanaticism that he would conjure up concerning every project he was ever involved with. The four soldiers following Colonel Colquitt and Spencer were all armed with assault rifles and looked as if they were pumped up on adrenaline and ready for action.

As Frank approached the group, he noticed that Dax held a large cigar in his mouth and had a crooked grin on his deeply creased face, with his hard, black eyes in a perpetual squint despite being indoors. Spencer was standing behind him with a look of caution and uncertainty on his face.

Dax was the first to speak, as he belted out words with his harsh, raspy voice when the men were within a few yards of each other. "Frank, what the fuck is this all about?"

"It's nice to see you too, Dax. I see you still have your charming personality. Haven't you talked with Hernandez or Bishop?"

"Of course, I talked with them. But I still don't understand what the fuck you think you're doing!"

"What I'm doing is taking a man out of the facility to avoid any further breach of security at Black Diamond."

"And you don't think we can control security breaches by locking his fucking ass up for the remainder of his stay?"

"I think it's preferable for him to be out of the facility ASAP."

"Well, I disagree and so do some higher ups in the Department of Defense."

Frank felt his heart sink because although he was in charge of the facility, his decisions could be superseded by some high-ranking officials in the U.S. government. Still, he decided to press the issue further, "Have you talked with them personally?"

"No, but Hernandez did."

"Well, I got off the phone with the Pentagon about twenty minutes ago, and they agreed with the plan for him to leave the facility in my custody." Frank could feel beads of sweat forming on his forehead."

"Who the fuck did you talk to?"

"Are you telling me that you think I'm lying?"

"Just tell me who the fuck you talked to."

"I talked to several people—the last one was Miles Beckham, who told me to get Spencer Montgomery out of Black Diamond immediately."

"Goddamit, Frank! Why are you feeding me this crock of shit?"

Fortunately, Frank was familiar with Colonel Colquitt's technique of discovering the truth, which usually consisted of accusing everyone of lying to him.

With Dax glowering at him, Frank calmly responded in a smooth, relaxed tone of voice, "Look, Dax, this is very simple. I'm in charge of this facility, and I made a decision. I even confirmed that decision with officials in the D.O.D. I've talked with them personally, but you haven't. Now quit giving me crap, and let's get on with our day."

Colonel Colquitt squinted even further, spit out his cigar, and stared viciously at Frank, with evidence of dark, malevolent thoughts brooding inside of him. Almost a minute passed without a word being exchanged, as the two men stared, unblinking, at each other.

Although remaining calm, Frank had tensed the muscles in his face and had a look of determination in his eyes, with a hint of malice as if to say, *you fuck with me Dax, and I'll make your life a living hell!*

When Dax finally broke his stare and looked away, Frank knew he had succeeded. "Alright, Frank, let me make a phone call to confirm this bullshit!"

Dax turned abruptly to walk back to the command center on Level 1, leaving Spencer staring at Frank with a peculiar look on his face. The other four men stepped forward so that they were within a few feet of Spencer, as the sound of Colonel Colquitt's footsteps reverberated in the large chamber.

After five minutes had passed, Frank reached into his pocket and pulled out his cell phone. "Let's get this show on the road." Because the huge door and ramp into the facility were open, cell phone reception was still possible. He punched in a number, waited for a few seconds, and then started talking when the call was answered.

"Hey, Dax, so what's the verdict? Do you believe me now? …Okay, Okay. I know you just had to confirm it for yourself. Can we go ahead and leave? …Okay. I'll tell them. Thanks."

With that, Frank turned to face the four soldiers and said, "Colonel Colquitt told me to pass orders on to Sergeant Boles and company that we're cleared to leave."

He motioned to Spencer and said, "Come with me, Dr. Montgomery."

As both Frank and Spencer started toward the Range Rover, one of the soldiers stepped forward, identified himself as Sergeant Boles, and said, "Uh, sir, you can't leave yet. Not until Colonel Colquitt returns."

Frank ignored him and kept walking.

"General Donner, sir. Please stop moving toward the vehicle." This, Boles said with more authority and urgency.

Frank continued to ignore him.

"General Donner!"

Frank could hear the ominous sound of safeties on the assault rifles clicking to the off position. He and Spencer were only ten feet from the Rover and about twenty-five feet from the soldiers. Frank stopped, turned to face Boles, and said, "What in the hell are you doing, soldier?"

"Sir, I can't let you leave until Colonel Colquitt is back."

"He just told me that I could leave, and that's exactly what I'm going to do. If you want to challenge my authority, then you'll have to shoot me in the back!" With that, Frank spun around and continued to the car with Spencer.

"Sir, please, sir!" Frank could hear panic in the soldier's voice. As he and Spencer climbed into the Range Rover, Frank gave a salute to the confused soldiers wielding the assault rifles. He could see that Spencer was also sweating profusely and had a look of extreme anxiety on his face.

When the doors were closed, Spencer said, "How can you stay so damned calm? We have four nervous soldiers with assault rifles breathing down our necks!"

"Relax, Spence. We're going to be okay."

Just then, they heard five loud, rapid pneumatic "pops" followed by a continuous mechanical buzzing noise, as if an enormous insect had just flown inside the large room. "Oh shit!" said Frank. "Now would be a good time to panic—that was the auto-tracking mechanism being engaged for one of the 125mm anti-tank cannons!"

Frank quickly jammed the key in the ignition, started the car, and slammed his foot on the accelerator, causing the Rover to shoot up the loading dock ramp. Without warning, a massive impact lifted the Rover off of the ground and almost caused it to flip. Instead, it landed on two tires and balanced precariously until the weight of the vehicle pulled the other two tires down to the ground.

Inside the vehicle, Frank and Spencer were recovering from the disorientation and pain of the impact. At first, Frank thought that an explosive had detonated near the car—perhaps a grenade. But then he realized that that they had been hit by one of the massive shells from the 125mm cannon.

As pain seared through his left arm and shoulder like a red, hot branding iron, he grasped the steering wheel with his right hand and tried to guide it up the ramp, while flooring the gas pedal. Pain was also tearing into his left ribcage, and he found it difficult to breathe. He glanced over at Spencer and noticed that blood was seeping out of his left ear, and that Spencer was clearly dazed and looking like he might pass out.

Once the Rover started moving forward rapidly, Frank was tremendously thankful that the tires appeared to be intact, despite the horrific impact. As they moved up the ramp at an increasing speed, another impact shook the vehicle, but did no damage as the shell missed the car and hit the nearby wall instead. By that time, the Range Rover had reached the surface and barreled out into the moonlit Nevada desert.

As they approached the front gate of the razor wire perimeter fence, Frank accelerated to eighty miles an hour, and they easily leveled the gate as they blasted through the opening. They met no resistance whatsoever from the guard, who was apparently unaware of this sudden turn of events.

The highway was dimly lit, but Frank pushed the car as hard as he safely could for the next five miles. Finally, he took inventory of the damage and noticed that the entire back third of the vehicle was missing, having disintegrated with the first round from the cannon. He had not noticed the increased noisiness created by the huge opening, because his ears were ringing so intensely that he was having a difficult time hearing anything. This started to slowly dissipate, and the ringing was replaced by a dull throbbing in his ears.

Spencer looked over at Frank, after clearing some of the fogginess from his head, and said, "That was one of the craziest fucking things I've ever seen anybody do. What possessed you to take a risk like that with your own life, not to mention ruining your military career?"

Frank shrugged his shoulders. "I just figured that with what you think might be going on, we need you alive to help us through the worst of it. Besides, I hate those crooked ass-hole politicians that I'm sure are behind the fabricated story about you jeopardizing our national security."

"Well, I guess I owe you one. Thanks."

"Don't thank me yet. When I told you this is the most secure military installation in the country, I wasn't just talking about the impenetrable underground monstrosity. We're in a shit load of trouble, because I'm sure they're tracking us with satellite surveillance, and I know that within another five minutes they'll have military helicopters in the air bearing down on us rapidly. The razor wire fence we blasted through means nothing. There's an *invisible* perimeter around Black Diamond encompassing about a hundred square miles with military personnel stationed every half mile at that perimeter. I'm sure they already have hundreds of soldiers closing in on us as we speak."

"So, how the hell do we get out of here?"

"There's only one possible way, and it's a long shot—but it's our only chance. That's where I'm driving now."

"Who did you call on your cell phone? I know you didn't call Colquitt."

"I just called my private office and talked into my voice mail. Thank goodness I remembered the name of Sergeant Boles. I knew I had to plant the seed of doubt in his mind or we were going to get our asses riddled with bullets. Shit! My left arm hurts like a son of a bitch!"

Frank pushed through his apparent pain for another four miles and then slowed the vehicle to exit the highway onto a small paved side road that was barely visible amidst the surrounding desert and rocks. Within a few minutes, they had arrived at an old, abandoned army bunker that was partially built into the side of a huge rock outcropping that marked the bottom of a mountainside.

"Hey, Spence, I need you to take over and drive us into this bunker. I'm having a hard time concentrating with my arm and shoulder feeling like this."

After he had opened a large, metal sliding door, Spencer returned to the Rover and traded seats with Frank, who then unbuttoned his shirt to get a better look at his injury. From where he was sitting, Spencer could see the large bruise covering most of Frank's left upper arm and shoulder, and he could also see exposed splinters of bone, with torn flesh surrounding it, just above Frank's left elbow.

"Oh, my God, Frank! That looks bad!"

"Well, it doesn't feel too good—but I'll live."

"We need to get you to a hospital."

"Let's just concentrate on surviving the next few hours, and then we'll worry about that."

As they drove into the bunker, Frank explained the plan to Spencer. "They can track wherever we go with satellite surveillance, but they can't see us when we're underground. There's also no way of getting past the invisible perimeter around Black Diamond, unless we bypass it by traveling underground. This bunker leads into a series of tunnels in the mountainside that were constructed during the Cold War when the

U.S. was paranoid about a possible nuclear strike from the Soviet Union. Some of the tunnels lead to a different exit route from the mountain away from the bunker. If we can find one of these tunnels, then we can exit in a location past the perimeter that they won't be expecting. By the time they figure out what we've done, we'll be long gone."

"How did you know this place existed?"

"I stumbled across it when I was out driving around one day. Then I did some research and found out more details about the bunker from military archives. The only thing I didn't do was to explore the tunnels, so let's hope that the archives were accurate, and that the tunnels haven't collapsed over time."

"Do you think that Colquitt or anyone else at Black Diamond knew about this place?"

"They do now. I'm almost certain they tracked us here with the satellite."

Colonel Colquitt looked at the large LCD video screen on the wall in the Level 1 command center. The mainframe computer had established a connection with the satellite and was now controlling the video display images, which consisted of side by side night-vision and infrared projections of the Nevada desert just outside the old military bunker.

The computer technician pointed to the building on the screen and said, "They've gone inside this bunker—only nine miles from Black Diamond—about a mile inside the perimeter."

"How much do we know about this goddamn bunker?" Colquitt asked.

All five of the men seated in the room remained quiet, but the only woman, Dawn Beeson, stood up and said, "We need to look up the bunker in military archives, so we know better what we're dealing with. It looks like the bunker is built into surrounding rock, and there may be an extensive network that could give them an escape route. If you block off the bunker, then we can flush them out at the other end. I can have all of that for you in thirty minutes."

Colquitt looked at Dawn admiringly. He knew how bright she was, and that was why she was part of his team, but he still had an issue with women in the military, so he had to bite his lip and ignore her gender.

"Okay," said Colquitt. "Get on the radio, contact the perimeter station closest to the bunker, and tell them I want ten soldiers at that bunker entrance in five minutes to seal these fuckers off. Dawn, you get your ass working on the archives immediately."

Ten minutes later, Colonel Colquitt was in one of the private offices on Level 1 with the door shut and locked, making a phone call on a secure line to Senator Clinton Wolfe.

"Clinton, it's me. We ran into some problems at Black Diamond. Spencer Montgomery got out of the facility, because Frank Donner decided to save his sorry ass and made up some bullshit about getting a go-ahead from the Pentagon."

"What kind of fucking morons do you have down there, Dax? Why did you even listen to the bastard?"

"He's a goddamn general for Christ's sake! I had to check out what he said. I'm *not* going to ignore orders from the fucking Pentagon, no matter how much money you pay me! After I went to check it out, he pulled rank on my men, and they freaked out."

"Can you put a lid on this bullshit?"

"We're working on it. We should have the fuckers within an hour."

"Dax, I want you to understand this very clearly. I don't want you to take them into custody. That will lead to too many questions, and this crazy destruction theory crap is bound to come out. I'm already getting way too much heat from the USGS. You need to personally make sure that both of them take a bullet in the head!"

Spencer knew that their odds of getting away alive was already slim but were decreasing with every minute. Frank's pain was steadily increasing with the inevitable swelling at the fracture site. Fortunately, there was little bleeding, but the pain alone was becoming incapacitating for him. The tunnels were easily large enough for the Range Rover, but they were pitch black and even with the headlights on, visibility was very limited. Several times, Spencer had to stop and move debris out of the way so that the Rover could pass. To make matters worse, the pain in Spencer's left ear was now substantial, and he was certain that he had sustained a ruptured eardrum from the blast.

The tunnels were similar to a maze, and there was no logical way to figure out the correct way to go. Spencer had already experienced a dead-end twice, which forced him to retrace his route and waste valuable time. Whenever he entered a tunnel that was descending, he would reach a dead end, so he decided to follow only tunnels that were level or ascending. Frank was of no help, because he had closed his eyes, and was utilizing all of his resources just to deal with the pain.

Dawn Beeson found Colonel Colquitt sitting in the lounge puffing on a cigar and quickly approached him with her findings. Before she could tell him anything, he escorted her to a private office, offered her a seat, and then locked the door.

"Colonel, I think I know where they might be heading, based on the schematics of proposed tunnels that were supposedly dug decades ago and connect the bunker with the mountainside. Now, I'm not even sure that all of these tunnels exist, but if they do, there are only a few places that they can exit, which are all on the opposite side of the mountain. I've drawn you a map that outlines the most likely route they will take, as well as the probable end point."

Dax gave her a hawkish grin. "Excellent work. This is very important for you to understand, so listen carefully. You are *not* to share this information with anyone else—this is a very sensitive issue, and I've been asked to take care of it myself. Do you understand?"

She nodded, and they left the office.

One of the tunnels seemed to be different from the rest; it had a steeper grade of ascent, and the walls appeared cleaner and smoother than the rough, irregular walls in most of the tunnels. For lack of any better criteria, Spencer decided to try his luck on this slightly different type of tunnel and followed it for a long distance, perhaps a mile and a half, before it split into two smaller tunnels. He arbitrarily chose the one on the right and continued his journey into the unknown reaches of the mountain.

Spencer had unnerving claustrophobia that was increasing the deeper they drove into the labyrinth. He had the distinct impression that the tunnels were becoming narrower, which added to his anxiety when he started considering the possibility that they might become impassable by car, yet there was no flashlight to use for travel on foot. He was also quite certain that Frank was in no condition to hike, and he knew he would be unable to carry or support Frank on foot for any significant distance.

The bleakness of their situation reached an even more ominous pitch when one of the tunnels narrowed to within two feet of the car on either side, and Spencer heard a few scraping sounds as the rock walls briefly contacted the side of the car in some irregular areas. He now had to decide if he should back up and try a different tunnel or take a chance that this tunnel would narrow further and possibly trap them in their vehicle.

Finally, he decided to get Frank's opinion before he was too incapacitated to respond. "Can you talk to me for a second?"

Frank grunted and shuddered in pain. "What do you need?"

"From your research, do you know why they would have narrowed these tunnels so that they were impassable in a vehicle?"

Frank remained still and quiet, slowly taking deep breaths, as if to muster up enough energy to talk. "I know that a few tunnels lead up to some overlooks on the other side of the mountain. These probably weren't meant for transport or storage, but ventilation." With that, Frank gave another grunt and closed his eyes again.

"Shit! I don't know what to do. Are you sure you don't have a flashlight in the car?"

"I do have one, but the batteries are dead."

Spencer felt trapped, disoriented, and confused, but he knew he had to put it together for both of their sakes. He decided to get out of the car and look for any clues that would help him decide what to do. He opened the door, leaving the headlights on high beam, and walked fifty feet down the tunnel, before he stopped and leaned against the rock wall. There was no question that the tunnel was even narrower here, probably impassable for the Rover.

As he took his hand away from the rock, he noticed some moisture on his fingertips and considered the implication of this for a second. Did this mean that they were in one of the ventilation tunnels? That was when he heard a very faint whisper of wind traversing the tunnel. Suddenly a glimmer of hope started forming in Spencer's thoughts. He walked another 200 feet further and felt a soft, cold breeze wafting toward him from the distant recesses of the tunnel.

He knew he might regret it, especially given Frank's condition, but he decided to abandon the Range Rover. It had driven them several miles into the mountain but was now useless for the final trek out, which he was praying would be a short one. Spencer was sure that they could use Frank's cell phone to call for help, but only after they had exited the tunnel. Right now, he was angry at himself for not thinking to call someone before they had entered the maze of mountain tunnels.

Spencer helped Frank out of the car and realized that they wouldn't make it very far with the degree of pain that Frank was experiencing. With every step, the agony on his face became more pronounced and, for some reason, his breathing was increasingly labored. They stopped after a few hundred yards, before the car headlights had completely faded in the tunnel.

Spencer unbuttoned Frank's shirt and looked at his chest. The entire left side was covered with a massive black bruise extending up to his neck and down to his waist. When he applied pressure to the skin, he could feel the crunching of shattered ribs, as well as air bubbles that had found their way through the shredded flesh of Frank's chest wall.

"Dammit, Frank, why didn't you tell me that your chest was in such bad shape?"

"What difference would it have made?"

"Because I would have driven to the perimeter and had them take you to the hospital instead of this spelunking crap that we're doing."

"Then they would have thrown you in a military prison or holding cell and made you conveniently disappear—forever. I'm dead either way, but this way, at least you have a chance to make it."

Spencer already had tremendous respect and admiration for Frank Donner, so his courage and selflessness were not surprising, but this did not make the situation any easier for Spencer. Frank suggested that Spencer should go on without him, but Spencer completely refused to even consider this. Instead, he put Frank's right arm around his shoulder and moved forward into the dark tunnel.

Within another hundred yards, there was complete darkness, and they were forced to walk along the right wall, so that Spencer could feel his way through the tunnel. He could feel a chill from the breeze that was now strong enough to intermittently cause his hair and clothing to flutter like butterfly wings.

After they had gone another three- or four-hundred yards, Frank's breathing was more of a gasping for air than anything else, and Spencer was in a panic to get them out of the mountain. As he looked forward, he saw a slight shimmer that he thought might indicate the end of the tunnel. As he approached this area, he realized that he was, in fact, seeing the reflection of moonlight off of a smooth surface of rock at the very end of the tunnel. They had actually found a way out!

When they reached the end of the tunnel, Spencer could see that they were close to the edge of a cliff, with only about fifteen feet of walkway between the edge of the mountain and the 500-foot drop-off. The walkway appeared to slope downward on the left side. He let Frank rest for a minute against the mountain, as they caught their breath, but as Frank drew in some deep, ragged breaths, he began to cough up large clots of blood.

After he had finished, Spencer leaned over to him and said, "Hang in there, buddy. It's going to be okay."

"No, it's really not!" said Colonel Colquitt, as he stepped out of the dark shadows near the edge of the cliff and into the moonlight. Spencer could see that the bastard was smiling and holding a handgun pointed directly at him.

Almost immediately, Frank stepped in front of Spencer and started talking to Dax. It was almost as if Frank had found some energy reserve that he had been saving for just this moment.

"Dax, can I let you in on a little secret?"

"Why, of course, you can, Frank. We're old friends."

"Well, then here it is: This isn't going to end the way you think it will."

"Oh, really—and why is that, Frank?"

"Because you've always been a piece of shit with a black heart, and you can't even comprehend what a true friend will do for someone he cares about."

With that, Frank jumped forward toward Dax, just as he unloaded three rounds into Frank's chest. With blood spurting from his wounds, Frank grabbed Dax in a bear hug and threw himself off of the edge of the cliff, taking Colonel Colquitt with him.

Spencer heard the Colonel shouting in rage as he slipped over the edge and screaming in terror as he fell to his death. Spencer sat down on the walkway and started to cry over the loss of his friend, but he knew that this was a fitting death for a courageous soldier like General Frank Donner.

He was later surprised to find that there weren't any other men with Colonel Colquitt, but he did find the colonel's car at the bottom of the walkway and started his long drive to Colorado. He had promised Stephen Hanson that he would head straight to his home in Denver as soon as he had left Black Diamond. Besides, he could think of no other place where he would be welcome right now.

Casper, Wyoming: September 14, 9:38 p.m.

Stephen stood up in front of Michael and Cassie in the living area of the bungalow and said, "I need to give you both some background, so that you can better understand the details of what I'm going to tell you. Michael, I've already talked to Mark about this, and he's planning on meeting you at my house in Denver."

"When will he be in Denver?"

"He's flying out tomorrow morning, so you'll see him there tomorrow afternoon."

"So when will you be heading back to Denver?"

"With the new information that I have, I really need to force the issue with the Geological Survey to make them understand what's going on here. That's the only way that we can get an adequate warning out to the rest of the country and to the world."

"The world! My God, Stephen, what's going on here?"

"I don't want to get ahead of myself, but let's just say that it's unclear if the human species will even exist a few years from now. I believe we're about to see an event occur that's on a scale that no one could even fathom in their most vivid imagination."

"So, why can't you deal with the USGS from Denver?"

"There's nothing that I want more than to be with my family right now, but all of my information is on the database at the Yellowstone Volcano Observatory. I'll head home as soon as I've made my case with the USGS."

Stephen sat back down on the couch next to Cassie and turned to face her and Michael. The look on his face was initially grim, but it softened as he cleared his throat and started talking. "Some of this is a little involved and complicated, so as we go through it, if you don't understand something or need more information, then I want you to stop me and ask questions, so that I can make everything clear."

Both Michael and Cassie nodded, and so he continued. "About five years ago, we started seeing some interesting things happening at Yellowstone National Park. The thing that most people don't understand about Yellowstone is that it represents a huge collapsed volcano crater that we call a *caldera*. This crater was formed when the Yellowstone Super Volcano erupted hundreds of thousands of years ago."

"You're calling it a super volcano," said Michael. "Does that just mean that it's bigger than a regular volcano?"

"It is dramatically bigger than a regular volcano, but the designation "super volcano" refers to the amount of magma that can potentially be ejected during an eruption. In this century, the largest volcanic eruption in the world was in 1912 at Novarupta on the Alaska Peninsula. This eruption produced fifteen cubic kilometers of magma, which is thirty times that of Mount St. Helens. In this case, Yellowstone has 25,000 cubic kilometers of magma. That's enough to cover the entire U.S. with about four feet of lava!"

"I didn't realize that a volcano existed that had that much magma."

"Most people don't even recognize the fact that Yellowstone has a volcano at all. Just to give you an idea of the size, the present crater is thirty miles wide and forty-five miles long. The reason people don't recognize this as a volcano is because regular volcanoes have a mountain peak formed when hot magma flows from the depths of the Earth out of a hole in the Earth's crust to the surface. That's when lava cools and over time builds up into a mountain.

"The volcano at Yellowstone is different—it's hidden because magma is blocked from reaching the surface and is contained within a huge magma chamber trapped below several miles of rock. This chamber has roughly the same dimensions as the caldera rim, so you can understand how it contains such a massive amount of magma. And it's this magma chamber that fuels all of the hydrothermal features at Yellowstone, including geysers, hot springs, and steam vents."

"So, if it's blocked from the surface, what makes it eventually erupt?"

"Well, they don't erupt very often, but super volcanoes, like Yellowstone, erupt because pressure is constantly building up in the magma chamber. Eventually, the pressure is so intense, that the entire surface of the underground chamber, which is sometimes several miles thick, is blown away by a huge explosion that is thousands of times more powerful than a regular volcano. The last super volcano eruption was 74,000 years ago in Indonesia that resulted in an explosion that was 10,000 times more powerful than Mount St. Helens."

Michael then said, "Stephen, can you remind me of a few details about the Mount St. Helens eruption. I just don't remember."

"Sure. Mount St. Helens in Washington erupted in 1980 and was the most violent American volcano eruption in recorded history, killing fifty-seven people. Now for comparison, the Indonesia super eruption resulted in the near extinction of humans, with their numbers being pushed down to a few thousand."

"Humans were really almost extinct?"

"Granted they were more primitive than we are today, but the answer is yes. You see, the thing you need to understand is that humans are relatively fragile."

"Can you explain how the extinction would occur?"

"Sure, Cassie, let's take the example of a theoretical Yellowstone eruption. I say theoretical, but I want you to know that an eruption at Yellowstone will occur, we just don't know exactly when—or I should say—we didn't know until recently. As a matter of fact, Yellowstone eruptions have occurred approximately every 600,000 years, and the last eruption was 640,000 years ago."

"So, we're overdue for an eruption?" said Michael.

"Oh, God, how I wish that was all that was happening here, but yes, you could say that. So, let's get back to Cassie's question: How could a volcano eruption at Yellowstone result in extinction of species? To understand this, you need to understand what would occur during a super volcano eruption. This is how it likely would happen: First, many large earthquakes would occur in the area just before the eruption, and one of the earthquakes would fracture the layer of rock between the magma reservoir and the surface. This would release the pressure that had been building up for 640,000 years in a cataclysmic explosion with the force of 1,000 atomic bombs—literally the loudest sound heard by man in 74,000 years. Magma would be flung thirty miles into the atmosphere and all life within 600 miles would perish within the first few hours."

"Would lava flows cause most of this death?" Cassie asked.

"No, it's not what you're thinking. Most deaths in the immediate vicinity of Yellowstone would be caused by a combination of several factors, including falling volcanic ash, pyroclastic flows, and the explosive force of the eruption."

"What is a pyroclastic flow?"

"The best way I can describe this to you is that there are two types of eruptions: A red eruption, which gives you a slow but destructive lava flow. Most people can walk faster than lava so this is only a danger to stationary objects. Just think of the volcanoes in Hawaii, and you'll understand a red eruption. The other type is what we're talking about, and it's called a gray eruption. With this type, magma under pressure turns to foam and gas and would blow upward at twice the speed of sound. This would be followed by a pyroclastic flow which consists of the spillover from the eruptive column that reaches temperatures of 500 degrees and can surge up to 500 miles per hour. This would incinerate and destroy everything in its path.

"But the worst damage and the greatest loss of life would be caused by the volcanic ash that would cover places even thousands of miles away. It would short out most electrical equipment, clog machinery, collapse roofs, blind people and animals, and combine with the moisture from the lungs to form cement, so that people and animals would literally drown in liquid concrete. Tens of millions would die in a few days, and there would be nothing we could do to stop it. An ash cloud would cover most of the U.S., water would be contaminated, hospitals would have power failures, buildings would collapse, and ash inhalation would be rampant."

"I see how that would devastate the United States, but how could this lead to a worldwide extinction?"

"Because thousands of cubic miles of ash would fill the atmosphere, blocking out the sun and creating a nuclear winter, with global temperatures falling dramatically. A large percentage of plant life would die due to lack of sunlight and the drop in temperature. This would then create massive food shortages worldwide, with subsequent starvation, disease, and death that could impact billions of lives. Not a pretty picture."

"So, is that what you think we're facing?" said Michael.

"Yes, but that will probably be the most minor part of what is about to occur."

Michael then responded incredulously, "Did I hear what you said correctly—the 'most minor part' of what is about to occur?"

"Unfortunately, the answer is yes."

Oh, my God, Michael whispered softly under his breath, as he and Cassie looked at each other and instinctively started holding hands.

"You see, the main reason that I spent all this time explaining to you about the Yellowstone Super Volcano eruption is so that you understand part of what is going to occur in the U.S., but even more importantly, so you can understand the severity and scale of a relatively *minor extinction event*, otherwise known as a *mass extinction* or *extinction level event* (ELE).

"We'll come back to this concept of extinction level event in a little while, because it's a crucial part of the theory about what is happening, but for right now, just understand that there have been twenty or thirty *minor* extinction events in the past 500 million years, but only five *major* extinction level events. I don't mean to scare both of you, and I know that some of this sounds unbelievable, but before I'm finished, I want you to understand what we'll be facing, and it's truly horrendous."

With that, Stephen took a break to retrieve more coffee and to stretch his legs, but more importantly to give Michael and Cassie a chance to relax. He didn't want to overwhelm them, but he could tell that they were a little rattled, and he knew that the worst news was yet to come.

When everybody was again seated on the couch, Cassie was the first to speak, "Stephen, at the very beginning, you said something about some interesting things that had been happening at Yellowstone in the past five years, but then you never mentioned what they were."

He smiled at her. "You'd make an excellent geologist—that's very observant. The changes at Yellowstone are where the story starts, but I decided to give you some background, before I hit you with the details of what we've been seeing."

"With all this talk about extinction events, does any of this tie in to the dinosaurs in some way or another?" Michael asked.

"Another excellent question," Stephen said. "The answer is yes, but probably not in the way you might think it does. We'll get back to this later on, but first let's talk about the interesting things occurring at Yellowstone.

"Since 1923, the ground in the Yellowstone Caldera has been progressively rising and until about five years ago, it had elevated approximately seventy centimeters. This indicated that the reservoir, or magma chamber, was filling with magma and subsequently swelling at a significant rate, forcing the ground upward. This is referred to as *ground elevation* or *ground uplift*. Starting five years ago, there was a sudden and completely unexpected shift downward in the ground level, by almost forty centimeters. We still don't know why this occurred, but in the few years following this unprecedented event, the ground has risen over twelve feet, and this has been accelerating dramatically over the past four weeks.

"You see, that's why they initially called me in as a consultant at Yellowstone—to help try and figure out what was going on and to decide if a super volcano eruption was eminent.

"Since I've been at Yellowstone for the past two weeks, several other dramatic changes have been occurring. First of all, we've seen a tremendous increase in hydrothermal events. In some areas, we've seen geysers and steam vents that have been dormant for forty years that have suddenly come to life. Overall, there has been a 5,000 percent increase in hydrothermal activity, which is truly remarkable.

"In addition, there's been a frightening increase in earthquake activity at Yellowstone. Earthquakes at the park are extremely common, sometimes as many as two or three thousand per year, although the last major earthquake was in 1975 and prior to that, 1959. In the past week, we've seen twenty times more earthquakes than at any point in the history of Yellowstone since seismic activity has been recorded."

"Stephen, the things that you mentioned—ground uplifts, hydrothermal events, earthquakes—do they accurately predict an impending eruption?"

"Most scientists would say no, Michael, because although these are indicators of possible volcanic activity, both earthquakes and volcanoes are notoriously unpredictable. But there is no question that we're seeing a series of unprecedented events occurring at an exponential rate and causing dramatic changes in the park."

"So, if these things are so difficult to predict, and all of this may mean absolutely nothing, then why are you so concerned about what's happening here?"

"Well, there's one more thing that I haven't told you about. You see, with the possible indicators that we've been talking about, the scientists at the Volcano Observatory and the USGS were concerned but most considered the changes a scientific or geological curiosity more than anything else. We've not seen any evidence of harmonic tremor on seismographs, which is the only sure sign of an impending eruption, because it indicates magma on the move.

"But one week ago, something happened that scared the shit out of everyone. We have the ability to measure the size and dimensions of the magma chamber with a technique called *seismic tomography*. It's performed using an array of seismographs planted around the park and is based on the fact that seismic shock waves generated by earthquakes will travel slower through molten rock (magma) than solid rock. The size of the magma chamber has been stable for the entire time that we've been measuring it, but in the past week, we've seen the bottom of the magma chamber expand in a downward direction by almost two miles!"

"That sounds like a fairly big change," said Michael.

"That is the understatement of the century. Do you remember when I described how massive the magma chamber was and how enormous the amount of magma that could be ejected during an eruption could possibly be?"

"How could I forget; you said it was enough to cover the entire U.S. with four feet of lava."

"With this new change in just one week, the magma chamber has more than doubled in size!"

"How could that happen?" said Cassie, a bit suspiciously.

"That is the key question, and we had absolutely no idea what the answer was, nor did we know what it meant, other than the fact that if the super volcano did erupt, we were in some deep shit."

Stephen could see that Michael had a peculiar look on his face, as if something was at the edge of his mind and he was trying to pull it into focus. Suddenly his expression changed, and Stephen could tell that a light bulb had just turned on in Michael's head.

Cassie also noticed his expression. "What is it? You look like you suddenly understand something that's important."

"I didn't realize until now the importance of what Kate told me on the phone. Remember how she talked about the strange, sudden ground uplifts that were occurring in Nevada, Utah, Idaho, and Wyoming— some of them almost a thousand square miles?"

Then Michael turned to face his brother again and said, "Stephen, Cassie and I both experienced sudden ground uplifts three times when we were in Nevada. We didn't know what was happening at the time, but they were very frightening events."

He paused for a few seconds, rubbed his chin as if in deep thought, and said, "What's happening involves something much bigger than the Yellowstone Super Volcano, doesn't it?"

Stephen replied, "Uh huh. I see you're starting to put some pieces together now. Honestly I was stumped until I received a phone call from a good friend and colleague, Spencer Montgomery. Michael, you've met him once or twice before. He's a very bright man, with a PhD in both geology and structural engineering, and he was being consulted by the military concerning some structural problems they were having at an underground base. He told me it was a top secret facility, so he couldn't give me too much information about it, but there were some problems with the exterior walls at the bottom of the facility.

"From what he described, something was causing them to collapse, and that it represented a truly mind-blowing amount of force, because these walls were massive and tremendously strong. It was actually Spencer who put it all together and figured out what was going on, after I told him about the dramatic events at Yellowstone.

"Now, before I talk about Spencer's theory, we need to spend a little time discussing dinosaur extinction. How much do either of you know about theories concerning the extinction of the dinosaurs?"

"It involved a large asteroid that hit in the Yucatan, didn't it?" asked Cassie.

"You're right; that is the most popular theory, but you should know that there are some problems with this theory."

"Like what?"

"Well, first of all, there's been a longstanding debate for the past twenty-five years about dinosaur extinction between two groups— one favoring a meteorite impact; the other favoring prolonged mega-volcanism or massive volcanic activity. We call this type of volcanic activity a *continental flood basalt*, and when it occurs, it can go on for literally hundreds of thousands of years."

Now, Cassie had a perplexed look on her face. "Stephen, what's the relationship between a super volcano and a continental flood basalt?"

"That's very good, Cassie. Another piece to the puzzle fits in place. By definition, every continental flood basalt results from a super volcano eruption, although not every super volcano eruption will lead to a flood basalt with prolonged volcanic activity. Most super volcanoes will erupt and then die out quickly. As we already talked about, the end result of even a single super volcano eruption can be devastating, although not nearly as devastating as a flood basalt, where the volcanic activity goes on and on."

Michael said, "What causes the volcanic activity to go on and on?"

"Most scientists believe that an event called a *mantle plume* is the cause of prolonged massive volcanic activity. The best way to think of this is a massive upwelling of abnormally hot rock within the Earth's mantle that occurs in an effort to cool the Earth's core. As the plume head rises into shallower areas, this causes decompression melting with the creation of huge amounts of magma. This can now rise into the Earth's crust and result in the creation of *hotspots* or volcanic centers that can then lead to flood basalts."

"So, tell me if I have this correct," said Michael. "Mantle plumes create massive amounts of magma, which form hotspots when they rise into the Earth's crust, eventually leading to prolonged volcanic activity (flood basalts), which erupts from a super volcano."

"You've got it. That's the right sequence of events."

"Okay, now I'm confused about where you're leading us. Are you trying to imply that super volcanoes and flood basalts, not meteors, caused the extinction of the dinosaurs?"

Cassie also spoke up, "And I thought you said that a super volcano eruption was probably the most minor part of what is about to occur."

"I understand why both of you are confused, but you'll understand shortly. I still agree with my statement about the super volcano eruption, but let me clarify something. This eruption is vital to understanding the theory about what's happening. Also, an impact event was very likely involved in the extinction of the dinosaurs, but many scientists believe that a single six-mile-wide asteroid could not have caused such a significant extinction of species as what was seen sixty-five million years ago—fifty percent of all species were wiped out, including all non-avian dinosaurs."

"So why did you say that an impact event was likely involved in the extinction, if we assume that an asteroid wasn't a factor?" asked Cassie.

"To answer that, let me give you some information on what we know about four of the five major extinction level events that have occurred in the last 500 million years. And really, let's limit this to the last 400 million years, because that's when most complex life started emerging on Earth. So, if we're dealing with the last 400 million years, then we're talking about four extinction level events that have all dramatically changed life on the planet because they all resulted in a sharp decrease in the number of species in a relatively short period of time."

Stephen started pointing to a graph that showed extinction intensity versus time. "Now, for each of these extinction events, we have evidence of prolonged volcanic activity, which is a very rare event occurring every thirty- to fifty-million years. We also have evidence of a large impact event for each of these major extinctions, which are even rarer, occurring every hundred million years."

"So, now I think you're saying that asteroids and flood basalts together caused the extinctions. Is that right?"

"Stick with me here, Cassie, because we're getting to the critical part, but the answer to that question is no, that's not what I'm saying. But the question does bring up something very important. Let's do some simple math. In the past 400 million years, what are the odds that a large asteroid or comet impacted Earth at the same time that a flood basalt occurred? That would be a one in eight chance. Now, what would be the odds that in that same time period that four large asteroids or comets impacted Earth at the same time as a flood basalt? That's one chance in 3,500—not very good odds at all.

"So, now we've come to the unexplained mystery that's been baffling scientists for a long time: Why do major extinction level events always coincide with both impact events and flood basalts? How is this possible? Based on chance alone, it seems very unlikely."

"Could a large asteroid that impacted the Earth cause a volcano to erupt?" asked Michael. "That would explain how the two events could happen at the same time."

"A large asteroid probably could, but that wouldn't cause prolonged volcanic activity that characterizes flood basalts. Remember that this is caused by mantle plumes, and an asteroid has nothing to do with that."

"So, it seems like we're at a dead end here," said Michael.

"We were, until some very bright scientists at Geomar, an Earth Sciences Institute at Kiel University in Germany, came up with a very controversial theory called a *Verneshot*. Although it's not a well known theory in the U.S. geological literature, Spencer Montgomery remembered reading about it after he studied data collected at the underground military base."

Stephen could see that Michael and Cassie were thoroughly intrigued and wanted to keep going, but he needed a break to get some more coffee and visit the bathroom, so he told them to relax for a minute. When he had left the room, Cassie took Michael's hand, looked at him for a few seconds with her lovely, blue eyes, and gave him a big hug.

He said, "What was that for?"

She then smiled warmly and said, "I just needed a hug. This is some pretty scary stuff, and I have a feeling that we're getting ready to hear the scariest part of it. Besides, I've hugged your brother, but haven't even given you a good hug."

"Did you really mean what you said earlier to Stephen?"

"About what?" she asked coyly, indicating that she knew exactly what he was referring to. Just then, Stephen entered the room, and this ended their discussion.

Casper, Wyoming: September 14, 10:33 p.m.

Winston Delk walked into the main concourse of Natrona County International Airport and quietly made his way to baggage claim. When he had retrieved his suitcase, he headed to the deli just off the main concourse and sat down after getting a large sandwich and Coke. He gulped down his meal in a few minutes and then made his way to the public restroom, where he entered a stall. Although the restroom had no other patrons, he was taking no chances until his job was completed. He didn't need any other bodies lying around in the airport arousing suspicion before his two targets were hit.

Afterwards, when he had disposed of the bodies, he would get a better look around the town of Casper and have some fun. He rarely allowed himself to indulge in the typical carnage and torture in his professional life that he enjoyed in his personal life. But there would be time for that later, and he was sure that he could find a young woman or even better, a teenage cutie, with whom he could explore his unquenchable desire for domination, torture, and death, mixed with a little hardcore sex.

He opened the suitcase and flipped the hidden latch, which opened a secret compartment. While he was staring at his tools of death and torture, he started to think about the conversation he had with Senator

Wolfe this afternoon. His current targets were a geologist and his brother, who was some hero ex-military asshole. Supposedly, he was a member of Force Recon with the Marine Corps. Winston had some military experience and had worked as a mercenary for a period of time, so he knew that Force Recon was composed of a group of elite military soldiers. He had heard that they were self-proclaimed "bad asses" who were sent on only the nastiest missions.

We'll see what a bad ass he is after he's tasted a few of the little surprises I have for him, Winston muttered under his breath.

Casper, Wyoming: September 14, 10:40 p.m.

"Alright," said Michael. "Tell us about a Verneshot. What is that?"

"First, I'm going to give you a simple description, and then I'll go back and fill in the details and explain how this fits in with recent events."

Stephen pulled out a diagram as he explained the theory. "A Verneshot is a massive volcanic eruption, which launches an extremely large rock into a sub-orbital trajectory that ultimately comes back to Earth causing a violent impact. The name is derived from author Jules Verne's book, From the Earth to the Moon, which featured a huge gun that could shoot objects into space. The beauty of this theory is that it explains the mystery that I alluded to earlier as to why major extinctions always coincide with both massive volcanic activity and impact events."

"Are you serious?" asked Michael. "That honestly doesn't sound like such a big deal. I guess with all of this build-up, I was expecting something worse."

"I'm dead serious. And you need to listen to the details of how this will happen. I think you'll change your opinion."

Stephen looked at Michael with the gravest expression and then began his more detailed description. By the time he was finished, Michael and Cassie were left speechless, with their mouths gaping open.

"First, a huge mantle plume, called a *super plume* occurs, which can have a diameter covering one to two thousand miles. When the plume breaks through into the Earth's crust, several things start to occur. Huge pools of magma—so-called *hotspots*—accumulate. Eventually these hotspots cause a super volcano eruption, but this eruption is prolonged and deadly. It could last for hundreds of thousands of years and might involve thousands of square miles. In addition, if the plume tries pushing up through continental plate rock, otherwise known as a *craton,* which is very tough and thick, truly massive pressure would build up from the release of explosive gases, carbon dioxide, and sulfur dioxide, which are generated from rising magma. If the pressure builds up to a critical level, the gases could crack the craton and hell on Earth would be unleashed."

Stephen then looked away from his brother and Cassie, sighed deeply, and continued. "This cracking of the Earth's crust would happen very quickly, probably in a week or less and would culminate in a catastrophic gas explosion, which would blast out at an astronomical velocity and trigger at least a Richter scale magnitude 11 earthquake. Just so you understand what I'm talking about, this would be *1,000* times stronger than the largest magnitude earthquake ever recorded and *32,000* times stronger than the Great San Francisco earthquake of 1906 or the Great China earthquake of 1556, which killed 830,000 people. An 11 magnitude earthquake would be capable of leveling entire mountain ranges in a matter of minutes! And of course the gases released would immediately start to poison the atmosphere.

"But what I've described so far is just a curtain-raiser. You see, the pipe through which the magma and gas has traveled is now empty and would cave in from the bottom upward. This collapse would happen at hypersonic speed, creating a shockwave that would blast upward and hit the remainder of the craton, pulverizing it, and ejecting huge chunks of the Earth's crust from the top of the pipe. The energy released would be equivalent to 120 billion tons of TNT or seven million Hiroshima type atomic bombs! The blast would spread out in all directions, obliterating everything within a thousand miles.

"The Verneshot impactor, which is the largest chunk of Earth's crust ejected, would then impact the Earth somewhere else. The impactor would be over 200 miles across and if it hit in the ocean, which would be most likely, it would generate mega tsunamis that would be over 2,000 feet high when they hit land and travel up to 500 miles per hour!"

Stephen sat, almost breathless, after his description of the catastrophe. Michael and Cassie sat in stunned silence.

Finally, Michael spoke up. "Okay, I heard what you said, but come on, Stephen. What kind of evidence could you possibly have that proves that this theory is correct, and that it's getting ready to happen again?"

"Believe me, Michael, I wish I didn't have the evidence, but let me give you what we know. First, there's the massive increase in size of the magma chamber under Yellowstone, which we now understand represents a hotspot. This is simply the weakest area in the Earth's crust, and it represents the tip of the iceberg, but you can also think of it as our earliest warning sign. We had no way of knowing the timeline on how quickly these events can transpire, but it now appears that the mantle plume reached a critical point about five years ago, when we first started seeing dramatic changes at Yellowstone. My guess is that we'll see volcanoes pop up for six- or seven-hundred miles around Yellowstone once this begins.

"Next, there's the sudden ground uplifting, that Spencer said represents the massive pressure of the explosive gas that has now cracked the craton under Nevada, Idaho, Utah, and Wyoming. Right now, we're sitting on top of the largest ticking time bomb in the last sixty-five million years.

"As of three months ago, according to some international connections that Spencer has, we now have definitive proof that this theory is correct—it just hasn't been published yet. Some field geologists in Russia have uncovered a deep, vertical "pipe" under the Great Tunguska Depression in Siberia, which is part of a huge crater and is the site of the Earth's most massive volcanic eruption 251 million years ago. This eruption lasted almost a million years and was associated with the worst mass extinction that the planet has ever seen. It's called "The Great Dying" because 96 percent of all life on Earth was wiped out.

"This recently discovered pipe fits the description of a Verneshot launch pipe with frightening accuracy. From history, we also know that in 1908, 2,000 square kilometers of forest at Tunguska were flattened by a mysterious explosion. Eyewitnesses were dismissed as probably crazy when they reported that they saw a large fireball shooting upward, not falling downward like a meteorite. This most certainly represented a micro-Verneshot, where the original pipe was reused in a smaller gas release event.

"But the most definitive proof we now have is from the Yucatan. We've always known that the Chicxulub crater is lop-sided, which would be consistent with a Verneshot impactor coming from the southeast at 20 degrees. This would fit perfectly with the Deccan Traps in India, the known site of the massive volcanic activity that occurred at the time that this crater was created sixty-five million years ago. But now they've uncovered small fragments of the impactor from inside the crater, and scientists have geo-chemically fingerprinted the fragments to show that they originated from the Deccan area in India. Like it or not, the theory is correct."

"Let me play devil's advocate," said Michael. "Okay, I'll concede the point that the Verneshot theory is correct and that these events have occurred millions of years ago. I'll even say that it seems likely that a similar thing is happening again, right now. But isn't the evidence still circumstantial? The increased number of hydrothermal events and earthquakes at Yellowstone, the significant ground uplift at Yellowstone, the dramatic increase in size of the magma chamber, and the sudden huge areas of ground uplift involving four states. I certainly see why all of this looks ominous, but how does it prove that we're about to see a Verneshot?"

"Well, there's one more thing that I haven't told you, but it is the final nail in the coffin. Spencer Montgomery's investigation into the events unfolding at the underground military base uncovered something completely unexpected. When he studied the piles of data that they gave him, he noticed an unusual trend. Based on sophisticated sensors on the exterior walls of the facility, they found an unusually high concentration of carbon dioxide and sulfur dioxide intermixed with the surrounding rock layers only at the bottom of the facility.

"Initially, he was unsure what to make of this, but after phone calls to the USGS, he discovered that the closest area of volcanic activity, the Long Valley Caldera, which is adjacent to Mammoth Mountain in eastern California, has had an event occur in the past week that is frighteningly similar to what has occurred in Yellowstone. The magma chamber for this super volcano collapsed dramatically 760,000 years ago, when a colossal volcanic eruption emptied most of the chamber. Now, in the past week, the collapsed chamber has re-expanded and has filled up with a similar volume of magma that it had 760,000 years ago! Keep in mind that the Yellowstone Super Volcano is 900 miles from the Long Valley Super Volcano.

"According to Spencer, if you connect the dots, the underground military base is between these two areas, although it is much closer to California. What is about to be unleashed is an enormous geological event, stretching from eastern California to northwestern Wyoming. These hotspots are apparently on the outer edge of the upcoming catastrophic event, and the reason that walls at the bottom of the military base are collapsing is because the craton is cracking from the explosive gases, carbon dioxide, and sulfur dioxide, which are leaking into the Earth's crust. That's why the gas concentration was so high under the military base. There is no mistaking what is happening here; we're facing the greatest catastrophic global geophysical event since the age of the dinosaurs!"

When he had finished, Stephen looked and felt utterly exhausted. It was as if he had unloaded a lifetime of painful memories in the past two hours, but they were not his memories, but his own internalization of the pain and suffering that the human species would have to endure if they were to survive.

Michael looked at his brother, softly patted him on the back, and said, "Thank you for taking the time and effort to help us understand what's going on here. I know this has drained you, but can you answer just a few more questions before we all retire for the night?"

Stephen smiled wearily. "Sure—go ahead."

"When do you think all of this will happen?"

"Spencer and I talked about this question for quite a while. Our best guess is that we have less than a week before the craton is cracked enough to let the explosive gases break through. The bottom of the military base is only a mile underground, and there's already evidence of cataclysmic pressure from gases at that depth."

"Is there any chance that the pressure could decrease before the catastrophe occurs?"

"Unfortunately no, Cassie. Spencer likes to use the term *domino theory* to describe the sequence of events that lead up to the Verneshot. Once these events have been set in motion, then there is absolutely no way that they'll stop until the horrible process is completed."

"What will happen to the U.S. when the massive earthquake hits?" Michael asked.

"Most likely, large portions of the Rocky Mountains will be leveled in a matter of minutes. A huge crevasse will form at the same time, splitting the continental U.S. in half from Canada to Mexico. In spots, the crevasse will be twice as wide and four times as deep as the Grand Canyon and will span over 1,500 miles!"

"Can you give us more specifics on the huge chunk of the Earth that will be launched?"

"This is definitely just a guess, but there may be a two- or three-hundred-mile-wide chunk of the Earth ejected, possibly near the borders where Nevada, Utah, and Idaho come together. The chunk will probably hit in the Pacific Ocean about thirty or forty minutes later and create mega-tsunamis that will fan out in all directions, eventually hitting the west coast of the U.S., the east coast of China and Russia, and the northeast coast of Australia. Japan, the Philippines, and much of Indonesia will be completely obliterated. Casualties in those areas may be close to 99 percent of all inhabitants!"

All three of them were now exhausted with the realization of things to come.

"You know, there is something very ironic about this," Stephen added. "There's a thing called the *extinction cycle*, which deals with a periodicity that exists for the Earth—in other words, mass extinctions are cyclical, probably because geological instabilities might allow heat to build up in the Earth's core every fifty- to a hundred-million years, which is released in mantle plumes, which then results in extinctions. The dominant group is often wiped out, as in the case of the dinosaurs sixty-five million years ago, leaving room for another group, the mammals, to take over.

"You can think of it as the Earth 'cleaning house.' Maybe that's really what's going on here—the time for the human species is over, and the Earth is hell-bent on wiping out our existence to open up room for another group to evolve and dominate."

Chapter 4

Endurance

Casper, Wyoming: September 15, 12:20 a.m.

Winston Delk sat down in the upstairs lounge adjacent to the administration and business offices of the small airport and started browsing several magazines. It would be a long night, because he never allowed himself to fall asleep within eight hours of an upcoming hit. Plans can change because people are unpredictable, and if you're asleep, you'll never even know that a target had slipped through your fingers.

Initially, Delk had planned on meeting up with Stephen as he drove back to Yellowstone from the Cody Municipal Airport, but when he was informed about the second target, Michael Hanson, he decided to take both of them out at the same time. Natrona County International Airport was the logical choice. He had already spent twenty-five minutes exploring every nook and cranny of the airport and devising three or four contingency plans, depending on where the two brothers headed when they were inside the airport and how many witnesses were present. Certainly having no witnesses was the easiest scenario; however, if he had to kill a few more people, then that would be just fine, as long as he was able to dispose of all the bodies to give him time to have "fun" in Casper. Besides, he enjoyed killing so much that any additional executions were a bonus to him.

As he stared at the magazine, he realized that he had no idea what he was looking at because his mind was elsewhere. After learning that Michael Hanson was ex-military, he could not stop thinking about a hit he made six weeks earlier on another ex-military special-forces asshole. Regular civilians were boring; you could make them cry and beg for mercy just by showing them a gun. But some ex-military were more of a challenge, and the man six weeks ago was an especially tasty treat. That was one of the few times that Winston allowed himself to savor the moment and not end the ordeal quickly.

At first, the man showed no fear and almost no response to the excruciating torture that Winston was making him endure. He even had the audacity to spit in Winston's face and call him a "chicken-shit little pussy." But eventually, he broke the man, when he brought out his ten-year-old son and started carving his name into the boy's back with a knife. Even though he couldn't get the man to beg for his own life, he could still hear the man wailing, crying, and pleading for his son's life and could still see the expression of terror on his face as he witnessed his son's torture.

As the excitement of that moment came back to him, Winston decided that breaking another ex-military man was too tempting to pass up if the situation unfolded as he envisioned it. Now, he had even more planning and preparation to keep himself busy over the next six hours.

The time spent in Casper just might be one of the best trips he had ever taken, not to mention one of the most exciting. He took out a few sheets of paper and started outlining his plans to make the encounter come to fruition as he hoped it would.

Casper, Wyoming: September 15, 12:22 a.m.

Michael and Stephen shared one of the bedrooms in the bungalow, leaving Cassie alone in the other one. At first, Stephen was confused as to why his brother chose to share a room with him instead of a beautiful, young woman, but Michael briefly explained how he had met Cassie only two days ago, and how events had transpired over the past thirty-six hours.

Stephen was embarrassed that he had put Cassie on the spot like he had at the restaurant, but Michael teased his brother. "Stephen, I didn't know you had the balls to be that direct, forceful, and abrupt. I always thought that Kate was the one in your relationship with big balls."

"Go screw yourself," said Stephen.

"Hey, you have gotten tougher."

"Well, the end of the world will do that to you."

"I guess I can see your point."

"So, do you think she meant what she said when I asked her my direct, forceful, and abrupt question?"

"I honestly have no idea. That woman is a complete mystery to me. She's thrown me for a loop several times in the past couple of days."

"I think that's just the plight of all men. After eleven years of marriage, Kate is still a mystery to me. But I'll tell you what I think about Cassie's response, based on what you've told me and what I've seen for myself. I certainly put her on the spot and made her say something long before she was ready to say it, but I don't think she's the type of woman who would say something that important if she didn't really mean it."

Michael shrugged his shoulders and turned the light out as he climbed into bed. There were things that he wanted to say to his brother, but he couldn't right now, because they sounded too much like the closure that loved ones would share on their deathbed. He was also in denial about the ominous feeling that he and his brother were sharing the last few hours together that they would ever have.

After he lay in bed for about thirty minutes, unable to sleep because his mind kept replaying the vivid descriptions that Stephen had depicted for them, Michael finally decided to get up and watch some TV in the living area of the bungalow for a short while. He could tell that Stephen was asleep by the raspy snoring he heard coming from the other bed, so he quietly made his way into the other room.

Although the only light in the living area was from the moon shining through the French doors overlooking the river, Michael could see that there was another person standing across the room. At first he was startled, but then he realized that it was Cassie, and so he turned on a lamp next to the couch.

Cassie looked over at him. "I thought I was the only one who couldn't sleep. Really, I should be able to sleep; I'm actually very tired."

"You can't sleep for the same reason that I can't—visions of what we heard tonight keep running through my mind, and I can't turn them off."

She nodded in agreement, and the two of them stood there staring at each other, knowing that neither one of them would ever see the world through the same eyes again. Every tree, every bird, every sunset, every flower, every mountainside, every lake, every person or living creature that they encountered would from this moment forward look infinitely more precious than they ever did before.

Cassie softly said, "Can you please turn the lamp off? I like to look at the moonlight on the water."

He turned off the lamp and then walked toward her as she turned to look out the window. When he was directly behind her, she reached back to grasp his hands and slowly wrapped his arms around her. He could feel her body heat, which instantly warmed and comforted him, and made him long to spend the rest of the night holding her. He found her feminine scent intoxicating, and even developed a mild swimming sensation in his head each time he inhaled deeply.

A part of him still felt foolish for having these feelings for a woman he had known for only two days, but he also understood that once in a blue moon, unusual circumstances allow a man and a woman to share a special bond that would take some couples a lifetime to form.

Cassie leaned back against him, and he could feel the rhythmic movements of her breathing. She pulled his hands closer to her soft breast. "The answer is yes."

Confused, Michael asked, "What?"

She paused, and then said, "The answer to your question earlier—did I really mean what I said to your brother at the restaurant—the answer is yes."

Casper, Wyoming: September 15, 7:24 a.m.

Michael and Stephen pulled into the parking lot, parked their vehicle, and walked toward the front entrance of the small airport. Cassie was still sleeping when they woke up at 6:45 a.m., and so they chose not to disturb her. Instead, Michael left a note saying he would be back in an hour.

They walked into the main ticketing/check-in area, and Stephen approached the counter with his driver's license and e-mail confirmation ready. When he had finished, the two brothers grabbed some coffee and headed down the short hallway leading toward the security check-in and terminal gate.

Before they passed through security, Stephen headed back to the restroom, but noticed a "Closed for Construction" sign on the door, which he curiously didn't remember seeing when they first walked into the main concourse. Michael recalled that there was another restroom upstairs near the administration area, so they both made their way to the second floor.

There were very few people in the airport at this time, but Michael did notice a large man, with jet black hair, deep pockmarks on his face, and wearing a brown leather jacket, heading for the stairs to the second floor about five steps behind them.

When they reached the second floor and turned the corner to head to the restroom, Michael heard the distinctive sound of two shots from a silencer-equipped handgun and turned to see Stephen falling to the ground. It was then, that he felt the sensation of two sharp objects penetrating the skin of his left chest, and he realized that he was about to get hit with a huge jolt from an Air Taser.

Winston Delk quickly dragged the two incapacitated men into the upstairs storage room, while he carefully looked both ways to ensure that he had no unwanted spectators. He used a towel to wipe up the blood that had poured out of Stephen Hanson's exit wounds, and when he was satisfied that his activity had gone undetected, he closed the storage room door behind him and turned the deadbolt lock.

He was surprised at how simple this was going to be; the two brothers walked right into his trap. A large, hideous grin creased his face when he thought of how well his newest toy, the Air Taser, had worked. Michael Hanson was still curled up in a fetal position from intense muscular contraction. This new Advanced Taser M-18 used compressed nitrogen to shoot out two darts attached to fifteen feet of high-voltage insulated wire. The device resulted in Electro-Muscular Disruption (EMD) where 50,000 volts were transmitted to the subject, which would completely override his central nervous system, directly control all skeletal muscle, and result in horribly painful, uncontrollable muscle contraction. With a higher instant incapacitation rate than a 9mm handgun, the device could debilitate any target, regardless of pain tolerance or mental focus. But the most beautiful thing about this device was that it was completely legal, and he had purchased it online, rather than through the black market, which he had been forced to use many times in the past to obtain certain weapons and torture devices.

He left Stephen lying on the floor of the storage room while he tied Michael's hands behind his back with a type of reinforced wire that had sharp barbs with wickedly bent ends so that any attempt to escape would result in the barbs becoming more deeply imbedded in his flesh. He then bound Michael's feet in a similar brutal fashion and propped him up in the corner of the room, where he secured his hands to a large metal pipe coming out of the wall.

Next, he dragged Stephen closer to Michael, so that the two brothers were within ten feet of each other. He was less concerned about the geologist being able to escape, so he bound him with duct tape because it was quicker than the wire. He then waited for Michael's extreme muscle contraction to relax before he started the "fun and games."

A few seconds later, he heard the latch on the dead-bolt click as someone unlocked the door. The door slowly swung open to reveal a maintenance man with the name "George" on his nametag. The man unknowingly walked into the room and stared in confusion at the two men who were sitting on the floor with their arms and legs bound.

Winston nonchalantly walked over to the man, raised his gun, and shot him in forehead, causing blood to splatter on the wall adjacent to the door. As the dead man crumpled to the floor, he glanced outside and saw that there were no more visitors to take care of, so he again closed the door and latched the dead bolt. This time, he also propped a chair against the door to prevent any further interruptions.

He sat on a chair directly in front of Michael, opened his suitcase full of goodies that he had hidden in the storage room, and started taking out some of the razor sharp knives, cleavers, and drills that he enjoyed using the most. By that time, Michael's muscles had almost completely relaxed, but he still had evidence of pain on his face, which thoroughly pleased Winston.

He stood up to command more attention from the ex-Marine and said, "I know everything about you. I know you think you're some kind of military hero, so we're going to see how much of a hero you really are. I also know that your wife and daughter died a few years ago, so I'm going to make this really simple for you. If you want me to kill you quickly and painlessly, then I want to hear you say: *My wife and daughter were bitches, and I hope they rot in hell.* Otherwise, I'm going to do things to you that will make that Taser seem like fun."

As Michael sat up straighter, Winston could see another surge of pain cross his face, and he knew that Michael had discovered the wickedly crooked barbs on the wire binding both his hands and his feet. He could also see some blood starting to pool near Michael's hands and the metal pipe. "Well, I guess that means we need to start the "fun" before you bleed to death trying to get free. Unless, of course, you want to tell me what I want to hear."

"Fuck you!" said Michael.

With that, Winston picked up a battery powered drill and started to slowly grind a hole into Michael's thigh as he gritted his teeth to keep from screaming out in pain.

Casper, Wyoming: September 15, 8:06 a.m.

Cassie heard someone knock on the front door to the bungalow, so she pulled herself out of her lazy slumber and headed toward to the door. She decided that it was either Michael, who was already back from the airport and had forgotten his room key, or room service with breakfast that Michael ordered before he left. She unhooked the security chain, and opened the door with a smile on her face.

Kyle McMurphy stood in front of her. "Good morning, sweetie. Have you missed me?" With that, he kicked the door completely open, briskly walked inside the bungalow, and had his huge hands around her neck in seconds.

"Do you remember what I told you I'd do if you ever ran from me?" he hissed. "Well, that's about to happen, you fucking bitch! Oh, and just so you'll know—your boyfriend and his brother are probably dead by now!"

After fifteen minutes of torture, which had been largely unsuccessful, Winston decided to switch tactics. He knew his time was limited, because someone would eventually come looking for the maintenance man. Also, Michael mystified him, because he seemed to show more evidence of pain on his face when Winston stopped the torture, as if he were enduring something worse when the drill and knives were not being employed. Besides, if he were going to use Stephen Hanson to break Michael, he would need to do this before Stephen succumbed to his gunshot wounds.

He dragged Stephen closer to his brother. "Let's see who you love the most—two dead bitches or your brother."

Although Stephen was lightheaded from blood loss, he looked up at Michael and said, "I know you love all of us. I don't care what he does to me; just don't let this sadistic loser mess with your head!"

Winston laughed. "That's the first time anyone's ever called me a sadistic loser. I really like that one."

Then, with a big grin on his face, he grabbed Stephen's right hand, held it down to the concrete floor, and slammed the meat cleaver with brutal force on his middle and index fingers, instantly reducing them to pulverized bone and shredded meat. Stephen cried out as the intense pain shot up his arm and made his entire right side spasm uncontrollably.

Winston looked imploringly at Michael, set the cleaver down, and said, "Look, hero, you can make this all stop if you just tell me what I want to hear."

He could now see tremendous pain on Michael's face, which gave him a sense that he might be close to winning the game, so he chose to drop another demoralizing bomb on Michael. "Oh, by the way, your girlfriend should be reunited with her husband, Kyle, by now. He arrived at the airport early this morning. Seems like a great guy."

Winston was pleased with the panic he could see spreading across Michael's face with this revelation, but suddenly all of the pain on his face seemed to rapidly diminish, leaving Winston thoroughly confused.

Michael looked up at him and said, "Do you know what it is that most people don't understand about blood?"

Winston frowned, which exaggerated his deeply pocked brow and forehead, and said, "What's that?"

"That's it's one of the best lubricants that exist."

This statement produced a perplexed look on Winston's face, which was quickly replaced with surprise and fear when he saw Michael reach out and grab the cleaver with his free right hand. Before Winston had a chance to react, Michael brought it down with bone-shattering force on the side of Winston's left knee. The impact was so brutal that bone fragments and tissue went flying across the storage room, as the lower portion of his leg was savagely forced sideways with an audible "pop" as all of the ligaments and tendons were instantly torn out of their bony attachments. Winston collapsed forward, landing on his shattered knee, sending further lightning bolts of pain up his spinal cord to his brain.

Michael quickly freed his left wrist and used one of Winston's torture devices to cut the wire binding his ankles together. Blood was profusely pouring out of the wound on Michael's right wrist from a six-inch section of shredded skin and exposed muscle, which he wrapped tightly with a piece of cloth that he had ripped from his shirt. He then reinforced it with duct tape to form a firm pressure dressing, which slowed the blood loss.

Winston's mistake was that he had severely underestimated Michael, who had used the sharp barbs on the wire binding him to literally tear a six-inch flap of skin off of his right wrist by rotating his arm repeatedly, allowing him to free his hand by sliding it under the skin flap, using his own blood as a lubricant. This de-gloving maneuver left some pieces of Michael's skin still attached to the wire.

He looked down at Winston, who was still writhing in pain on the floor, and said, "That, you *sadistic loser*, was for my brother!"

Then, he raised the cleaver above his head and slammed it down with formidable force on Winston's right hand. The man started wailing and crying out in pain, as he rolled onto his back.

"And that is for my wife and daughter!"

Next, Michael raised the cleaver over Winston's head and listened as the man pleaded for mercy and for his life. Tears were running down his blood-streaked face as he looked up at Michael, sobbing and crying.

Finally, Michael said, "I'm going to make this really simple for you. If you want me to kill you quickly and painlessly, then I want to hear you say: *I'm sorry for all of the people that I terrorized, but I know I'm a piece of shit that is going to rot in hell.*"

Five seconds later, Michael said, "Time's up," and brought the cleaver thundering down on Winston's left hand, shattering it to a pulp. The wailing, screaming, and crying reached a crescendo, and so Michael finally slammed the cleaver down on the man's forehead, flattening his skull like a broken eggshell and instantly ending the cacophony of pain.

"But that," said Michael "is for all of the other people that you've tortured and murdered before you fucked with the wrong guy."

Kyle dragged Cassie by her neck and right arm into the second bedroom and threw her on the bed. "Let's make another baby. The last time was fun, don't you think? But this time, I'm gonna make it rough to teach you a lesson, you fucking cunt!"

Although Cassie was terrified, when Kyle released his grip by throwing her on the bed, her initial reaction was dictated by more anger than fear. When he moved forward and tried to climb on top of her, she attempted to kick him in the crotch, but missed and hit his inner thigh instead, which infuriated him. He threw himself on top of her, and the impact of his weight knocked all of the breath out of her lungs, leaving her gasping for air. Then, he grabbed her neck with one of his hands in a stranglehold and started pulling down her pants with his other hand.

As the blood supply to her brain from the carotid arteries was cut off by his crushing grip, she could feel herself slipping into unconsciousness, with darkness rapidly descending on her peripheral vision. She knew she had less than fifteen seconds before darkness engulfed her entire field of vision and her state of consciousness, so she closed her eyes and allowed her body to go limp.

After a few seconds, Kyle sensed the change and released her neck, so he could use both of his hands to remove her pants and panties. When his gaze was transfixed by her naked lower body, she carefully reached over to the nightstand for her cosmetic bag. With one swift motion, she grabbed the nail file and thrust it into Kyle's left ear canal, which caused him to roll off of her howling in pain. Blood started flowing freely out of his ear, as he grasped the pointed, metal object and dislodged it from his lacerated ear canal and ruptured eardrum.

Cassie rolled off the bed and pushed up to a standing position, but felt so lightheaded that she almost fell down again. She had to stabilize herself before attempting to flee the bedroom.

Kyle was now looking over at her, while he held his bloody ear with one hand and grasped the nail file with the other hand. She had seen him angry many times in the past and had endured the brunt of his rages more times than she liked to consider, but there was a new expression on his face that was infinitely worse than anything she had ever seen from him before.

She bolted for the door just as Kyle swung the nail file at her, and it sliced her right forearm, tearing a jagged laceration into her flesh and breaking off the tip of the nail file in her arm. Relying on her adrenalin to ignore the pain, she ran through the doorway, slamming the door shut on her way out. As she continued her sprint to the front door of the suite, she heard him tear the bedroom door open and looked back to see him emerge from the doorway with the door knocked off its hinges from the impact with his body.

His face was beet red with spittle at the corners of his mouth, and he screamed in a murderous rage, as he started to thunder across the room toward her. She reached the front door and frantically opened it, but by that time he was within five feet of her and grabbed a piece of her long hair, yanking her backwards. Although her forward momentum carried her through the doorway, his grip on her hair caused her to lose balance, as the lock of hair was ripped from her head. This slowed her down dramatically, allowing him to grab her by the neck from behind.

At that exact point in time, as if the great clock that governed all things had suddenly stopped to give her a moment of clarity, Cassie realized that no matter what happened, she could no longer be the victim. She had crossed the point of no return, dictating that she would, from this time forward, become a warrior even if it resulted in her own death. Her epiphany also gave her the realization that she was meant for something more than being raped and murdered in a bungalow bedroom by an abusive monster.

When Cassie's lower body started shifting back towards Kyle, as he lifted her off of the ground by her neck, she pulled her right leg up to her body and kicked backwards with as much force as she could muster, hoping to catch him in the stomach. Instead, this time she connected with his crotch, which caused him to immediately release his hold on her neck and reflexively bend forward.

After landing on her hands and knees, she could see that he had also dropped the broken nail file, which she scooped up as she scrambled to her feet. Without even giving it a second thought, she jammed the jagged piece of metal upward as hard as she could, directly into Kyle's left eye, which it penetrated easily.

Kyle screamed in pain, now on his knees, and flailed his head from side to side, as he reached up to pull out the nail file. Cassie had impaled him at an angle, which penetrated not only his eyeball, but the side of the orbital bone, therefore the file was now deeply imbedded, and he could not dislodge it.

Cassie ran across the parking lot, heading toward the main entrance and check-in area. Although she was naked from the waist down, she was way past modesty, so she didn't hesitate to rush under the porte-cochere, through the main doors, and into the lobby. She ignored the shocked look on the faces of the four guests and two front desk attendants as she approached the desk. "Please call the police and security! A man just tried to rape and strangle me in my bungalow!"

One of the front desk clerks handed Cassie a towel, which she wrapped around her waist. She had chosen not to mention that the man was her husband, because she didn't want to explain the entire complicated story to these bystanders. She would save that story for the police who would be here shortly.

Michael rapidly cut the duct tape binding his brother's hands and feet and lifted him out of the pool of blood that had formed from his oozing gunshot wounds. When Michael started running to the door with his brother in his arms, Stephen spoke up, although his voice was so weak that it was barely audible. "Michael, please put me back down."

When he had placed Stephen gently on the floor, Michael knelt down so that he could hear what his brother was saying. "You need to leave me here and go help Cassie. I'm not going to make it."

"There is no way in hell that I'm leaving you here, so don't ask me to do that." With that, he unlocked the door and scooped Stephen back up, and they exited the storage room. Despite a few strange looks from other patrons in the airport, the two brothers made it back to Michael's car quickly and without incident and started speeding back to the bungalow as fast as Michael could drive.

During the drive, Michael called the front desk of the Casper Private Suites and found out that Cassie was safe, but that Kyle was nowhere to be found. After getting directions, he then rushed to the Wyoming Medical Center, where he literally ran into the emergency room with Stephen in his arms, handing him to the E.R. staff as he explained about the gunshot wounds and the blood loss. They quickly started intravenous lines and within minutes, Stephen was being taken back to the operating room for exploratory surgery to try and save his life.

The E.R. staff had assumed that the blood covering Michael was all from his brother, because Michael failed to mention any of his injuries, but a nurse noticed the multiple tears and punctures in his clothing, and the duct tape and cloth wrapped around his right wrist. She insisted that one of the E.R. doctors take a look at him. When he removed his clothing in an exam room, what they found was shocking even for the seasoned E.R. staff.

More than forty lacerations and puncture wounds were distributed over his entire body, not to mention one of the worst de-gloving injuries on his right wrist that the E.R. doctor had ever seen. He had sustained such a severe blood loss that the physician had a hard time believing that he was able to walk very far without collapsing, and he refused to believe that he had carried his brother into the E.R., despite eyewitnesses that confirmed this event.

After receiving a blood transfusion, almost 200 stitches, IV antibiotics, and extensive care to his right wrist, Michael refused admission to the hospital and instead met Cassie in the waiting area for the operating room. She had also received medical attention for her forearm laceration and minor strangulation injury.

Casper, Wyoming: September 15, 1:26 p.m.

After almost four hours of surgery, the general surgeon, Dr. Scott, entered the waiting area and approached Michael and Cassie with a serious look on his face. The tall, lanky surgeon approached the couple slowly, as if he regretted having to talk to them. Cassie reached over, grabbed Michael's hand, and placed it in her lap.

When Dr. Scott finally spoke, it was very slow and deliberate. "He's in the ICU right now and is in critical condition. He's actually very lucky to be alive at all. In addition to the massive blood loss, he sustained multiple bowel perforations, which has caused peritonitis, where bowel contents have leaked into the abdominal cavity. He also had a significant liver injury from one of the bullet fragments. We've cleaned this up as best we can, but it will still be touch and go for the next few days. I assure you, he'll get the best care possible anywhere, but I'd be lying to you if I didn't tell you that his chances aren't good."

"When can we go in and see him?" said Michael.

"He's just waking up from surgery right now. I'll have the nurses come out and get you when he's ready for visitors."

"Thank you for everything that you've done."

"You're welcome." Dr. Scott gave a sad smile and started to turn and walk off, but then faced Michael and said, "I think you should know that there are a lot of rumors circulating around the hospital right now. The only reason your brother survived at all was because of your efforts to get him here. With the injuries that I hear you sustained, it's amazing that you made it to the hospital at all." He hesitated, looked away from Michael for a second, and his expression changed to that of curiosity and wonder, before he continued.

"I understand that they found a known hit man and suspected serial killer dead at the airport. They say they've been looking for this man for a long time, and he was apparently one of the most brutal killers that have ever graced the Earth. I also understand that you're not giving a lot of details about how you sustained your extensive injuries, and I have a feeling that what you did was more amazing than we'll ever know.

The police need to take a statement from you, but I want you to know that we're good people here in Casper, and we appreciate what you've done today."

With that, he nodded at Michael and walked off. Cassie cocked her head and looked inquisitively at Michael. "What's he talking about? You said you had a few minor cuts and bruises."

"They're making a big deal out of nothing. You know how people always want something amazing to talk about. Now, how you fought back against Kyle—that was amazing."

Cassie didn't buy his story and knew that the doctor was probably right, but she decided to let it pass. Next, Michael had the difficult task of calling Kate to let her know what had happened. When he explained the severity of Stephen's condition, Kate insisted on flying to Casper, and Michael agreed to meet her at the airport. Fortunately Mark had already arrived from New York and could stay with the children while she was gone.

"So, how well did she take it?" asked Cassie.

"She was crying, but she's a very strong woman—sort of like you. I think she'll be okay."

"You actually think I'm a strong woman?"

"Are you serious?"

"Of course, I'm serious. Why would you say that?"

"Anyone who has been through what you have in the last two years and can make the turn-around that you've made in the past two days is truly a remarkable person. When I first met you, you seemed like you were broken, but you've continued to surprise me with things you've said and done. How you defended yourself against Kyle was truly phenomenal. I know you must have been terrified, but you still summoned the courage to fight back like a demon."

As she looked back at him, she could feel emotions welling up inside of her that she had been suppressing for years. The man who sat in front of her had saved her life, had taken her away from an abusive situation that she felt trapped in, had listened to her darkest confession and had not judged her, had put his own heart on the line by revealing it to her, and now had revealed how remarkable and courageous he thought she was. And all of this happened in only a few days.

As she sat there, tears began welling up in her eyes. She could instantly see concern on Michael's face, as he reached over to gently wipe the tears off of her cheek. She turned her head and softly kissed his hand and then leaned over to lay her head on his chest, letting the tears fall on his shirt. There was no need for words as they sat in that waiting room; they were content to sit and feel the warmth of each other's bodies and to block out all other things in the world for a little while. The setting could not have been less romantic, with the rather plain waiting area half filled with family members waiting on surgeries to end. But the emotions were just as strong for the two of them, so the setting really didn't matter.

Casper, Wyoming: September 15, 5:10 p.m.

Cassie drove Michael's car to the airport, leaving him at the hospital, because Stephen had finally recovered enough from his surgery to allow visitors and had been almost frantic with his insistence on talking to Michael immediately. This just happened to coincide with the arrival of Kate's plane flight from Denver, so Cassie was given a detailed description of her and even made a small sign with the name "Kate Hanson" written on it, although Cassie felt certain that she could identify her without it.

She was sure that Kyle was no longer in Casper, but just to be safe, she brought the Air-Taser with her that Michael had confiscated from

Winston Delk's collection in the storage room. She also made sure that she constantly remained alert and aware of her surroundings, so that she couldn't be taken by surprise. Michael was still concerned about her safety, although he realized that she could be a surprisingly resourceful adversary.

Cassie waited for Kate in the baggage claim area. She instantly recognized her from Michael's description. Kate was about four inches taller than Cassie at five-six and was very attractive, with piercing green eyes and dishwater blond hair. She had a warm but sophisticated manner about her, and Cassie instantly liked her from the moment they met.

After introducing herself and explaining why Michael was not there, Cassie was surprised and pleased when Kate stepped forward and gave her a hug. She thanked Cassie for picking her up and allowing the two brothers to be together at such a critical time.

As they were walking to the car, Cassie described what she knew about the ordeal with Winston Delk that Stephen and Michael had endured at the airport earlier this morning. Then she described the interesting revelations and insight that Dr. Scott had revealed earlier.

Kate smiled with understanding as she said, "If I know Michael, the surgeon's insights were correct. Did you ever find out what his injuries were?"

"He just mentioned a few cuts and bruises."

"Don't feel bad—he told me and Stephen the same line of bullshit when he returned from Somalia. Did he tell you anything about what happened there?"

"He mentioned that the Marines sent in Special Forces to rescue some hostages in Mogadishu and that one Marine died and two were injured. I know that the Marine that died was his best friend, Darius, but that all of the hostages lived, thanks to Darius' actions."

"Cassie, I'm going to tell you the entire story while we drive to the hospital, so you can gain some understanding about this man. The only reason I know what really happened is because Stephen and I met one of the Marines in Force Recon at the military hospital, when we were visiting Michael. Stephen suspected that Michael's version of the story was missing some details, but neither one of us were prepared for the incredible story that the Marine recounted for us that day."

As she started driving to the hospital, Cassie listened intently as Kate told her the story that was never revealed to the press or the public, because of strong political pressure.

> Apparently, the three American missionary families just happened to be in the wrong place at the wrong time. They were actually passing through the East African country of Somalia on their way to Ethiopia and made the mistake of straying outside of the airport in Mogadishu, because at the time it happened to be one of the most dangerous cities in the world.

> Mogadishu is the largest city and capital of Somalia and has been plagued with political unrest, civil war, and violence since 1991, when warlords ousted former President Mohamed Siad Barre. Since that time, multiple different warlord alliances had formed, all in an effort to gain control of the city and the country, and this resulted in almost continuous bloodshed.

> This seemed to reach a peak about ten years ago, when an especially fanatical and violent Islamic warlord named Abdullah Hassan Jabadda attempted a major coups in one of the largest alliances by assassinating all other warlord leaders in that alliance, so that no one could usurp his power or question his authority. The United States was keeping close tabs on Jabadda, because they considered him an extremely dangerous leader, especially with his history of violent fanaticism

in the name of religion and his suspected ties with international terrorism.

Just as he was taking control of the alliance, the U.S. started secretly funding another competing alliance of warlords through the CIA, in an effort to balance the power and prevent Jabadda from taking over. These efforts were relatively successful, although the U.S. knew it was treading on thin ice, in order not to violate the international arms embargo of Somalia established by the United Nations. When Jabadda's power started slipping, he became frantic and started a campaign of terrorism aimed at all Americans, in an effort to get some leverage on the U.S. In just a few weeks, Jabadda had orchestrated six car bombings which resulted in the death of fourteen American citizens.

It was at the height of this violence that the three American missionary families, which included six adults and eleven children, had flown into Mogadishu on their way to Ethiopia. They had an eight hour lay-over, so they decided to see some of the culture in a market area which was close to the airport. When they arrived at the market, they were instantly recognized as Americans by some of Jabadda's men and were subsequently abducted at gunpoint and taken to an abandoned warehouse in an industrial area of Mogadishu.

At the warehouse, all of the men and women were bound and gagged, and the children, who ranged in age from two to fourteen, were kept in a separate locked room with only one doorway and no windows. Jabadda thought that he finally had the leverage he needed to end the U.S. support for opposing factions, but the U.S. flatly denied any funding of rival warlords, so he sent U.S. officials in the area a severed ear, supposedly from one of the adult missionary women. The U.S. later discovered that the ear was, in fact, from one of Jabadda's concubines who had displeased him.

It was then that Jabadda threatened to begin a systematic slaughter of the missionaries if the U.S. continued their denial of any funding. In a now famous quote, he told the local press that he would "slice off pieces of flesh from the hostages, starting with the youngest children, and mail them to the President of the United States in plastic baggies." He also warned the U.S. not to send a rescue mission, because this would prompt the immediate execution of all missionaries.

This was viewed by the U.S. military as a no-win situation, until one of Jabadda's men secretly defected because he could no longer tolerate "the persecution of innocent children" and started sharing information about the location and layout of the warehouse.

Force Recon was chosen for the difficult mission, and the twelve Marines were immediately flown to Mogadishu, where they were given a detailed layout of the large warehouse. With multiple entrances into the building, they were relatively certain that they could quickly eliminate any guards or lookouts, break into the facility, and save the adults, but there was no easy access into the room housing the children, because there were no windows. To make matters worse, the room had thick concrete walls, so any attempt to use explosives to enter the room was likely to injure or kill some of the children.

In addition, there were always two guards inside the room and four guards outside, all armed with automatic weapons. They were instructed to immediately start killing the children in the event of a military siege on the warehouse. The final complicating factor was that the only door into the room was a heavy iron monolith that could not be penetrated easily enough to instigate a surprise attack on the guards inside. Apparently Jabadda understood that the warehouse was a stronghold only because of the threat of injury or death to the children.

After considering every possible option, Force Recon decided to proceed with an extremely risky plan that would have to be executed to perfection in order to work. At the precise time of a late night shift change for the guards overseeing the children, snipers would eliminate all lookouts and guards, and then Force Recon would knock out both the power grid and back-up generator for the warehouse. In the confusion created by the total darkness of the power loss, they would then storm the building using night vision goggles and tear gas and quickly incapacitate or kill all guards before they had a chance to injure any of the children or adults.

The only hitch to this plan was that they would need to know the exact time of the shift change, which would require a member of their team to be inside the building to give visual confirmation. In order to achieve this, the U.S. arranged a meeting with Jabadda to "negotiate." They assured him that they would cooperate with his demands, but only if one of the male adults who had been severely beaten, according to their intelligence, was released to receive medical attention.

The U.S. agreed to exchange the hostage for another adult male, which is how Darius, Michael's best friend in the military, entered the warehouse. He had been chosen for this task because of his uncanny ability to pick locks and free himself from ropes or handcuffs, giving him the nickname Darius "Houdini" Johnson. When this maneuver was decided, he was surgically implanted with an undetectable wire he could use to alert Force Recon of the precise time of the shift change. Even if he was unable to break free from the handcuffs or ropes binding him, he would still be able to coordinate the time sensitive siege.

When all Force Recon operatives were in place that evening, Darius gave the signal at 11:35 p.m.. that he suspected a shift change in the next few minutes. When that was confirmed several minutes later, snipers instantly took out all six exterior guards and lookouts, and power was immediately shut down.

Michael led the siege into the warehouse, as he and the other eight Marines easily wiped out fourteen of Jabadda's men in less than one minute. When they reached the central room, which was adjacent to the children's room of confinement, they incapacitated the six guards, freed the five missionary adults, and found out that Darius had escaped his handcuffs and went bolting for the children's room just seconds before the lights went out. The adults didn't know why he ran into the room, but they heard automatic weapon fire after the lights were extinguished.

Michael quickly entered the children's room and found Darius barely hanging on to life with three gunshot wounds to the abdomen and a huge pool of blood surrounding him. Next to him, with his neck broken, was the unsuspected third guard that Darius had seen inside the children's room that did not exit the room for the shift change, prompting Darius to enter the room and try to avoid catastrophe because of the incorrect information they were given. The other shock was that the children were nowhere to be seen!

Darius pointed to the floor. "Down there." When Michael looked down, he noticed a large wooden trap door, which they immediately opened, to reveal stairs leading down into a large basement, dimly lit with torches. Feeling time running out for the children, Michael threw off his night vision goggles and dashed down the stairs with reckless abandon, followed by another marine, Jacob Cambron.

The corridor at the end of the stairway quickly turned into a large central basement area with multiple small rooms around its perimeter, all with barred windows resembling prison cells. They heard a child's cry coming from one of the small rooms on the opposite side, so Michael ran across the central area, with Jacob staying back to cover him.

When he was halfway across the room, three separate doors on his right side suddenly opened, revealing men with assault rifles who immediately opened fire on Michael, with bullets passing through his right upper arm, grazing his scalp, and penetrating his right hip and left lower leg. This caused him to stumble and fall, and his own assault rifle went sliding across the floor, out of his reach. He immediately rolled twice to dodge oncoming bullets and threw his knife at the closest man, hitting him directly in the neck. Jacob opened fire on the other two men, riddling both of them with a slew of bullets before they time to react.

As Michael limped over to the doorway to free the children, he pulled his knife from the dead man, grabbed the keychain hanging on the wall, and slid the large key into the lock. It was too dark for him to see into the room, but when he pulled the door open, he could see all eleven children huddling in the corner. As he stepped into the room, he heard shots fired from behind him and instinctively pulled the door shut to protect the children.

Force Recon's military intelligence had been compromised with inaccurate information about the interior of the warehouse and the number of guards overseeing the children, but the most important piece of information that they lacked was that Abdullah Hassan Jabadda had a secret entrance and exit to the warehouse, which connected directly to the basement.

When Michael looked back through the barred window, he could see Jabadda and four of his men standing over Jacob Cambron in triumph. As the power hungry warlord approached the cell, he exclaimed, "Children must die!"

Michael knew what was coming, so he quickly had the children line up single file, so that he could block all of them from the line of fire with his own body. When Jabadda reached the barred window, he put his assault rifle up to an opening between the bars and unleashed a massive barrage of bullets into Michael's back, trying in vain to slaughter the children.

Although Michael was wearing an advanced technology bullet proof vest designed specifically for military Special Forces, the impact from bullets at close range was still devastating, but somehow he continued to shield the children after being hit with over a hundred rounds at close range, including multiple shots that penetrated his already injured extremities. By the time the remainder of the Marines arrived, Michael was on the verge of collapsing from the pain.

In a last ditch effort, because he knew he was defeated when his four men were torn to shreds by the Marines, Jabadda opened the cell and walked up behind Michael, hitting him in the head with the butt of the rifle, which caused him to collapse sideways. He then stepped over Michael and aimed his assault rifle at the group of terrified children, yelling to the other Marines, "I will kill them all unless you let me leave unharmed!"

As Michael lay on his side just behind Jabadda, he regained consciousness long enough to realize that there was only one thing he could do. He pulled out his knife, and in one motion, sliced cleanly through the warlord's Achilles tendon on both feet. When he tried to step away from the pain, Jabadda collapsed forward, at which time Michael expended his last reserve of energy to drag himself on top of the man and slam his knife as deeply as he could into the vile bastard's left chest.

The members of Force Recon carried Michael, Jacob, and Darius out of the building, and they were flown by military helicopter to the closest hospital and trauma center. Michael held Darius' hand in the helicopter and his dying friend smiled when he said, "I love you, brother." Those were the last words that the two men shared before Darius closed his eyes and took his final breath.

By the time the story was over, the two women were sitting in the hospital parking lot, and Cassie had a look of awe on her face. Kate touched her right arm, and said, "I hope the story gave you a little better understanding of Michael Hanson. Without knowing the details, I'm sure that something phenomenal must have happened this morning. I also know in my heart that the only reason Stephen is still alive is because Michael was there."

There was one more thing that Cassie desperately wanted to ask about Michael, but she had already monopolized a lot of Kate's time, and she knew that Kate needed to see her husband. Cassie decided to save the question for a later time.

Michael had been sitting in a chair beside Stephen's bed for thirty-five minutes watching his brother sleep, when he finally reached over to hold his hand gently. Stephen opened his eyes, looked up at him, and smiled, but Michael could still see significant concern dwelling within his facial expression. Stephen's face and hands were pale white, which was a disturbing contrast to his normally ruddy complexion. When he started talking, his voice was still very weak, so Michael leaned over the bed to hear him more clearly. "I told you to leave me, but I guess it doesn't surprise me that you didn't. You've always been so damn stubborn. How is Cassie?"

"She's fine. Did you hear that she fought back against Kyle and actually got the better of that big gorilla?"

"I told you she's an incredible woman. I could tell that after only knowing her a few hours. She's part of what I wanted to talk with you about. But, first, please tell me that Kate isn't flying out here to see me."

Michael sat in silence and looked away from Stephen, effectively answering the question without saying a word. Not really knowing what else to say, Michael answered his brother as best he could. "Look, Stephen, what was I supposed to do? She's your wife, and I had to let her know what was going on. What would you have done if the roles had been reversed?"

Looking at his brother with irritation in his eyes, Stephen said, "I'll tell you what I would have done. I would have tried to convince her not to come. You know what's about to be unleashed here, and we're right in the middle of the blast zone for the upcoming catastrophe. This city is way too close to the Verneshot launch pipe; in fact, anywhere in the continental U.S. is too close."

Michael looked sheepishly at Stephen. "Do you really think I could have convinced her not to come?"

Some of the irritation faded from Stephen's eyes, as he sighed, and said, "Knowing Kate, I guess you're probably right. She's even more stubborn and pig-headed than you are."

"Hey, I heard that," said Kate from across the room. She and Cassie had arrived at the room just moments before and now approached the bedside. When Kate stood next to Michael, she looked down at Stephen. "Wow, you look like shit!"

"It's good to see you too, honey."

Kate immediately smiled and bent over to kiss Stephen. "I guess you're still cute, even when you look like shit."

With that, Michael and Cassie walked out to the waiting area to give Stephen and Kate some time to be alone and talk. Michael knew that Stephen was anxious to discuss what was going on with Kate, so that he could quickly convince her to fly back to Denver.

They drove back to the Casper Private Suites, grabbed a quick bite to eat at a nearby restaurant, and told the front desk that they would be staying another night. They were given a different suite and felt relatively safe because the entire complex had been carefully inspected by the police. In addition, four officers remained close by to ensure that Kyle did not cause any more problems in Casper.

By that time, it was almost 8:00 p.m., and Casper Mountain was silhouetted against the beautiful orange, violet, and dark purple hues of the setting sun. A cold breeze was now drifting down from the mountain, carrying with it the scent of mountain forests and unspoiled wilderness. Although Michael found this invigorating and wanted to stay and relish the moment with Cassie, he knew that they needed to get back to the hospital.

When Michael and Cassie entered the ICU waiting area, Kate was waiting for them and approached Michael with tears in her eyes. She put her arms around him and kissed him on the cheek. "Thank you for what you did—and thank you for calling me. I know he gave you a hard time about that, but I needed to be here with him."

"Has something happened to him?"

"No, he's about the same. I was just sad thinking about everything. You know he wants me to go back to Denver with you and Cassie."

"He loves you, Kate."

"I know he does."

"So, what are you going to do?"

"I don't know. I just don't know."

"We're not leaving until tomorrow, so why don't you just think about it tonight."

She nodded her head. "He really wants to talk with you again, so Cassie and I will go get some coffee and meet you back here in a little while."

He agreed and started walking toward Stephen's room, as the two women turned around to leave.

When Michael entered Stephen's room, two nurses were checking monitors and administering medication. When they finished, he approached the bed and pulled the chair closer so that they could talk.

Stephen was the first to speak. "I don't know if I'm going to be able to convince her to go back with you. When are you leaving?"

"Not until tomorrow, so you still have time to work on her."

"I don't know why I was always attracted to the strong willed type, but she is so frustrating some times. For every point I made about why she should leave, she had a reasonable argument to the contrary."

"She wants to be with her husband. That's pretty reasonable."

"I understand that, but we have two children to think about."

"She's between a rock and a hard place, Stephen. She has a husband in critical condition in the hospital, although he's not so critical that he can't argue with everyone. Then she has two children that she loves very much at home, with the entire country about to be blown off the map. There aren't any great options here."

Stephen gave a grimace of intense pain for a moment, and his breathing and heart rate became more irregular. Michael was about to summon the nurse, when the pain appeared to subside, and Stephen said, "I know all that. But when the word gets out on what's happening there will be the largest transportation crisis and panic that the world has ever seen, with everyone trying to flee the country. The U.S. government will have no choice but to shut down all air travel and put the country under martial law in order to restore some semblance of order. Then it will be virtually impossible to get out of the country."

"We're going to face that in Denver, too."

"Mark is in Denver with his corporate jet at his disposal. I want all of you to get the hell out of this country and at least over to Europe before the news breaks."

"And what about you?"

"If I recover enough to travel and if I have enough time before this hits, then I'll hook up with all of you later."

"I don't want to leave you here."

"I know that, but you don't have a choice right now."

"Well, then, we'll wait here until you can travel. You said yourself that we don't know exactly when this will happen."

With exasperation in his weak voice, Stephen said, "Dammit, Michael! You're not getting this! If you don't get your asses out of the country right now, then you're going to be stuck here in the middle of this damned apocalypse when it does occur! We're talking about something that's going to annihilate billions of people worldwide and quite possibly 90 percent of all people in the U.S.!"

Stephen's heart rate increased significantly on the monitor, and his breathing again became irregular, which prompted his nurse to enter the room, but by that time he had calmed down again, so she left after double-checking his vitals.

Both men remained silent for a few minutes, but finally Stephen said, "Michael, I want you to get back to Denver tomorrow, and I want you to get my family out of this country. I'm entrusting you with the lives of my children. I don't know if you know this, but you've always been my hero. When you were cavorting around the world with Force Recon, I was so proud of you, and I knew that the U.S. had the best man in the world to protect us against power hungry monsters and terrorists.

"Somehow, I knew you would find a way to save us from that psychotic sociopath at the airport this morning. Now, the human species is facing the biggest threat to its survival that it will probably ever encounter. Even after the volcanoes have burned out, and the earthquakes and tsunamis are over, and the sky has cleared, humans will still be on the endangered species list because most of our crops and livestock will have died, food shortages and starvation will be rampant, chaos and anarchy will rule supreme, and the most violent and fearsome barbarians will temporarily seize power and rule the Earth—the innocent will be subjected to their will.

"This is not what I think will happen, but what I know will eventually become a reality. In this terrifying world of the near future, there's only one man on the planet that I would want protecting my children—and that's you—my older brother and my only hero."

By this time, there were tears in both Stephen and Michael's eyes, but Stephen continued to lay his thoughts and emotions on the line. "You know that I love Samantha and Christopher more than life itself, and so I'm entrusting you with the most sacred thing that I possess, which is the love I carry in my heart for my children."

"Stephen, you know I love your kids."

"I do know that—and if I'm not around…"

"I'll treat them like they were my own children."

"You know that there's a chance that Kate won't be around either, especially if I can't convince her to return to Denver with you."

"I don't want to think about that, but the thought has crossed my mind."

"You know what that means…"

"That Cassie might have to be a surrogate mother and inherit two children that she's never met before?"

"I just think we need to consider all possibilities. I think you need to talk to her about this to make sure you're both on the same page. That's one hell of a responsibility to dump on someone you've known only a few days."

"I'll talk to her about it tonight."

"Thank you for everything, big brother. I love you."

"I love you too," said Michael.

When Cassie and Kate reached the visitor's lounge on the first floor of the hospital, they each grabbed some coffee and sat in high-back leather chairs next to a coffee table. They looked out the window and marveled at the small, manicured garden area.

"Stephen really talks highly of you," said Kate. "It sounds like both you and Michael have been through quite an ordeal."

"We definitely have been through some life-altering things in the past few days. By the way, I think your husband is wonderful."

"He is a great guy, but I wish he wasn't so stubborn."

Cassie smiled and in a good natured tone, she said, "You know he says the same thing about you."

Kate smiled back. "Isn't it pathetic how married people start to act like each other and even start saying the same things?"

"I don't know; I think it's kind of sweet."

"I guess so—pathetic and sweet. Say, do you mind my asking what the deal is between you and Michael?"

"It's hard to explain; so much has happened in such a short time. I don't know how much Stephen has told you, but I am married."

"To some abusive monster who tried to rape and kill you; I don't consider that a marriage."

"I don't either. I just thought it's best to be honest with you. I've made some very bad choices in my life."

"We all have, Cassie. So, back to my question, I guess I should tell you that I don't think two people need to know each other for a long time in order to share a special bond."

"What you're asking me is the same thing that your husband asked me yesterday—just in a different way."

"You see, there's that creepy married couple thing again."

"To answer your question, Michael and I do have a special bond. I'm not sure that there's going to be much of a world left for us to share our life together, but that is what I want."

"That really makes me happy to hear that. He suffered so much when Amy and Tabby died. I know there may not be much of anything left for any of us, but he deserves someone like you, and with how I feel about Michael, that's one of the biggest compliments I can give."

"Thank you," said Cassie, as she and Kate gave each other a hug.

"That reminds me, Kate, can you please tell me what happened with the car wreck that claimed his wife and daughter's lives. You know he still blames himself for their deaths."

"My God, I had no idea! How could he blame himself for what happened?"

"What he said, when we talked a few days ago, was that he was the one responsible for their deaths. I didn't really buy that, but I also didn't want to churn up any painful memories for him by asking a lot of questions."

"Cassie, it was horrible tragedy, but there was nothing he could have done to prevent the accident, and no way he could have saved their lives in the ten minutes following the wreck."

"You mean they weren't immediately killed in the crash?"

"That was the most horrible part of the entire nightmare. You see, Michael, Amy, and Tabby were driving home from San Francisco to Sonoma on Highway 101 North late one Sunday afternoon in April, after spending the day with friends in the city. What Michael could not have known was that a rancher pulling an empty horse trailer with his pickup truck had fallen asleep behind the wheel and was barreling right for them at over ninety miles per hour.

"Just as Michael reached the top of a small hill, he realized that he was seconds away from a head-on collision with the truck, which had crossed into his lane. They were unfortunately on a small two-lane bridge, with a thirty-foot drop and guardrails on either side, so Michael tried to do the only thing that he could, which was to dodge the oncoming truck by quickly veering to the left into the opposite lane. This probably would have worked, but the rancher woke up at the last second and in a panic slammed on his brakes, which caused the truck and horse trailer to jack-knife. This swung the trailer out wide to the right and directly into the passenger side of Michael's SUV at extremely high speed, instantly crushing the side of the vehicle where Amy was sitting in front and Tabby in the back. The SUV spun around twice before colliding with the guard rail, which caused it to roll over once, finally landing on its roof in the middle of the bridge.

"I can't imagine the kind of horror that Michael must have experienced, when the vehicle came to a stop upside down, and he looked over to see the battered bodies of his beloved wife and daughter, who were both trapped and partially crushed by the deformed metal shell of their car. Both were still alive but unconscious for the first few minutes. As Michael tried desperately to free both of them, Tabby regained consciousness, and when she saw Michael, she started crying out, "Daddy, please help me!"

"Because Amy was still unconscious, he focused all of his efforts on freeing his daughter for the next ten minutes, unfortunately in vain, because Tabby's crush injury was fatal, and she died in the car with Michael holding her hand and looking into her frightened eyes.

"He was able to free Amy after about five minutes, but she never regained consciousness and died in the hospital two days later. Tabby was so severely crushed by the wreck that it took a crew of men with heavy equipment almost an hour to extricate her body from the SUV, and even though they were careful, she was almost torn in half by her injuries.

"I know that Michael was haunted by several things about this tragedy. First was the look of fear and pain on his daughter's face. Second was the fact that Tabby was calling out for help, but he was unable to do anything but hold her hand and watch her die. But third was the fact that Tabby's injury was fatal, but he wasted most of his efforts in the first ten minutes trying to free her because she was conscious, and maybe Amy would have survived if he had focused on freeing her instead.

"These were all things that we knew were tormenting Michael, because he talked about them frequently, but we never knew that he believed he was the one responsible for their deaths. Why in God's name would he come to that conclusion?"

Cassie said, "Based on your description, I think I might know why."

When Michael returned to the waiting area, Cassie and Kate met him at the check-in desk and after exchanging hugs, Kate said she would be staying at the hospital that night. As Michael and Cassie walked out to his car, he said, "It's almost 9:30 p.m., but I'd really like to get a drink and a bite to eat before we go back to the hotel. Does that sound okay to you?"

"Sure. Where do you want to go?"

"I don't want to be too boring, but I really liked that bar and steakhouse that we went to the other night. Is that okay?"

"Sounds good to me—that place was great! Hey, you're not choosing a bar because you're trying to get me drunk, are you?"

She said this with playfulness in her voice, but Michael seemed confused by the question, and simply said, "Why would I do that?"

At this point, Cassie became very embarrassed and changed the subject quickly.

After ordering dinner, Cassie scarcely uttered a single word. A few minutes later, she noticed a big grin on Michael's face as he said, "Why don't we order some mixed drinks."

Now, Cassie was confused and even more embarrassed, so she gave Michael a peculiar look but said nothing. He then switched seats so that he was sitting next to her instead of across from her, leaned over with his arm around her back, and whispered into her ear, "So, do you get frisky when you're drunk?"

She looked at him with aggravation in her eyes and some irritation evident in her voice, and said, "You did that on purpose!"

"What was that?" Michael said in a coy fashion.

"Acting like you didn't understand what I was saying earlier about getting drunk."

"I don't know what you're talking about," he responded innocently.

"That was so mean!" she said, as she punched him with only a little force on his right side, but this resulted in Michael grimacing in pain. At first, Cassie was concerned, but then a look of amusement washed over her face. "I'm not falling for that act any more."

He looked at her and shrugged his shoulders, just as the waitress brought their dinner to the table.

They made their way back to the bungalow around 10:55 p.m., and Michael immediately slumped down on the couch. Cassie sat on one of the love seats adjacent to the couch and said, "You know I'm still mad at you for teasing me tonight."

Michael smiled. "Sorry, but I couldn't resist. You know you're adorable when you're mad."

She moved over to the couch, sat close to him, and raised her hand to give him another soft punch in the side, but this time, he held her hand and said, "Hey, that does hurt when you do that."

She responded by saying, "Don't give me that baloney, tough guy. I barely hit you."

She put her hand down and leaned back on the couch. At first, both of them sat quietly, but then Cassie turned to face Michael and took both of his hands in hers. "Michael, can we talk about something important for a minute?"

"Sure thing, tough girl."

"I'm serious."

"Okay, go ahead."

"I want to talk about the car wreck several years ago, but only if you're comfortable with it." She could see the muscles in his neck and shoulders tense up as soon as she mentioned the word wreck. "What do you want to know about it?"

"I want to know why you told me you were responsible for the deaths of your wife and daughter."

"Did Kate talk to you about the wreck?" he said with some apprehension.

"She did. She explained what happened in detail, and both of us were concerned that you still blame yourself for something you couldn't have prevented."

"You just don't understand what happened," he said, as he looked away from her. She reached over and gently grabbed his face, turning it so that they were looking into each other's eyes again.

"I think I do understand. Will you let me give this a try?"

He nodded, so she said, "When that truck was coming at you, you veered to the left, which exposed the passenger side of the car to the impact, but if you had chosen to veer to the right, you would have exposed the driver side instead."

She saw tears forming in his eyes, as he nodded again to let her know that she was right. Cassie took a deep breath, and then said, "Michael, have you considered what would have really happened if you had veered to the right instead?"

He remained silent, so she continued, "You're not stupid, and you're not naïve, so I know you can't really believe that everything would have turned out perfect for your wife and daughter if you had veered the other way."

"I exposed their side of the car to the area of greatest force and therefore the greatest danger and peril. From my military training, I knew all of this by heart."

"And from your training, you also understood that *every* decision in a dangerous situation is a calculated risk."

"But this was different."

"Why?"

"Because the calculated risk was with my wife and daughter's lives; I never should have taken that chance."

"You didn't have a choice!" Cassie had very distinctly raised her voice in order to get her point across, and this immediately caught Michael's attention.

"Now you listen to me, Michael! From what Kate described to me earlier, let me tell you what I think would have happened if you had veered the other way. First of all, the truck would have impacted the driver's side at very high speed, which would have slammed the passenger side into the guard rail with severe force. This "sandwich" effect would have crushed the car from both sides and probably caused it to flip over the guardrail, falling off the bridge, with a devastating impact thirty feet below. That would have resulted in three fatalities and possibly four if the man in the truck died, instead of the two fatalities that actually occurred.

"What you did, in reality, was the only possible way that you could have saved your wife and daughter, and it would have worked if the rancher hadn't awakened and jackknifed the trailer. But with him either awake or still asleep, you would have been slammed into and over the guardrail if you hadn't veered left."

"There's no way you can prove that you're right about this."

"And there's no way you can *prove* that I'm wrong!"

Michael sighed, wiped his eyes once, and said, "Okay, I see your point. It's just that with the hundreds and hundreds of people that I had spent my life saving with Force Recon, I couldn't even save the two people that I loved most in this world."

Cassie held his chin up so that he was looking into her beautiful, compassionate eyes. "Michael, you saved a lot of people, but you can't save everyone in every situation—not even if they're the ones that mean the most to you."

She said this with both tenderness and emotion in her voice and then leaned over and gave him a soft kiss on the cheek before sitting back again. He kept his eyes focused on her lovely face, held her hands more tightly, and replied, "Thank you. You know, it took me a long time to work through a lot of these things, and I'm a lot better, but I still feel like I failed them."

"I know you do—and because of the type of man you are, you probably always will. But in reality, you didn't fail them. And right now, they're probably looking down at you, and they're really pissed at you because you're putting yourself through this!"

Her attempt at humor produced a small smile from him, and his posture appeared to relax. "While we're on the subject of important things," he said, "there's something I really need to ask you."

"I'm all ears," said Cassie.

"Stephen's going to try and convince Kate to go back to Denver with us tomorrow, but there's a chance that she'll choose to stay with him instead. If that's what she chooses and Stephen doesn't recover before the catastrophe begins, then neither one of them will make it out of here alive. The reason I'm telling you this is because my brother is very concerned about his children, especially if both he and Kate don't make it."

Suddenly Cassie's face showed a look of understanding. "Are you trying to ask me whether I'd be willing to fill in as Mommy for Samantha and Christopher, if Kate isn't around anymore?"

"Well, it is a huge responsibility, and I didn't want to be presumptuous about such an important thing."

"Michael, I know for sure I'd love those children with all of my heart."

"How can you know that?"

Cassie paused and moved close enough to Michael that she could feel the warmth of his body pressing against her, and said, "That's simple—because I'm in love with their uncle."

Michael suddenly had a surprised look on his face, backed away from Cassie, and said, "When did you meet Mark?"

Cassie moved closer to him again and raised her right hand playfully as if she were planning on hitting him. "You better quit messing with me, Buster, or I'm going to give you one of my devastating punches in your right side again."

"Please don't—that last one really did hurt."

"What a wimp," she said mockingly. "Let's see what damage my dangerous fist did to your right side."

With that, she reached over and started unbuttoning his shirt. When she had all of the buttons undone, she pulled the shirt sideways over his shoulder and gasped in shock at the sight. Almost every inch of his chest was covered with horribly bruised, swollen, and badly inflamed skin. He had seven long lacerations in a crisscross fashion and over thirty nasty gaping puncture wounds. On his right chest alone, there must have been over fifty stitches holding the lacerated skin together.

Tears started filling Cassie's eyes. "Oh, my God, I had no idea. I'm so sorry."

He looked at her, and with a grin, he said, "You sure do have one hell of a devastating punch. I never realized one punch could do so much damage."

When he saw that this failed to produce a smile and she still had some tears in her eyes, he reached over and slowly pulled her toward him. Then he leaned forward and softly kissed her on the lips. When he started to lean back again, she put her arms around his neck and pulled him closer so that their mouths were almost touching, and then she softly caressed and teased his lips with her tongue, until he opened his mouth and pressed his lips against hers for a passionate, deep French kiss that seemed to make everything else fade away.

As Cassie's passion intensified, she gently ran her hands across his chest, and down his abdomen, which caused him to wince in pain when she reached a particularly red swollen puncture wound on his left side. This made her almost jump off the couch, but he held her tight, and said, "I guess you'll believe me when I say something hurts now."

"I'm so sorry. I thought you were just teasing me when you said it hurt earlier."

"Oh, that's okay. I know how you can make it up to me," he said with a devilish grin on his face.

She stood up while holding one of his hands, gave him an innocent, little girl smile, and started leading him to the bedroom. Then she looked at him with her big blue eyes and in her sweetest, most innocent voice, she said, "I just can't imagine how I'm going to be able to make this up to you, but I'd love to do *anything* that would make you feel better."

The maid had left the window in this bedroom cracked open an inch so that a slight chilly breeze swept across the room, mixing with the air from the heater, to produce a pleasant cool draft that instantly produced goose bumps on Michael's arms, back, and shoulders. Cassie flipped off the light switch, but left the bedroom door open so that shadows danced across the room from the undulating window curtains.

As they stood there in the soft light, she quickly slipped out of her jeans, shirt, and bra, so that only her panties were still clinging to her lovely petite figure. She slowly slid her fingers inside her panties and said, "Is there anything I could do to make it up to you?"

Although Michael's injuries were significant, he was way past the point of feeling any pain, as he let passion dictate and consume his actions. He reached over and gently picked up Cassie and laid her softly on the bed. He undressed and stood at the foot of the bed staring at the stunning woman who lay before him, slowly rubbing her inner thighs together and softly moaning.

Although he had sutures, lacerations, puncture wounds, and bruises covering much of his body, she could see the firmly sculpted muscles, which were now tensed in excitement and anticipation of feeling her soft feminine curves next to them. He reached down and slid off her panties and stared at the smooth, soft skin between her legs, as she slowly spread her legs apart for him.

Finally, he moved forward and lowered himself on top of her, and pleasure started overwhelming the pain of his injuries, as he felt himself swell deep inside this adorable and amazing young woman. He never really believed that he would have feelings like this for another woman after the death of his wife, but he could now see that he had been granted a second great love in his life.

As Cassie moaned with pleasure, Michael softly whispered into her ear, "I love you, Cassie, and I want to spend my life with you."

He could feel the goose bumps on her arms, as he caressed them with his fingertips. Then, she pulled his hips toward her and pushed up with her pelvis, which forced him more deeply inside of her and caused her to moan loudly with intense pleasure. She then whispered back to him, "I love you too, Michael, and I want you next to me and inside me every night for the rest of our lives."

Jackson Hole, Wyoming: September 16, 12:47 a.m.

Senator Wolfe lay awake on his bed staring up at the ceiling. He had sent his girlfriend home earlier, after a particularly violent session that had been strangely unsatisfying. He was convinced that it must have been related to the multitude of things that were giving him anxiety and preventing him from falling asleep for the past hour.

The first troubling issue was the fact that the USGS was preparing a statement, which was to be released to newspapers, radio stations, and television news stations throughout the country in the next twenty-four hours. Second was the fact that Colonel Colquitt, General Donner, and Spencer Montgomery were nowhere to be found as of yesterday evening, when Frank Donner made a daring escape with Spencer from Black Diamond. But most disturbing was the fact that Winston Delk was found dead in a storage room at the airport just outside of Casper, Wyoming. In their statement to the media, police officials had commented that it had likely been a "failed professional hit." They noted that Winston Delk had been linked to over seventy professional hits in the past fifteen years and possibly another eighty or ninety abductions, rapes, and murders, especially involving teenage girls.

Clinton Wolfe realized that there was now a chance that he could be linked to Winston Delk, because of the four times that he had used Delk's "services." This entire debacle was now becoming a huge destructive force aimed directly at his political career.

As he was contemplating his options, he started considering something that he hadn't thought of before. What if these fucking scientists were right about all of this doomsday stuff? Based on the taped phone conversations, he now had information that even the U.S.

Geological Survey couldn't know about, unless they had already talked to Spencer Montgomery or Stephen Hanson. What if he released this information, and it resulted in an evacuation that saved millions of lives? He would be perceived as a hero and a leader with true vision who was bold enough to release information that others were unwilling to consider. Yes, there would be an economic catastrophe in this country, but when the dust cleared, he would be hailed as the savior of millions and would be a forerunner for the next president of the United States.

While he was considering this grandiose scheme, his front doorbell rang. Who would be visiting him at this time of night? If his bitch girlfriend was back, he was suddenly feeling much better and was certain that their time together would be much more enjoyable for him. He grabbed his bathrobe and went to the front door. When he opened the front door, much to his surprise, an extremely large man with an eye-patch over his left eye, stood in front of him.

"Who the hell are you and what are doing at my door this time of night?" barked Clinton.

The stranger replied, "You should know who I am, Senator Wolfe. I talked with you on the phone yesterday concerning the whereabouts of my wife."

A look of understanding and sudden recognition filled Clinton's eyes. "You're that sheriff from Nevada, Kyle McMurphy. Your face has been plastered all over the news—that bitch wife of yours has the police in Wyoming looking for you with charges of attempted rape and murder."

As Kyle pushed his way past Clinton to enter the house, he exclaimed, "What the hell do you think you're doing? You can't stay here—you're a wanted man!"

"Excuse me, Senator, but I don't think you're in any position to tell me what to do."

"Leave my house immediately or I'll call the police!"

"Well, you just do that and when they get here, I'll let them know that I had a long conversation with a certain gentleman named Winston Delk that I met at Natrona County International Airport. Apparently, you wire-tapped a phone conversation between Michael and Stephen Hanson, and that was how you knew that my wife was in Casper. From what I understand by watching the news, Winston was a very bad man—a known hit man. Hmmm, I wonder what he was doing in Casper and how he knew about the wire-tapped phone."

"You fucking bastard, I knew I shouldn't have called you about your bitch wife!"

"Calm down Clinton." Kyle was now seated on the couch, looking over at Clinton with a big grin on his face. "I need a place to stay, and I think we can both help each other so that things work out in our favor."

Casper, Wyoming: September 16, 9:10 a.m.

When Kate didn't call them for a ride back to the bungalow, Michael and Cassie assumed that she simply chose to remain at the hospital, for fear that something would happen to Stephen. In the morning, they went to the hospital and when they entered the ICU waiting area, Kate was pacing the floor, with a look of fear and anxiety on her face.

As Michael approached her, he could tell that she had been crying earlier, because her eyes were still bloodshot, and her nose was still slightly red. "Kate, what is it—what's wrong?"

With a tremulous voice, she replied, "I don't know. He did well last night, but this morning, he started having intense abdominal pain and his heart rate became very irregular about thirty minutes ago. The nurses sent me out of the room, and the doctor has been in there with him for the last fifteen minutes."

Michael convinced her to sit down with him and try to relax. Cassie sat on the opposite side and held Kate's hand to try and lend some support.

In a little while, Dr. Scott emerged from Stephen's room and cautiously approached them. Again, he was very direct, calm, and deliberate in what he told them. "He may be having another leak of bowel contents into his abdominal cavity, causing his condition to worsen over the past few hours. We repaired all of the visible perforations, but sometimes a portion of the bowel isn't perforated, but is damaged or loses its blood supply enough to cause it to perforate later. If things don't improve in the next half hour, I'm going to have to take him back to the operating room and explore his abdomen again."

"Doctor, can we see him?" asked Michael.

"Go ahead. He's doing a little better now, so this would be the right time to visit in case we need to go back for surgery soon."

As they entered Stephen's room, his eyes were open, and he immediately motioned them over to his bedside. When he talked, his voice was even weaker than before, and he looked at Michael and Cassie. "Kate and I have decided that she'll go back with you to Denver today. The sooner you get on the road, the better."

Michael said, "Stephen, according to what the doctor said, you may be going back into surgery within the hour. We can wait and leave after you're out of surgery, and we know you're doing okay."

Stephen looked at him beseechingly and said, "Michael, this is a wish of mine that I'm begging you to honor. Please leave now so that you can be there for my children in case things go to hell in a hand basket. I've been watching the news closely last night and this morning, and something's getting ready to happen. There have been a truly frightening number of small scale earthquakes that have occurred in the past twelve hours—more than has ever been seen in the history of seismic recording. The ground uplifts had stopped, but are now steadily increasing in certain areas of Nevada, Utah, and Wyoming. This thing is going to blow very soon. You have to leave now!"

Michael realized that there was no point arguing with his brother, and that he needed to honor his request. He held Stephen's hand, and with tears in his eyes, said, "We'll leave now, little brother. I want you to know that I'll be thinking of you, and I want you to know that I'll protect your children with my life."

He leaned over so that the two brothers could have one final hug, which lasted for several minutes, because both of them knew that this was the last time that they would see each other in this life. Cassie and Stephen then exchanged a kiss and when they hugged, he whispered something in her ear, which produced a big smile, and more tears instantly started flowing. Finally, Kate gave Stephen a brief peck on the cheek, which puzzled both Michael and Cassie, and the three of them walked out of the room together.

When they had reached the waiting area, Kate put a hand on Michael's shoulder to get his attention, and when he turned around, she said, "Well, he's not going to like this, but I can't leave him here alone. Especially with him possibly going into surgery, so I've decided to stay."

"Kate, you do know what that means...."

"Of course, I do," she said without hesitation. But, as they stood there, the impact of her decision hit her all at once, and she started crying.

Michael put his arm around her at almost the same time that Cassie did. "I may never see my children again," Kate said. "I'm so afraid for them, but I don't know what else to do."

The pain and sadness in her eyes was so profound that Michael could almost feel her anguish. They sat down on the couch for a few minutes, so that she could calm down, but by this time, Cassie was also crying and Michael was teary eyed. After a few minutes, a firm resolve re-emerged on Kate's face, and she stood up. Michael and Cassie followed her lead, as she walked out to the car with them.

When they reached the car, she kissed and hugged both of them, giving her best attempt at a smile. When both Cassie and Michael were seated, she walked around to the passenger side of the car, and Cassie lowered the window. The two women held hands tightly. "You take care of my babies—tell them I love them."

Cassie nodded her head. "I will."

Kate turned back toward the hospital entrance and started walking, but before she reached the door, she turned her head to look back at the car as it drove away.

Part 2

The Countdown Begins

———◆———

Chapter 5

Panic and Flight

Monty Tipton was recovering from a hangover, as he and three of his college buddies headed home after a wild weekend in Vegas. They all attended the University of Colorado at Boulder, although Monty was originally from Waco, Texas. Monty's father was a Baptist preacher in Waco, and Monty had disappointed his parents terribly when he chose to attend college so far from the Bible belt and the God-fearing people of central Texas. His father strongly believed that his son had to find his own way in the world, however, so they agreed to the University of Colorado, with the stipulation that he maintain at least a 3.0 grade average and that he continue his Bible study on a weekly basis.

Monty became the pet project for his roommate, Travis, who was determined to show him the ways of the world. Travis had introduced Monty to his first beer, first mixed drink, first porn magazine, first strip-poker game, first gambling, first vandalism, first adult video, and

191

now his first wild weekend in Vegas. Although Monty had been a willing participant in the weekend's activities, he had fallen so far into debauchery over the last thirty-six hours that he now had recurring voices of his parents plaguing his guilty mind.

He remembered the final talk that he had with his father, just before his parents departed the college campus for their long ride home. "Son, you'll have many temptations at college, but you need to stay strong despite this, because God does not look favorably on those of us who give in to our desires. Remember that *his* wrath is both strong and severe. We will all eventually be judged, and I pray that you stay on the straight and narrow path, because if you stray too far, God can open up the Earth so that you will fall into the depths of hell!"

This message was being replayed in his mind over and over again, like a broken record, as he thought back on the binge of alcohol, marijuana, cocaine, gambling, and prostitutes. He knew he had crossed that line that his father had been talking about, and he felt a huge weight on his shoulders, as he drove the car north on I-15. His college friends, including Travis, were all sleeping soundly, so he had no one to help him with his guilty conscience, and so his father's voice became louder and louder.

"*...if you stray too far, God can open up the Earth so that you will fall into the depths of hell! If you stray too far, God can open up the Earth so that you will fall into the DEPTHS OF HELL! IF YOU STRAY TOO FAR, GOD CAN OPEN UP THE EARTH SO THAT YOU FALL INTO THE DEPTHS OF HELL!!! OPEN UP THE EARTH...FALL INTO THE DEPTHS OF HELL!!! OPEN UP THE EARTH...FALL INTO THE DEPTHS OF HELL!!! OPEN UP THE EARTH...DEPTHS OF HELL!!!*"

When the voice reached a crescendo, Monty thought that he might have to pull the car off the road, but before he reached this decision, he started feeling a peculiar vibration in the steering wheel, that extended up both of his arms, until he was unsure that he would be able to maintain control of the car. Within a few seconds, he realized that the entire car and all of its occupants were shaking in a similar fashion, and that all of the boys were starting to emerge from their slumber, because of the intense jostling. There were seven other vehicles on the road in front of them, and Monty could now see that the other cars and trucks were weaving uncontrollably on the road.

He started to slow the car down to bring it to a controlled stop, when something about 300 yards in front of him caught his attention, but he could make no sense of it whatsoever. From his vantage point, it appeared that three of the cars in front of him suddenly disappeared. But that made no sense at all—the road was flat for the next ten miles, with no hills or depressions. The intense shaking continued, making him feel disoriented. Could this be an optical illusion? Could it be a mirage? Could it be a hallucination from one of the drugs he'd taken the previous night?

As he continued to contemplate this, three more vehicles disappeared, including a very large eighteen-wheeler, leaving only one pickup truck about fifty yards in front of him. He continued to slow down, but was still traveling faster than the truck, so in another ten or fifteen seconds, he was within fifteen yards of the truck.

Despite the continual shaking and subsequent disorientation, he now had a clear view of the road ahead, and what he was looking at sent a lightning bolt of fear through his body that initially paralyzed him. Approximately a hundred feet in front of his car, the road abruptly ended in an enormous crevasse that split the highway in half with at least a sixty-foot gap before the highway continued on the other side. The whole scene had a surreal, dreamlike quality, and it seemed as if everything was unfolding in slow motion. As he watched the strange and terrifying scene unfold before his eyes, he could see the truck in front of him dive off of the precipice and fall into the deep abyss below.

Monty finally pulled himself out of his paralysis and slammed on the breaks, which caused the car to go into a slide. As he stared in horror at the apocalyptic nightmare in front of him, the words started circulating through his brain once again…*If you stray too far, God can open up the Earth so that you will fall into the depths of hell! OPEN UP THE EARTH …FALL INTO THE DEPTHS OF HELL! DEPTHS OF HELL! DEPTHS OF HELL! DEPTHS OF HELL!*

The car swung around into a full 360-degree spin-out, as it gradually slowed to a stop. By this time, his friends were aware of the precarious situation they were facing and were on the edge of their seats with terror in their eyes, as the car rapidly approached the edge of the crevasse. Monty had lost all control of the car and had completely given up keeping his hands on the steering wheel. Instead, he was holding his hands over his mouth and repeatedly saying, "I'm sorry for straying, God…I'm sorry for straying, God…I'm sorry for straying, God…"

"SHUT UP!" screamed Travis from the passenger seat, as he reached out to grab the wheel.

When the car finally came to a stop, Monty found himself staring into the dark abyss, because the car was again facing forward, and the front two tires were hanging over the edge. From what he could see, there was no visible bottom to the crevasse, and he knew that he was teetering on the edge of a gateway leading to hell.

Travis snapped into action, popping the gear shift into reverse from the passenger seat and screaming at Monty to floor the gas pedal. When he did, the car remained stationary which initially confused the boys, but then they remembered it was a front wheel drive vehicle. They felt the car lurch forward slightly, as the demolished highway at the edge of the crevasse began to crumble from the weight of the vehicle.

"GET OUT NOW!" screamed Travis, as he pushed the passenger door open and scrambled out of the vehicle. The other boys followed his command and within a few seconds, they were standing outside of the car, staring at the massive crevasse, which extended as far as the eye could see in either direction. All of the tremors had ceased, but they could still see huge pieces of rock falling off of the edge in certain areas.

"Holy shit!" said one boy, as he stared at the amazing sight.

"Jesus Christ, it's a mini-Grand Canyon!" said another.

Monty stared at them and said with some emotion, "Stop using the Lord's name in vain!"

"Shut up, Bible boy!" said Travis. "You almost got us killed!"

Suddenly, without warning, a five-foot ledge of rock in front of them broke away from the edge, causing the car to shift forward and slide off into a freefall. Although the boys were startled, they were standing far enough back that there was no immediate danger. They let out some nervous laughter and stepped back another fifteen feet from the edge.

"Goddamn, that was the scariest shit I've ever seen," said Travis. They all breathed a huge sigh of relief, except for Monty. When another tremor suddenly hit, and a twenty-foot section of the edge collapsed, carrying the boys with it, they were surprised, except for Monty.

As they fell into the depths of purgatory, the other boys screamed. Monty was silent, because he was listening to those prophetic words repeated over and over again: *Stray too far…open up the Earth…depths of hell…Stray too far…open up the Earth…depths of hell…*

Las Vegas, Nevada: September 16, 11:34 a.m.

Sydney Morgan had a significant fear of heights, so if anyone had asked her what she was doing at the top of a 1,149-foot tower, she would have been unable to give a reasonable explanation other than her own stupidity and her intense attraction to Bobby Sims. Bobby worked as a blackjack dealer at the Mandalay Bay Hotel and Casino, and Sydney met him shortly after she started working as a cocktail waitress there. After going out with her for only a few weeks, he discovered her fear of heights when she was unwilling to step out on the balcony of his condo on the fifteenth floor.

Bobby became convinced that he could "cure" Sydney's phobia concerning heights with a technique he had read about called *flooding*. With this technique, one simply exposed the phobic person to massive doses of whatever they feared, so that they could become desensitized to whatever it was that triggered their fear. That was how they ended up at the top of the Stratosphere Tower, which, at 113 stories, happened to be the tallest free-standing tower in the United States.

At first, Bobby had suggested that they should simply dine at the Top of the World restaurant, with Sydney sitting next to the window overlooking the Vegas strip. But when she seemed to tolerate this without incident, with the help of some Valium she had secretly obtained from a friend, the entire fiasco had escalated into a trip to the outdoor observation deck at the very top of the tower to attempt to go on the three highest thrill rides in the world.

When she broke down and started crying, Bobby took this as a sign that they were finally having some success at breaking through her defense mechanisms and became even more insistent that they complete the task of going on all three rides. As he dragged her up the stairs, she quickly decided that no man was worth this and that this would probably be the last date that she would ever go on with Bobby Sims. The more that she thought about it, the angrier she became with Bobby's sudden interest in psychology and using her as his first guinea pig.

When she tried to reason with him, he refused to listen to her and started talking in a patronizing tone. When she became angry, he told her that it was normal for her to react this way. As they approached the top of the stairs, she gave him a vicious look and said, "You're a fucking blackjack dealer, not a psychologist!"

"Sydney, after this is over, you're going to thank me," and he held an even firmer grasp on her arm, as he lifted her up the last few steps.

They were now on the platform to access the rides, and she could feel her heart beating wildly as her anxiety reached a fever pitch. She knew she could raise hell, make a scene in front of the other people waiting in line, and get someone to take her back down the stairs. However, she hated conflict, and Bobby was too stupid to reason with, so she decided to close her eyes and concentrate on how she would exact her revenge on this idiot when she got herself out of this horrendous situation.

After they went on *XScream*, which has a track that hangs down over the edge of the huge tower and shoots riders repeatedly to the edge of the track, Bobby then dragged her onto the newest and possibly scariest of the rides, called *Insanity*. It has a huge mechanical arm that swings passengers sixty-four feet out over the edge of the tower and spins them around, reaching three G's of centrifugal force, as the cars rotate to a seventy-degree angle facing downward. Despite hanging almost 900 feet in the air, Sydney was so angry at Bobby at this point that her anxiety was actually manageable, as long as she kept her eyes closed.

After the arm had fully rotated outward, so that they were now hanging in mid-air, but before the ride started in full swing, Sydney felt a sudden drop, as the huge arm lurched forward unexpectedly.

Bobby laughed wildly. "That was just the arm being positioned for movement. Isn't this great?"

A few seconds later, there was another sudden movement, followed by a rocking sensation that started gradually increasing. Sydney still had her eyes closed, but unfortunately she couldn't avoid hearing Bobby talk with false bravado. "Hey, I'm sure that's normal, too. Did you know that this tower was built to withstand hurricane force winds and even major earthquakes?"

Sydney wanted to tell him to shut up, but instead she remained silent.

"You may not have been aware of this," he said, "but the tower has a natural sway of fifteen to twenty feet to each side…"

Bobby's voice was interrupted by a movement that was so abrupt and chaotic that it could not have been part of the ride. They were now swinging erratically and starting to feel the huge arm tilting slightly to the side.

"Did you feel that? Now, that must have been some of the sway I was talking about…" Sydney could now hear fear in his voice, as it started becoming progressively more tremulous and high pitched, but he continued his nervous banter. "You know, I always thought it would be wild to be on one of these rides when an earthquake hit—completely safe of course, because of how it's built, but what a blast that would be. You know, I wonder how much sway would happen during an earthquake. I bet it would be just wild…"

"Shut up, you moron!" screamed Sydney. She opened her eyes to look back at the tower and see if she could get anyone's attention if she called for help, but she immediately wished she had kept them closed. The entire tower was now bending precariously from side to side, and she could see that a large section of glass and metal from the indoor observation deck was tearing loose from the edge of the tower, as it was subjected to tremendous external shearing forces.

As she watched in terror, six people on the outdoor observation deck lost their footing, fell down sideways and slid to the edge of the deck, where they grabbed frantically at the low railing, which broke loose. When they grabbed the surrounding high rail at the tower's edge, a large section of it tore loose from the tower, causing two of the people to slide off the edge with their arms and legs flailing in mid-air as they screamed in vain on their way down. The other four people desperately hung onto the remaining rail hanging over the edge of the tower and swinging with each movement of the huge structure.

Then, Sydney felt the entire tower tilt even more dramatically toward their side, followed by the fearsome sound of metal buckling and tearing from the sideways movement of the thousand-foot-tall structure. Just as suddenly as it started, all movement ceased, other than the back and forth rocking of their seats. When she looked over at Bobby, he had tears running down his face, as he sobbed, "I don't want to die!"

While looking down, she could see that midway up the tower, the structure was severely damaged, and pieces of the exterior were breaking free, with the gigantic steel supports bending from the weight of the upper half of the tower. She watched in a state of disbelief, as the top part of the tower continued to tilt, until it finally broke off from its lower half, carrying the Top of the World restaurant, all three thrill rides, Sydney Morgan, Bobby the "psychologist" and approximately 200 other people with it, as it fell almost a thousand feet to the Vegas streets below.

Interstate 25 South en route to Denver, Colorado
September 16, 12:50 p.m.

Michael and Cassie were only about forty-five miles from Denver when he realized that he was going to need to stop at a gas station soon or risk running out of gas on I-25. He had been pushing the car fairly hard but was still surprised at how quickly it had sucked up gas. After stopping at the next Exxon station he reached, he leaned over and gave Cassie a soft kiss on the cheek.

"What was that for?"

"Because you were such a sweetie and were so good to my family under really bad circumstances."

She beamed a beautiful smile that would have melted the coldest of hearts and said, "I absolutely adore your family, Michael."

"Well, they adore you, too, and so do I."

When he started pumping gas, Cassie got out to stretch her legs. He looked across at her and said, "Hey, maybe I shouldn't ask, but what did my brother say to you when he whispered something in your ear at the hospital just before we left?"

She gave him a bittersweet smile and said, "He told me that he loved me and considered me his sister-in-law, even though he had only known me for a few days. He also said that he knew Kate probably wasn't going back with us, and that I would make a wonderful mother for his children."

"That's so strange that he knew Kate would change her mind at the last minute."

Michael could sense that there was something else, so he encouraged Cassie to continue. After a brief hesitation, she said, "The last thing he told me was that you and I should have a baby, and he wanted me to give his future nephew or niece a big hug and kiss from Uncle Stephen."

Michael considered the words that his brother had conveyed to Cassie and realized what a double-edged sword all of this was going to be. On one hand, he was feeling euphoria with his new found love for this beautiful woman, but on the other hand, he was going to lose his brother and sister-in-law and, even more importantly, two children that he loved very much were going to lose their parents. And of course, they were merely one of millions of families that would be fractured and devastated by the loss of loved ones. What a horrendous, unfair tragedy this was going to be for everyone! A feeling of despair reared its ugly head and forced its diseased form into his heart, with a wave of melancholy that washed over his face.

When she sensed the change in his mood, Cassie wanted to ask what was troubling him, but she already understood his sadness, because she was experiencing similar feelings and mixed emotions. Just as she was about to share her feelings with him, she heard a loud gasp, followed by the words, "OH, MY GOD!" coming from an elderly woman standing near the door leading into the station's convenience store.

This instantly caught Cassie and Michael's attention, and both of them quickly walked over to the doorway along with five other people. After stepping inside, they found the cashier and an elderly couple standing in front of a TV that was mounted on the wall. They could hear sounds of shock and disbelief coming from them.

When he approached the screen, Michael could see a news reporter standing in front of a hotel on the Vegas strip. A few seconds later, the camera panned to the right, and he could see a scene of massive destruction in the background. He reached over and held Cassie's hand as they listened to the reporter:

> "…according to early reports, there is substantial damage to many of the resorts on the strip, with significant structural collapse involving nine of the largest casino resorts, with loss of life estimated in the thousands, and thousands more injured or unaccounted for. Perhaps the most dramatic structural collapse involved the Stratosphere Tower which, according to eyewitnesses, literally tore in half from damage inflicted by the massive earthquake, causing the upper half of the tower, including the restaurant and observation deck to fall almost a thousand feet to the street below, crushing as many as 30 vehicles and hundreds of pedestrians.
>
> "According to authorities, there are tens of thousands of people still trapped inside many of the hotels and

casinos, and emergency crews will be working around the clock for the next 24 hours to hopefully rescue the majority of them…"

Cassie leaned over to whisper in Michael's ear, "What does this mean? Is this the beginning of the nightmare?"

He whispered back to her, "I'm not sure, but I hope to God this isn't what it looks like. We're not even back in Denver yet." With that, both of them again focused on the television set.

"…the huge crevasse that formed 15 miles outside of Las Vegas spans a distance of 120 miles and is almost 80 feet wide in certain areas. It's unknown at this time how many vehicles inadvertently have plunged into the crevasse…"

While they all crowded around the television screen, a real sense of fear became more pervasive the longer that the news broadcast continued.

"…according to scientists at the U.S. Geological Survey headquarters in San Francisco, the earthquake registered 9.0 on the Richter scale, the same intensity as the largest magnitude quake ever recorded. There have also been reports of hundreds of smaller magnitude earthquakes throughout Nevada, Utah, and Wyoming in the past two hours, although we're now getting reports that there may have been several other large magnitude quakes in the neighborhood of 7.5 to 8.0 on the Richter scale that fortunately hit in some relatively unpopulated areas.

"Scientists, at this time, are unsure why so many earthquakes have hit almost simultaneously, but they think it may be linked to the huge ground uplifts that occurred earlier today. Although these uplifts have been occurring for the last few weeks and have involved hundreds of square miles of Nevada, Utah, Idaho, and Wyoming, this morning there was an uplift of 14 feet in certain large areas of these states—wait a second… I'm now getting reports that another large earthquake registering 8.2 on the Richter scale is hitting Salt Lake City and the surrounding vicinity—that's the same magnitude as the Great San Francisco earthquake of 1906…"

"Oh, shit! It's beginning," said Michael.

The other people in the room were too entranced by the TV to even notice Michael's exclamation. He grabbed Cassie by the arm. "We need to leave now!"

Both of them walked rapidly out of the store and ran to their car, jumped in, and tore out of the parking lot. When Michael was on the highway, he pushed the car over a hundred miles an hour, as they sped toward Denver. He handed his cell phone to Cassie. "We've got to get into Denver as fast as possible, and then get Mark and those children the hell out of there. I don't know how fast this thing is going to unravel, but I have the distinct feeling that the clock is ticking and our time is running out."

He told her the phone number for Stephen's house in Denver, which she called hoping to reach Mark, so that they could make plans for a rapid evacuation. Unfortunately, no one answered the phone, so Michael pushed the car to 120 miles per hour. He knew that if he arrived too late, it would be a death sentence for the entire family. A part of him could not see past the futility of trying to preserve only a few lives when millions and possibly billions would be lost in the catastrophe; however, with two children that he loved and had promised to protect, Michael was determined to reach them before the spreading apocalypse did.

Denver, Colorado: September 16, 1:38 p.m.

After they pulled into the driveway, Michael and Cassie went running into the house desperately hoping that Mark and the children were at home, but Michael became frantic when there was no sign of anyone.

Cassie looked at him with concern. "I know that the clock is ticking, but certainly we have at least a few hours before the situation becomes critical, right?"

"Cassie, this is what we're facing: When panic sets in, our ability to get out of here becomes significantly more challenging. If the news media gets wind of what's going on, and everyone starts to understand that these devastating earthquakes are just the tip of the iceberg and that we're facing loss of life on a truly cataclysmic scale, there are going to be 250 million people trying to flee the country at the same time. I don't want to be around when that happens—airports will be shut down, riots will be rampant, and the country will be put under martial law in order to organize an orderly evacuation. That is if, in fact, the government can actually be convinced that an evacuation is necessary, but it will be too late for all that. What they'll actually end up doing is trapping everyone inside of the U.S. which will condemn all of them to death."

"Okay, I understand now, so how do we find them?"

"I wish I knew how to find them, and I sure as hell wish I knew why I can't reach Mark on his cell phone!"

"Why don't you try him again—maybe he had it turned off."

"We've already tried about ten times, but I guess we have no other option."

This time, when Michael dialed Mark's cell phone, both he and Cassie could hear a phone ringing in the kitchen, where they found the cell phone sitting on the breakfast table. Now Michael was completely exasperated with the situation. "Oh my God, he's the owner and CEO of a billion dollar company, and he doesn't have enough sense to keep his damn cell phone with him when he knows that the world is facing the greatest catastrophe in the last sixty-five million years!"

Just as Michael's frustration was reaching a peak, the home phone rang, which he picked up immediately. Cassie could see a wave of relief quickly take over his facial expression. After Michael finished the brief conversation with Mark and hung up, he turned to Cassie. "Well, my genius brother decided that it would be a good idea to take the kids out for ice cream at Baskin Robbins, because he didn't want them to watch too much of the doom and gloom that presently is the only thing they're showing on television. He just didn't think it was that important to bring his cell phone. Mark always has been a free spirit, but sometimes it's so damn frustrating because he walks around with his head up his butt. You know, it's times like this that I find it hard to believe that he's as brilliant as I know he really is."

"So, how did he know to call home?"

"Well, that's the surprise. Stephen just got a call from Spencer Montgomery, who presently is with Mark and the kids. Stephen had a cow when he heard that Mark had taken the kids out for ice cream, rather than waiting at home for us. All of them should be back here in a few minutes."

"Thank God," said Cassie.

"I'll second that," said Michael.

Ten minutes later, the entire entourage walked in the front door, and before Michael had a chance to share his dismay with Mark's nonchalant attitude, Samantha and Christopher came running up to him and threw their arms around his neck. He picked them both up in a bear hug, and the children squealed with laughter and delight.

Samantha was the first to speak. "Uncle Michael, I missed you soooooo much!"

"I missed you, too, sweet pea," said Michael.

"I'm not pee. That's gross!" she exclaimed, with her innocent, high-pitched voice.

"He meant pea like the vegetable. Duh!" said Christopher.

As she pointed at her brother accusingly, Samantha said, "He thinks he's soooooo smart!"

"I'm smarter than you, you little doofus!"

"I'm not a doofus! That's so mean. You're gonna get in soooooo much trouble for calling me that!"

"Oh, I'm soooooo scared," he said mockingly. "At least, I don't say soooooo before everything."

At this point, Michael glanced over at Cassie, who had an amused look on her face, and decided to interrupt the banter between the two children because he could see that this wasn't going in a positive direction. "Hey, kids, can you do me a favor? We're going to go on a little trip, so can you run upstairs and get anything special that you'd like to take with you, because we'll be gone for quite a while."

Samantha leaned her head forward and whispered in Michael's ear, "Uncle Michael, who's that lady standing behind you?"

He smiled and whispered back in her ear, "That's my friend Cassie. Don't you remember? You talked with her on the phone."

"Of course, I remember. I'm not a doofus."

"I know you aren't, sweetie."

When Michael set both of the children down, Samantha bounded into the living room and returned with a picture in her hand and excitement in her voice. "Uncle Michael, I drew a picture for you!"

As Michael examined the picture, Christopher disgustedly said, "It's supposed to be a dog but it looks like a deformed alien cow."

"It does not. You are soooooo mean!" Samantha gave Christopher a shove and he shoved back.

Cassie quickly stepped forward to distract the children from their ongoing sibling rivalry. "Can I see the picture?"

Samantha handed it to her, and Cassie studied it carefully, as if examining a precious piece of art. "You know, that is a beautiful dog, but it looks very big. I guess that's why Christopher thought it looked like a cow."

She winked at Christopher and then said, "Hey, kids, can you take me upstairs and show me the special things that you'd like to take with you. I can even help you pack if you show me where your suitcases are."

Both children almost immediately reached out to hold her hand, and the three of them turned to walk upstairs together. On the way up, Cassie looked back at Michael and the other two men, and winked.

"Wow, I wasn't expecting her. She's something!" said Mark.

Michael smiled and nodded. He shook Spencer's hand. "It's been a long time, but it's a pleasure to see you again, Spencer."

"Same thing here, but I wish it was under better circumstances."

Michael then turned to give Mark a hug and said, "I'm still pissed at you for going to get ice cream, but it's great to see you, Mark."

As they hugged, Mark said, "Give it a rest, Bro; I already got bitched out by Stephen fifteen minutes ago."

The three men sat down on the couch and started discussing the most recent news that had been hitting radio and television. They were now reporting that casualties from earthquakes were estimated at almost 20,000 people and that disaster relief was being organized in record fashion, but that they wouldn't know exactly how many deaths had occurred for several days.

"We all know what's really going on here," Michael said, "and we've got to get these children out of this country before it's too late. Spencer, how much does the USGS know about all of this?"

"I spent almost three hours earlier today talking with them, but the problem is that they will never be able to confirm my findings at Black Diamond, because that's all classified and will never be released by the military."

"Typical government assholes," Mark said. "The possible death of 250 million people takes a back seat to keeping their stupid military secrets, which will be meaningless after this thing hits."

Michael turned back to Spencer and said, "So what you're telling me is that you don't think there will be any upcoming press releases that will precipitate crisis and panic to evacuate the country, because they can't substantiate your conclusions."

"You've got it. Unless there's something I don't know about, I don't think we're about to see the transportation crisis that would occur if this did get out. Obviously, we still need to exit the country in a timely fashion, but I don't think we have to go rushing out of here in the next hour. I guess I should take credit for some of the nonchalant behavior that you were upset with Mark about, because he and I talked earlier about some of these things."

"You see, I've been unjustly accused. It's the story of my life!" Mark said, with some animation in his voice.

"Give me a break!" said Michael, while rolling his eyes. "You actually want me to feel sorry for you, Mr. Doogie Hanson, computer genius and mega-gazillionaire?"

"Well, I guess not. I just really like being the underdog."

"Oh, brother, I guess now we know you're the doofus," said Michael.

The brothers looked at each other and started laughing, but they could see that Spencer still had a serious look on his face, so they returned their attention to him, because it was obvious that he still had something important to share with them.

When they were both quiet and staring at him expectantly, Spencer spoke. "I know that Stephen gave both of you a detailed explanation concerning what's about to occur, but there's something that I didn't tell him, because it represents classified military information. At this point, I don't think it matters anymore—and if I don't survive what's coming, someone else needs to know what I found out at Black Diamond, because it will be crucial if anyone is to survive the nightmare that's about to be unleashed..."

Mark interrupted, "You mean to tell me that we haven't heard the worst of this? How could it get any worse than what we've already been told?"

"It's what I call the proverbial *double whammy*. The dinosaurs were lucky because they had small brains and were too stupid to create weapons of mass destruction, so they lasted for almost 170 million years before the Earth wiped them out. Man, on the other hand, has been trying to create devices to wipe himself out for as long as he's been able to conceive of them. He's only been around for two million years, but remember that mammals have been the dominate species for sixty-five million years.

"Now, the human species has finally advanced its technology so that it has the ability to wipe itself out with one single virus that they call DM-19. Who needs an extinction level event when you have a doomsday virus instead? So, man, in his infinite wisdom, decided to hide this virus inside an impenetrable underground fortress called the Black Diamond

Military Base. Of course, the only problem is that this fortress is located in the same geographical region as our impending extinction level event, which can generate forces that far exceed anything they ever could have conceived of when they were constructing this "impenetrable" fortress."

"Holy shit!" said Michael. "This sounds like the Titanic all over again, and we know how that experiment turned out."

"Good analogy, Michael, only this time the population at risk is the entire human species instead of a few thousand people."

"So, didn't they have any contingency plans for potential catastrophes?" Mark asked.

"That's exactly what I became concerned about when I discovered the geologic cataclysm that we're facing. On the final day that I spent at Black Diamond, I first tried to research catastrophic contingency plans for the virus. What I found out was that they have an automated system, controlled by their mainframe computer, for destruction of all biological agents in the event of a substantial structural breach. All agents can be vaporized in a matter of seconds using their built-in Plasma Disintegrator, which instantly heats up the specimens to 10,000 degrees. The computer program designed to control this destruction process starts with the most dangerous agents, first, and DM-19 tops the list by a long shot."

"That all sounds pretty good, but I'm sure there's a hitch that we're getting ready to hear about—there always is," said Mark.

"You're right—the best laid plans of mice and men. Here's the problem. The laboratories housing the agents are located at the bottom of the facility. Obviously, this was by design, because the most likely point of a breach would be at the surface. For the exact same reason, the mainframe computer is also at the bottom of the facility. No one had considered that the structural breach might come from forces generated below the mile deep facility. In addition, as a worst case scenario, even if the computer failed to destroy the agents before it was destroyed, the fact that these agents were housed so deep underground would ensure that they were entombed below a mile of rock. But with the scenario that we're facing, massive forces are already trying to push the facility up to the surface—and we know it's going to get a lot worse. In fact, it's possible for the entire facility to be blown sky high into our atmosphere, depending on where the Verneshot occurs."

At this time, Cassie came back downstairs because the kids were content playing a board game upstairs and she wanted to be updated on what exactly was going on. After she was seated on the couch and given a summary, she said, "So, if there's a good chance that the virus will spread out of the facility to cause a massive epidemic, is there anything we can do to increase our chances of surviving? Does the virus have any weaknesses?"

"When it became obvious to me that the containment might fail, that's exactly what I wanted to know," said Spencer, "so I spent the remainder of my time researching the biological agents, especially DM-19, and its effects on the host. A lot of what I found out is not worth going into right now, but it does have one major weakness. You see, the viral transmission tends to rapidly decrease after the acute phase of the epidemic, so that after a number of months, the spread of the virus falls to zero.

Unfortunately, during the acute phase, it spreads more rapidly than any disease we've ever encountered, such that all large areas of population—in other words—all continental land masses will likely be 98 to 99 percent infected before the virus passes out of this acute phase. The virus will be lethal for most people infected, but there will be some individuals that may have a different fate—something I don't want to even consider right now. We'll cross that bridge when we come to it, and hopefully we never will."

"So, if I'm hearing you correctly," said Michael, "we need to stay away from all continental land masses or any areas with a significant population density, at least for a certain period of time."

"You hit the nail on the head," replied Spencer.

"All of this seems so unfair and unlucky for the human species," said Cassie. "I mean, we're facing not one but two apocalypse scenarios at the same time."

"I agree, but maybe it was inevitable that this would happen."

"In what way, Spencer?" said Cassie.

"Well, maybe the human species is an evolutionary dead end for the mammals, because of our inherent nature that makes us want to destroy each other. That's a very poor quality to have if you want your species to last for a long time."

"You know, the way I've always thought about it," said Mark, "is that humans have the capacity for great deeds and the capacity for great evil. The final outcome just depends on which side is going to predominate in the end. Maybe the evolutionary dead-end that you referred to is not so much a dead-end for all humans, but more of a dying branch on the tree of life that will end life for many, but if some humans can survive this ordeal, then maybe we can finally rise above our human strife in the future."

Everyone quietly contemplated Mark's words. Finally, Mark spoke up again. "I bet you guys didn't know I was a computer guru and a philosopher—just call me Doogie 'Socrates' Hanson."

This produced a smile from everyone and significantly lightened the mood. As Cassie looked at Mark, she could definitely see his resemblance to Michael, although Mark had a slighter build and wore his hair longer. He did have the same warmth and charm that was so evident in his older brothers, and she found him as instantly appealing as his brothers, just in a different, quirky way. The only thing that she found disconcerting about Mark was the fact that he seemed to approach everything with a "no big deal" attitude, but that was beginning to grow on her, along with the humor that he seemed to find in everything around him.

Cassie wrinkled her brow as if in deep contemplation and said, "Spencer, I know this might sound crazy, but couldn't we destroy the virus and the other agents if we could get control of the mainframe computer?"

Spencer shrugged his shoulders. "Well, I guess it would be possible if the person was a computer expert and was inside the facility, but there's no way at all to get into the facility. A good friend of mine, General Frank Donner, died getting me out of there."

"You don't have to be inside the facility to take control of the mainframe," Mark said matter-of-factly. "I could probably do it from Stephen's computer in his study. It's no big deal."

Everyone in the room turned to Mark, with incredulity written all over their faces. Spencer spoke first. "You're telling me that you could hack into and take control of a mainframe computer at a top secret military installation that harbors all known agents of biological warfare?"

"Sure."

"So, why haven't any of the enemies of the U.S. been able to hack into this computer and disrupt the research or destroy the agents?"

"I don't know—that's their problem."

Spencer glanced over at Michael. "Is he shitting me or is he for real?"

"If it has to do with computers, then he's for real. As for philosophy, I'd rather listen to Barney the Dinosaur."

"Low blow, Bro, my philosophy is damn good for a computer geek."

Spencer ignored the brothers' banter and said, "Mark, how long would it take you to do this?"

"With no access codes, about a week."

"Shit! We don't have that much time. I'm guessing we only have a day or two."

"Then get me the access codes."

"And just how in the hell am I supposed to do that?"

The men were stumped, but Cassie leaned forward and directed her attention to Spencer. "Didn't you meet someone in the facility that has access to those codes—someone that we might be able to persuade into getting them for us?"

Spencer shook his head at first, but then said, "Wait a second. There was this one lady that I met whose name was…Dawn—Dawn Beeson. She was a young computer expert who helped anyone at the facility who was having a computer problem. Because she was very bright, they often called her in to solve other issues as well."

"Would you repeat that again," said Mark.

"That they often called her in to solve…"

"No—not that—tell me her name again."

"Oh, it's Dawn Beeson."

"Well, folks, if we can contact Dawn, then our problems might be solved." Mark said this as he stood up from the couch and headed into the kitchen.

"Where are you going?" said Michael.

"To get my cell phone and give Dawn Beeson a call. She worked for my company about four years ago. I think I still have her number."

A look of surprise and hope glimmered in Spencer's eyes as Michael looked over at him.

Mark then added, "Oh, and I went out with her on two dates."

"Well, then that means we're doomed," said Michael.

After three unsuccessful phone calls, Mark finally called Dawn's parents in Los Angeles and was informed by her mother that Dawn would be coming home later that day, but she refused to give him Dawn's cell phone number. When he hung up, he immediately started heading for the door. "I'll be home tonight. I have to go meet Dawn at her parents' house in Los Angeles and try to convince her to come back with me. Wish me luck."

When he reached the door, he turned around and said, "By the way, Cassie, you're not only a hottie, but you're really smart. Thanks for helping us."

Then he looked at Michael, gave a thumbs-up signal, and said, "Strong work, Bro. You always did have good taste in women."

Then, without another word, he promptly walked out the door, leaving Spencer and Cassie with confused looks on their faces. Michael smiled and said, "He definitely marches to a different drummer. Let's hope that Dawn is a little weird, too, because then he may have an easier time convincing her to come back with him."

Spencer, still somewhat confused, said, "How is he going to get her back from Los Angeles by tonight? That's about 2,000 miles round trip."

"I guess he didn't tell you—he owns a Gulfstream V corporate jet."

"Are you serious?"

"Yeah, he bought it about a year ago off the Internet for fifty million dollars."

Spencer shook his head. "I feel like I'm in the Twilight Zone."

"Don't worry, you'll get used to it. Mark makes everyone feel that way when they're around him long enough."

Los Angeles, California: September 16, 4:58 p.m.

Mark walked up to the front door of the attractive two-story Spanish style house in a small suburb of Los Angeles and knocked on the door. He had obtained the address on the Internet and had also uncovered Dawn Beeson's unlisted cell phone, but he decided that his best chance for success would be to meet with Dawn in person, so he was hoping that she had already arrived at her parents' house.

When the door was opened, an attractive fifty-something-year-old woman with white hair, and a stern look on her face stood there staring at Mark as if she was sizing him up.

"Hi, my name is Mark Hanson. I was wondering whether I could please speak with Dawn—if she's here."

The woman stared at him for a short while and then said, "Are you that man that tried to get her cell phone number from me today?"

"Well, actually I am."

"I thought you said you were calling from Denver."

"I was calling from Denver."

"So, you just flew out here because I wouldn't give you her cell number?"

"Well, I actually decided it would be better to talk to her in person anyway."

"How did you find our address? I never gave it to you."

"Uh, so, is Dawn here?"

"You didn't answer my question. How did you know where we lived?"

"Please, can you just tell Dawn that…"

"She isn't here," she said coldly, "and if she was here, you wouldn't be welcome in our house anyway!"

The veins on the woman's temples started to bulge as she became more agitated, and she almost started hissing when she talked. Mark was completely caught off guard by the woman's interrogation and belligerence and found himself at a loss for words, which for him was unusual.

He quickly regained his composure and said, "Look, it's very important that I talk to Dawn. I'm unable to give you more information because this is highly classified. Certainly you must be aware that Dawn deals with critical military information on a daily basis. Just tell her that an old friend of hers is here to discuss recent events at the Black Diamond facility and that this concerns a matter of national security."

He said this with a grim, serious look on his face, and an authoritative, "all business" tone of voice. The woman was now caught off guard and asked, "You work with Dawn?"

"I used to," said Mark.

Just then, Dawn pulled the door completely open and stood alongside her mother. "Mom, it's okay. Let me talk with him. I know this guy, and he's harmless."

Her mother promptly turned around and walked back into the house, leaving the two of them standing at the doorway. Mark looked at her with huge concern in his eyes and said, "You called me "harmless." That's sounds so pathetic and wimpy. I've always thought of myself as a man of international intrigue with a glint of danger in my eyes."

"Mark, you haven't changed one bit—still a perpetual smart-ass. And what was this crap about highly classified information and matters of national security?"

"I thought that sounded pretty good. I think I'd make a good CIA agent, don't you?"

"Oh, brother, is that what you're here for, to harass me with your bullshit?"

"No, I just needed some sex and thought that you'd be up for some hooking on the side—like a moonlighting gig."

Dawn stepped outside and shut the door quickly. "Would you shut up! My Mom will hear you!"

"Dawn, I really don't think you should be embarrassed about your second profession. Be proud of what you are!" Mark said with evangelical exuberance in his voice.

"You're such a juvenile asshole. I can't believe I ever went on a date with you."

"You went on two dates with me."

"That's because I was twenty-four and stupid."

"Ouch! That hurts my feelings!"

"Sorry, I didn't know you had any feelings!"

"Ouch, again!"

"So, enough of the bullshit. How did you know about the Black Diamond facility?"

"Well, I met a friend of yours who had a charming stay there recently—Spencer Montgomery. According to him, there are some interesting things going on there that I'd like to talk with you about."

Dawn grabbed Mark by the arm and pulled him in the direction of his rental car parked at the curb. When they were both seated in the car with the doors shut, she looked over at him and said, "We can't talk here. There's no telling who's listening to us, and I can't put my parents in jeopardy. Let's drive."

"Damn, I thought you'd decided to take me up on the hooker thing."

Dawn gave him a look of disgust and said, "Asshole!"

After an animated forty-minute discussion while driving around L.A., Dawn and Mark dropped the rental car off at the airport and made their way to his corporate jet at the private aviation terminal. When they boarded the eight-passenger plane, Dawn was surprised at how luxurious the interior was, with large, comfortable leather chairs in the mid-section and a bedroom equipped with a comfortable bed, a built-in TV cabinet, and dresser in the back, not to mention the full bar and custom-built computer station.

The pilot and co-pilot, Jack Tally and Mitchell Bell, were friends that Mark had known for ten years, before he had made his fortune. Now, they worked for Mark full time and were always on stand-by in case they were needed to fly the Gulfstream anywhere in the world. The jet had a range without refueling of almost 8,000 miles, so there was nowhere on the globe that couldn't be reached non-stop.

As Dawn and Mark sat down in two of the leather chairs, the plane started taxiing over to the runway. He offered her a drink from the bar, which she declined, so the two of them sat staring at each other with quizzical looks on their faces.

Dawn was one of those women who tried to pull off the plain Jane look, but was too pretty for it to work effectively for her. She had big brown eyes, medium length dark brown hair, and even with no makeup her face was pretty enough to make most men give her a double take. She usually wore unisex clothes, but today, she was dressed in nice jeans, a cute blouse, and a stylish denim vest.

Mark finally broke the silent stare and said, "How come you never dressed like that when you worked for my company?"

"Dressed like what?"

"Dressed so cute—just like right now."

"I never dress like this when I work. I prefer to receive accolades based on the quality of my work, not how good I look." She said this with some irritation and contempt, which Mark recognized instantly as something straight out of the "Women's Movement Manual of Conduct."

Mark responded with his most serious voice and a look of deep sincerity. "I am so sorry that I offended you with my chauvinist pig comment. From now on, I'm going to have a new dress code at my company, where I give everyone burlap sacks to wear, so that every person is judged solely on their work and never on their external appearance."

This produced a smile from Dawn, and as she pictured a day at the office with hundreds of burlap sacks, she started to laugh, but Mark somehow continued to keep a straight face. "No, I'm serious. Everyone will be required to shave their heads, and women will need to wear tight binders around their breasts, and men around their groin, so that there can be no discrimination based on sex. And if that doesn't work, then I'll make the women go braless and the men will parade around in leopard skin Speedos."

He still managed to keep a straight face, which produced more laughter from Dawn. Finally, when she stopped laughing, she shook her head at Mark and said, "You're such an asshole—although I will admit you're actually funny sometimes."

"I guess a funny asshole is better than a smelly one," said Mark, which produced a disgusted look and some more laughter from Dawn.

"Hey, sorry that my Mom was running interference for me," she said. "I've had a few obsessive boyfriends over the past year, and she just worries about me."

"No problem. How about we start working on the computer. You know if we finish before the plane lands, we could always go into the bedroom for a quickie."

"Dream on, computer boy!"

"Well, it was worth a try."

Denver, Colorado: September 16, 7:04 p.m.

After dinner, prepared almost entirely by Spencer who wanted to showcase his cooking talents, Cassie took the kids upstairs to finish packing for the trip, so that Michael and Spencer could stay abreast of new developments in the news on TV and radio. Spencer made several more phone calls to discuss issues with scientists and colleagues, and Michael called Kate to check on Stephen's status.

According to her, Stephen was doing better and hadn't required surgery, although he remained in the ICU. She said she was really struggling with what she would tell the children when she talked to them and that this, in combination with the fact that there was no important news concerning Stephen, was why she hadn't called. Reluctantly, she said she needed to discuss things with the kids, and so Michael took the phone upstairs, so that she could talk to them.

Christopher took the phone first. "Hey, Mom, are you okay?"

"I'm fine, sweetie, how are you doing?" she said with a slight tremor in her voice.

"Oh, I'm good. Did you know that both Uncle Mark and Uncle Michael came to visit us?"

"I sure did. Say can you put the speaker phone on so I can talk to both you and your sister at the same time?"

"Sure, Mom."

Kate had debated for a while as to whether she should talk to the children individually in light of their age difference, with Samantha, six, and Christopher, eight, or together. She finally decided that emotionally she would be able to do this only one time.

"Samantha and Christopher, can you both hear me?" she said on the speaker phone.

When they both responded, Kate started her difficult talk. "First of all, I want you both to know that I love you very, very much and that I already miss you, even though I've only been gone one day. I want you to just listen right now, and after I'm finished, I'll talk to each of you alone on the phone—okay?"

"Okay," both of them responded.

"Right now I'm with your Daddy at a hospital in Wyoming. Yesterday morning, he was hurt badly when a very bad man shot him in the airport. The bad man is dead now, and I think your Dad will be okay, but there's something else that I need to explain to you that's very important. Do you remember when we talked about the dinosaurs and how they just disappeared?"

"Sure, Mom," Christopher said. "They died off after a huge meteor hit the Earth."

"That's right, sweetie. That's what we talked about because that's what scientists believed, but the scientists were wrong. What really happened is much worse than a huge meteor, and that same thing is about to happen again. Now, I want you to not be afraid, because you're with Uncle Michael, and he'll take care of you. I'm sure you've met his friend Cassie—she's really nice, isn't she?—and she'll also be helping to take care of you.

"Very soon, all of you will be flying away on Uncle Mark's airplane, so that you can be safe when this happens. Daddy and I have to stay here while he recovers, and we may be able to join you later, but if all of this happens too quickly, then you may need to go on without us. If we can't join you, I don't want you to be too sad, because Daddy and I will always be with you—even if we're not there in person, we'll be in your hearts."

Michael could hear that Kate was now softly crying as she spoke. "I want you both to be strong, and I want you to be good for Uncle Michael and Cassie—if you want, you can call her Aunt Cassie, because that's how I think of her. I love you both more than anything in the world, and I wish I was there to kiss you good-night, but always remember that I'll be watching over you."

Both of the children were now teary eyed, and Kate took time to talk to them individually, starting with Samantha. Somehow, at the end of the talks, Kate had worked her magic, and both of the children were smiling.

After talking with Kate, the children seemed to approach the task of packing and picking out favorite toys from their rooms with more urgency and determination. With Cassie and Michael's help, the children were completely packed for the trip within thirty minutes.

Michael and Cassie then started packing for the adults, using selected pieces of clothing from Stephen and Kate's closet. They also collected any items that they deemed useful for survival—canned foods, knives, matches, rope, tents, etc. They started compiling a list and shortly thereafter made a trip to Wal-Mart, where they purchased over $5,000 worth of merchandise, which filled eight shopping carts. Michael also stopped at a gun shop, where he bought an impressive arsenal of firearms—some legal and some straight off of the black market. They were hidden in a locked vault in the basement of the store and were offered only after Michael pushed for something better and flashed $25,000 in cash.

By the time they made it back to Stephen's house, it was past nine o'clock, and Spencer was upstairs with the children reading a storybook to them. He told Cassie and Michael that Mark had called and that both he and Dawn would be at the house in thirty minutes. When the children were asleep, the three exhausted adults went downstairs and plopped down on the couch.

"Do either of you know why the kids kept talking about Leonardo, Michelangelo, Donatello, Raphael, and Fred?" asked Spencer.

"The first four are the names of the Teenage Mutant Ninja Turtles," said Michael.

"The what?" Spencer asked.

"You're so out of it, Spencer," said Cassie. "It's a popular children's animated program, but the real reason that the kids keep talking about them is because that's also the name of their four hamsters."

"So who is Fred?"

"That's their dog. He's staying at the neighbors, because Kate didn't want Mark to have to worry about feeding and taking care of him while she was gone."

"Cassie, how do you know all of this?" said Spencer.

"Because I asked and they told me," she replied.

"Well, you must have the Midas touch because they just giggled at me when I asked," said Spencer. "Isn't Fred a strange name for a dog?"

"Samantha named the dog, and his full name is Fred "Flintstone" Hanson," said Cassie.

The three of them shared a brief laugh and then decided to catch up on the television news after first getting a cup of coffee from the kitchen. While they were sitting in the kitchen, the phone rang. Michael answered and immediately recognized Mark's voice. "Hey, Bro, are you guys watching the TV?"

"Not right now. We just got the kids in bed and were relaxing over coffee. Where are you guys?"

"We're in the car driving to the house. Which do you want to hear first: the good news or the bad news?"

"I guess the good news."

"Well, there is no good news. You only get bad news or worse news."

"Okay, the bad news."

"Five more major earthquakes have hit in the past *thirty minutes* and destroyed large parts of several cities, including Ogden and Cedar City, Utah, as well as Twin Falls, Idaho. In addition, another quake hit near Salt Lake City which has completely decimated it, with an estimated death toll of over 100,000 just in the Salt Lake area alone. To top it all off, they're reporting a type of seismographic reading called harmonic tremor at Yellowstone, which indicates magma on the move and almost guarantees an impending eruption. Bottom line is I think this zit is just about to pop."

"So what's the worse news?"

"I think you should be sitting down for this."

"Don't keep me hanging here, Mark." At the same time he motioned for Cassie to turn on the television, as they made their way into the family room.

"Some senator from Wyoming has called for a press conference that they've been airing on all the major networks. This is also hitting most radio stations and is all over the Internet right now. According to this dickhead, he has discovered a huge cover-up concerning a devastating natural disaster that's destined to follow on the heels of this wave of earthquakes that we've been seeing. He used the term Verneshot over and over again in the press conference and guess who he said were the main scientists involved in the cover-up?"

"Oh, shit!" said Michael.

"You guessed it—Stephen Hanson and Spencer Montgomery. Immediately following the senator's speech, they aired a separate press conference with the president of the United States, who said that they had been informed by the USGS that a large geological event was a possibility, but that they were still gathering data. He urged people to avoid panicking and said that the National Guard had now been deployed. I'm betting that the transportation crisis that we feared is taking place as we speak."

"How quickly will you be here?"

"In about fifteen minutes. All of you should head to the airport right now."

"It will take us another fifteen minutes to finish packing, so we'll just see you when you get here."

"There's one more thing that you need to know. Based on a conversation that Dawn overheard when she was at Black Diamond, this same senator is most likely the wonderful guy that ordered the execution of Stephen, Spencer, and you."

Spencer stared in disbelief at the picture of him on TV, as he was portrayed as a brilliant but disturbed scientist who, according to wiretapped phone conversations, learned of the upcoming natural disaster months ago but refused to reveal any of this information to anybody because of personal gains that were yet to be determined. Fortunately, Senator Wolfe had the phones at the Yellowstone Volcano Observatory monitored because of his fears concerning a possible super volcano eruption and his dedication to the welfare of the people living in Wyoming. When the senator learned about the cover-up, he decided to come forward with this information, despite threats on his life that he had received in the past few days.

Senator Wolfe was shown talking to a room full of reporters, as he said the words that had been repeated on multiple television and radio stations over the past hour, "The safety of fellow Americans and good citizens of this country far outweigh the threats on my life, and I consider it my duty to try and save as many lives as possible by coming forth with this information."

Michael stared in silence at the senator, who appeared to be in his mid-fifties, with clean shaven good looks and a full head of hair with distinguished graying sideburns. He then listened to Senator Wolfe as he mentioned the other scientist, a geologist named Stephen Hanson, who was a known anarchist who reveled in the possible destruction of the most powerful country in the world and the cleansing effect of the massive loss of life that was sure to follow the cataclysmic event.

Michael listened as the senator maligned his brother, and he considered the type of man who would hire a psychopathic killer like Winston Delk to do his dirty work and then try to make himself out to be a hero by revealing a dangerous cover-up. He decided that this man was worse than any of the terrorists or megalomaniac "monsters" that he had dealt with during his Force Recon days. Senator Wolfe was the hidden malignancy that poisoned the world while smiling and claiming to have everyone's best interest in mind.

When Mark and Dawn arrived at the house, Michael, Cassie, and Spencer were waiting with the two sleepy-eyed children in the family room. The Suburban had already been loaded up with all of their supplies and the firearms, and there was anxiety and tension in the room that you could cut with a knife.

As they all headed toward the garage, Samantha suddenly had a look of alarm on her face and went running upstairs saying she had forgotten something. The adults looked at each other, shrugged, and waited for her. She came bounding down the stairs a minute later with a small duffel bag in her hand. Then, she whispered something to Christopher, who went running out the back door of the house and returned to the kitchen a few minutes later and joined the group once again, huffing and puffing.

Cassie leaned over to look in the duffel bag as they made their way to the garage and saw eight tiny eyes staring up at her, which initially startled her, until she realized that it was only the four furry hamsters.

When they reached the car, everyone quickly realized why Christopher went running out of the house, because sitting in the back seat of the SUV, panting and wagging his tail, was Fred, a three-year-old black Lab-golden retriever mix.

Michael looked at the children and said, "Hey, kids, we barely have enough room for all seven of us because of all the stuff we have to take with us. I know you want to take him, but I don't think we have enough room for Fred. Michael felt his heart drop as he saw the sadness welling up in their eyes.

"You'll have enough room in the car, because Dawn and I aren't going with you guys," said Mark.

"Why not?" Michael asked.

"Because we haven't successfully hacked in to the mainframe computer yet; that's the reason that I didn't just meet you guys at the airport. We need to use the array of computers that Stephen has in his office to help us hack the mainframe."

"Can't you do that on your plane?"

"We tried, but Dawn and I each need to be working on a computer console at the same time to crack this bitch. You need to hit the road right now because I think it's going to take you two to three hours to make it back to the airport with what I could see on the road driving here. Panic has already set in, and millions of people are trying to get out of the city. Time is critical here, Bro, and we need these two hours to try and get control of that mainframe."

"So, how will you guys get there if the roads are that bad?"

"We'll take Stephen's motorcycle; that should allow us to bypass most of the traffic."

"But what if time runs out?"

"Then you guys need to take off without us. Shit happens, Bro.

Michael was definitely not happy about this turn of events, but he knew that he would never be able to convince Mark otherwise. So they hugged, wished each other luck, and set off on their separate tasks—Mark with his band of two trying to save the world from its own technological arrogance, and Michael with his band of five humans, four hamsters, and one dog, trying to hold his family together.

Black Diamond Military Base, Nevada
September 16, 10:43 p.m.

Thomas Pierce sat at his desk contemplating the current situation. Spencer Montgomery was nowhere to be seen, nothing had been solved concerning their structural problems at Black Diamond, the huge columns at the bottom had telescoped so much that virtually no buffer zone remained, and all hell was breaking loose at the surface with huge earthquakes hitting everywhere. He was aware that the facility was probably doomed, but he couldn't force himself to destroy the biological agents, and it was too late to move them out of the facility.

He was caught between a rock and a hard place, and he could see no obvious solution. On one hand, if they didn't destroy the agents, and the facility inadvertently unleashed some of them on humanity, then the results could be disastrous. On the other hand, if they did destroy the agents, over a hundred billion dollars of research would go down the tubes, and enemies of the United States with biological weapons would suddenly be in a position of power.

As he sat there wondering what to do, one of the computer technology experts, Jon Henlein, knocked on his door and entered the small room with a sense of urgency.

"Dr. Pierce, there's something going on that you really need to know about right now. The mainframe computer is going into structural alert mode, and I can't seem to stop it. It's probably hackers, but everything I've done short of powering down the entire mainframe hasn't worked—the hackers are too good. I've never seen anything like it. They know all of the access codes, and they're fast as hell. We've never had anyone successfully hack into our system; it's supposed to be impossible."

"How long do we have before the destruction of biological agents begins?"

"Maybe ten minutes."

"Then shut down that mainframe right now!"

They ran down the hallway, and Pierce took the express elevator to the labs, while Henlein sprinted to the secure room housing the mainframe computer. When he was inside the room, Henlein quickly flipped all of the power switches to the off position and waited as the computer went into shut-down mode. In another twenty seconds, all of the lights on the mainframe turned off, and Jon breathed a sigh of relief. However, ten seconds later, the computer turned back on again and indicated that it was now in auxiliary power mode, which Jon now remembered would happen if the primary power was shut down while there was a structural alert.

"Oh, shit!" he exclaimed, because he also remembered that there was no way to turn off auxiliary power with a structural alert.

Denver, Colorado: September 16, 11:07 p.m.

"That was too damn much fun!" said Mark as he hugged Dawn. They had successfully hacked into a secure mainframe Department of Defense computer that had probably never been penetrated before. They had taken control of the computer despite attempts by computer techs at the facility to thwart their activity. They had fooled the computer into thinking that there was a critical structural breach at the facility, which had caused it to shift into automatic structural alert mode. And finally, they had confirmed that all biological agents had been destroyed, including DM-19.

"What a kick!" said Mark. "I think I like saving the world. How about some quick celebration sex before we head to the airport?"

"You just don't give up, do you?"

"Sorry, I can't help myself—you're so damn cute. I just can't seem to turn my libido off."

"Oh, brother, what a cheesy pickup line that was."

"Well, I've tried everything else—the direct approach, humor, offering money—none of that worked, so I decided to try cheesy flattery."

"Keep trying, computer boy. Maybe you'll eventually get it right."

Within ten minutes, they were on Stephen's motorcycle heading to the airport. Even at that time of night, traffic was almost at a standstill on most roads, but Mark simply told Dawn to hang on as he began weaving in between cars. At times, he drove on the median as well as embankments and even waved as he passed by a few police cars that were just as stranded as every other vehicle. Although they were making better time than anyone else on the road, he could still sense that precious time was ticking away, and he hoped that Michael was past all of this horrendous traffic.

When he arrived at the Denver Airport, Michael knew that they were in trouble. He parked in the drop-off area for departing passengers at the private aviation terminal and saw armed men in military uniforms scattered everywhere. He was supposed to meet the pilot and co-pilot, Jack Tally and Mitchell Bell, in the ticketing/check-in area. He'd met them once before when he had flown on Mark's jet and was sure that he could recognize them. But when he walked into the building, he gasped at the sight before his eyes—the chaos and panic was almost suffocating.

People were standing in lines that appeared to have no beginning and no end. Children were crying. Adults were screaming at each other and at their children. People were pushing each other down and hitting one another to get a better place in line. Almost everyone was sweating profusely despite the air-conditioning.

Most ticketing counters could not even be seen through the turmoil, and the angry noises from the crowd were so deafening that it was difficult to hear conversation from someone standing nearby. An elderly man was screaming, as his wife was being trampled by a surging crowd of frightened people who, like scared cattle, had no concern for the individual being stomped to death. This is how he envisioned hell on Earth. It had all of the elements necessary—chaos, fear, anger, indifference, and pain. The only thing missing was total destruction and massive doses of violent death, but that would soon be provided to all of these doomed people in a manner that none of them could really understand until it happened.

Michael tore himself away from this scene because he realized that he couldn't find the two pilots in this state of confusion and chaos. He wasn't sure whether the jet would be in a hangar because Mark had returned from Los Angeles only a few hours ago, but he decided that a systematic search of the private hangars and surrounding tarmac was a much better idea than trying to fight through the crowd. As he exited the ticketing area, he noticed that some of the armed military personnel were hovering around the Suburban, looking suspiciously into the rear of the vehicle.

When he approached them, one of the men held up his gun. "Is this your car?"

"Yes, it is," Michael replied. He was already considering options at that point, because Cassie, Spencer, and the two kids were still inside the car, and the arsenal of firearms was in the back of the vehicle under a blanket.

"We need you to open up the rear of the vehicle, so that we can search it," the same man replied.

"Why are you concerned about my car?" said Michael.

"Because we've seen what appears to be the barrel of a gun sticking out from under that blanket in the rear of the vehicle."

Now Michael knew that they were in some deep shit. "Okay, let me get the keys from my wife. I left them with her."

He started to walk to the driver's side of the car, and the man barked out, "Unless you want to get shot, have your wife open up the front passenger door and give you the keys!"

Michael shrugged. "Okay, whatever you say." He started back over to the passenger side. There were three armed men—one at the front passenger door and two at the rear of the vehicle. Michael knew that he didn't want to open the passenger door, because Cassie might get pulled into this dangerous situation. He also knew that he needed to diffuse the situation quickly or the children could also be put into harm's way, and he didn't have time to argue with these men. He was sure they would be detained or held for questioning if the arsenal was discovered.

As he approached the passenger door, Michael tripped over the curb next to the door and fell onto all fours. This prompted the man nearest the door to step toward Michael and bend forward slightly with his gun pointed down, at which time Michael rapidly swung his right arm around the man's legs and pulled them forward while pushing up forcefully with his left hand on the man's chest. The end result was that the armed man was slammed down onto the street with enough force that his head hit the concrete, and he was instantly knocked out.

Michael grabbed the assault rifle and quickly slid himself under the Suburban. When the other two men became aware of the scuffle, they carefully walked over to the passenger side of the car to find the unconscious man lying beside the car, but no sign of the other man. Before they had time to decide on a course of action, they heard the click of a safety being released directly behind them, and they realized that they'd been flanked.

Michael had slid sideways under the car and then backwards behind the rear tire so that he could re-emerge on the passenger side directly behind the men. "Put the guns down," he said calmly. Before they had time to react, he stepped forward and hit them both in the back of the head with the butt of the rifle, which caused them to fall to the ground beside the other man. He grabbed all of their rifles and ran around to the driver's side and got in.

"Oh, my God," Cassie said, "when I saw those armed men, I didn't know what to do."

"Right now we've got a bigger problem," said Michael. "I don't know where the plane is, and I can't find the pilot and co-pilot in this hell hole!"

"That was so cool, Uncle Michael," said Christopher with enthusiasm. "That was just like the movie *Die Hard*!"

As Michael drove off, he handed the assault rifles to Cassie and Spencer. "With the current state of things at this airport, you may need these."

He described to them how to flip the safety off, but Spencer looked warily at the weapon and said, "I've never shot a gun in my life."

"Give it to me," Christopher responded quickly. "I know how to use it."

"No," said Michael, "I'm sure you'll figure it out, Spencer."

"I bet Fred knows what to do with it," said Samantha.

"Shut-up, doofus!" Christopher responded.

"Enough, kids," said Spencer. "I think I'll be okay. Christopher, you're my consultant. If I can't figure it out then I'll ask you." He smiled at Samantha and said, "And if the two of us can't figure it out, then we'll ask Fred."

Fred, having heard his name several times, started wagging his tail more vigorously as the car approached the first hangar.

Mark and Dawn had reached a stretch of road where even though there was still a massive traffic jam, the median was wide enough to allow him to increase his speed to 35 miles per hour. Several times he almost lost control when he hit some sizable bumps on the median, but he quickly compensated each time there was a change in road surface.

He could feel Dawn clinging to him tighter now as she sensed the brief periods of instability. He was not usually driven by anxiety, with his "no big deal" approach to life, but he could feel something urgent pressing down upon him and the ticking of the clock counting down to doomsday. Not so much for himself, but for his family he sensed something wrong, which made him feel even more urgency in making it to the airport faster. He pushed the motorcycle up to 45mph and prayed that there were no more large bumps.

After searching eight hangars, Michael finally got lucky and found Mark's jet. Now, the only problem was that they had no pilot to fly it, which was not much better than having no jet at all. After the lights were turned on, and they started to unload the supplies and the firearms from the Suburban, Jack Tally, the pilot, emerged from the back of the hangar. "Where's Mitchell?"

"You mean Mitchell Bell?" said Michael.

"Yeah, he set out to meet up with you at the check-in area about an hour ago, while I stayed back here with the plane."

"I didn't see him when we were there, but the place was a real madhouse. Maybe we just crossed paths."

They decided to get the plane loaded up and ready to go; then it would be a simple waiting game for Mitchell Bell, Mark, and Dawn. When everything was set, Michael called Mark on his cell phone to find out his location. He was surprised when Dawn answered and, for the first time, he actually became encouraged when she told him they were less than ten minutes away. If Mitchell hadn't returned by the time Mark and Dawn arrived, they decided that they should leave, because they were already pushing the envelope very close to a breaking point.

As Cassie, Spencer, and the children were walking toward the plane to board, Michael opened the large hangar door and started walking back to the plane. When he looked up at Cassie on the boarding ramp, she turned back toward him, and he could see a look of panic suddenly take over her facial features. He turned around to see four armed soldiers pointing their rifles directly at him and ominously at the children.

"STOP RIGHT THERE!" barked the same man that Michael had slammed down on the concrete right next to the Suburban. He then said to the other men, "Keep your distance from him, and if he comes closer, then shoot to kill. I think he's either a mercenary or ex-special forces."

Because of the excellent lighting, Mark could see the four armed soldiers a hundred yards ahead, standing in front of the hanger, and he instantly knew what he had to do. He stopped so Dawn could get off, and then he sped toward the men as fast as he could push the motorcycle. When he was within fifteen yards, he pulled the bike hard to the right, while he leaned to the right as hard as he could. This caused the motorcycle to go into a sideways slide, and Mark was yanked away from it as the concrete caught hold of his jacket and pants. The bike hit all four soldiers with enough force to send them flying twenty feet.

Although Mark's jacket and jeans were badly torn, he had avoided any serious injury, so he quickly returned to his feet. He could tell that the soldiers were not in any condition to give them any more problems, so he walked to his brother just inside the hangar.

"That's what I call bowling for soldiers," said Mark.

"Boy, am I glad to see you, little brother!" said Michael. "Where's Dawn?"

When Mark looked back toward her, he could see a military truck loaded with soldiers barreling directly at her.

"Oh, shit!" exclaimed Mark, as he ran toward the motorcycle. He then yelled so that Michael could hear him, "Get in the damn plane, Bro, and get the hell out of here! I'll give you a diversion, but it won't work for very long, so hurry!"

"Mark, but that will mean…"

"I know what it means. Just go now; it's your only chance!"

By that time, Mark had the bike upright and was speeding toward Dawn. He reached her seconds before the truck did, and she grabbed hold of him as he slowed down the motorcycle. Once she was securely seated behind him, he sped off away from the hangar, and the military truck turned to pursue them, which allowed the plane just enough time to exit the hangar and taxi off toward the runway.

By the time the men in the truck realized what had happened, the Gulfstream V was already streaming down the runway to take off, and the motorcycle was just a blip in the distance, which was fading away fast.

When he reached a safe distance, Mark slowed down to stop and catch his breath. Dawn pulled off her helmet and said, "Thanks for coming back for me, computer boy. You definitely gained some brownie points for that."

He smiled at her, and then could feel his cell phone vibrating, so he answered it. "Mark, what if we meet you in another airport and pick you up there?" asked Michael from the plane.

"It won't work, Bro. All of the airports will be just like this. You're on one of the only planes that's ever going to get out of this country. It's a one-way flight, and you need to keep going until you find some place safe for all of you."

"I love you, Mark."

"I love you too, Michael—big Bro."

"You take care, okay?"

"Don't worry about me. Dawn and I are going to go have some fun."

"You do that, Doogie Hanson. I want you to know you'll always be in my thoughts."

"Same thing here, Bro."

When the brothers had ended their call, Mark wiped tears from his eyes. "Let's go do a little car shopping, Dawn. I think this bike is on its last leg."

Ten minutes later, Dawn and Mark arrived at a Hummer dealership and were surprised that the lights were on inside the showroom at this time of night. Even more surprising was the fact that the door wasn't locked, and that there was a lone salesman sitting at his desk.

Mark approached him. "You're working fairly late tonight. What's the deal?"

"I have no interest in the craziness that's going on out there. I'd rather stay here tonight."

"Well, then, can I buy a car?"

"You're kidding, right?"

"Not at all, I really like the newest H2—fully loaded, of course. Here's my American Express Black card. I have a ten-million-dollar limit on it, so that should easily cover the car."

The man stared at Mark with disbelief in his eyes, until Mark produced the black card. After confirming that the card was legitimate, the confused man showed them a fully loaded H2, which Dawn and Mark both liked and within ten minutes, they had completed the transaction and were driving away in their new Hummer.

They decided to head toward Colorado Springs and found that the highway was deserted, because every car on the road was heading for the airport. They easily made the seventy-mile drive in an hour and found that Colorado Springs was nothing but a ghost town.

After stopping at the first decent hotel that they came to, they found that the lobby was deserted, so they grabbed one of the room keys and went to a nicely appointed suite with one king-sized bed. After getting some ice, Cokes, and snacks from a vending machine, Mark returned to the room to find Dawn lying on the bed in a T-shirt and panties, with a big smile on her face.

"So, does this mean what I think it does?" said Mark.

"I don't know what you think this means, but this is what I always sleep in."

Mark looked at her with a dejected look on his face. "Come here, computer boy, and I guess I'll let you have a little kiss."

"Can you not call me 'computer boy' for at least ten minutes?"

"What do you want me to call you?"

"How about computer man? That sounds so much more masculine."

"How about just Mark?"

"I'll go for that, too."

"So, come here Mark, and I'll let you have a kiss." She motioned him toward her with her right index finger.

When he was on the bed, they kissed softly for a few minutes, and then he said, "I have a proposition for you. How would you like to be the highest paid hooker of all time?"

"What!" she said, not believing he was ruining the moment with such a rude comment.

He pulled something out of his pocket, grabbed a pen from the nightstand, and scribbled something that she couldn't see from where she was lying. Then he handed her the piece of paper, which she recognized as a check that he had filled out and signed. It was made out to her in the amount of $742 million.

"That's my entire net worth as of the last time I checked a few months ago."

Dawn was still irritated at him for ruining the moment, so she just stared at him with an angry glint in her eyes.

"I'm pretty sure that you would have had all of that anyway, Dawn, because if I were to spend my life with anyone, it would have been you."

Her angry flash immediately melted, and she reached over and pulled him toward her. "You are an asshole, but you're a sweet asshole, and somehow I feel the same way about spending my life with you."

"Better a sweet asshole than a…"

"Shut-up," she said and kissed him passionately.

He soon found himself so lost within her that he could think of no more jokes, and he never wanted to be found again.

Aboard Gulfstream V Corporate Jet
September 17, 3:08 a.m.

The children had finally fallen asleep in the comfortable bed at the rear of the plane with the help of Fred, who was lying beside them with his nose nuzzled at their feet. Earlier, Michael had called Kate to let her and Stephen know that they were in the plane with the kids, and everyone was doing well, but that Mark was still in Colorado, due to his heroics at the airport.

Kate and Stephen had talked with the children, because Stephen was feeling better now and was finally starting to tolerate some food without subsequent abdominal pains. Although Stephen and Kate both tried to remain as upbeat as they could for the children's sake, Michael could sense a deep sadness in their voices when he talked with them. A few times, the kids each started crying, but they were quickly cheered up by Stephen and Kate's professed optimism that everything would be okay and that they would all be reunited soon. It was a little white lie that they deemed necessary at this time to prevent the children from falling into a state of deep despair with what they would be facing.

Cassie walked over to Michael's seat, softly ran her fingers through his hair, and when he looked up, she said sweetly, "Can I sit with you?"

He smiled wearily back at her and nodded, so she sat next to him in the large leather chair and snuggled her body up close, laying her head on his left shoulder. "I'm not hurting you, am I? I know you must still be extremely sore."

"No, I'm fine."

"That's good, because I don't think we have enough privacy for me to make it up to you again."

Instead of responding to her playful talk, he remained quiet. She could tell that deep thoughts were imprisoning him, so she tried to see if she could get him to open up to her.

"A penny for your thoughts; are you worried about the children?"

He remained quiet for a minute, but then he kissed the top of her forehead and said, "I am worried about the children, but what's really eating me is leaving my brothers and the women that they care about to simply die in this damn cataclysm. It just doesn't seem right that I live, and they die."

"I know it doesn't seem fair, but it's not our choice who lives and who dies. You know that you're doing what both of your brothers wanted you to do, which is to get the children to safety."

"I know that's right, but I still feel like there's got to be something I could do."

Cassie knew that he would have to exorcise these demons himself, so she remained quiet as they both drifted off to sleep and simply provided her support by the warmth of her body and the beating of her heart, as she lay next to him.

Spencer sat next to the computer station and TV, so that he could keep abreast of any new developments while everyone else, except the pilot and him, slept soundly. Something had been tickling his brain for the past thirty minutes about one of the conversations he had with Thomas Pierce at Black Diamond. He remembered that they had been discussing containment procedures for biological agents and the automatic function of the computer concerning destruction of agents in the event of a structural breach. He had asked Pierce if there was any method of foiling the computer's attempt to destroy the agents, once the process was begun.

Pierce's answer was definitive. "No, we set this system up for the protection of the human species. We didn't want any scientist potentially putting the world in jeopardy because they try to save the product of their research."

He certainly agreed with Pierce's statement, but there was something that still bothered him about what Pierce had said, almost as if he were reading it out of a manual of military procedure. And there was something in the way that he said it that bothered Spencer, as well, as if it were difficult for him to get the words out of his mouth. In fact, he had decided that Pierce must not have had any military background or belief in the military system, because of his comments at one point concerning the "stupid military hierarchy" that governed everything.

The more that Spencer pondered over these statements, the more that he became suspicious concerning the "complete destruction" of all biological agents. If there was one man at the facility who would have left himself a *backdoor* method of preserving biological agents, it would have been Thomas Pierce. These doomsday agents were his *babies*, and his fatal flaw was his extreme arrogance concerning military procedure.

Spencer was now faced with a critical decision, because they were headed for Central Europe—probably Switzerland or Austria, which he had determined would be one of the least likely areas that the Verneshot impactor would hit. He had made this decision based on several probability models that he formulated, after he heard that the biological agents were completely destroyed by Mark and Dawn. He realized that everyone was counting on him to make the correct decision on where they should go, but now he was second guessing himself based on a hunch.

He finally decided that it was crucial to talk to Stephen Hanson one more time, so he called Stephen's cell phone, hoping that he would answer at this time of morning. To his surprise, the phone was answered by a sleepy sounding woman that he realized must be Kate.

Spencer said, "Kate, I'm so sorry for calling you at this time of morning."

She responded, "Is there anything wrong, Spencer?"

"No, everything's okay. It's just imperative that I talk with Stephen, and I'm sorry, but it can't wait until later this morning."

"Okay, hang on."

There was silence on the phone for a few minutes, and then Stephen answered, "Spencer, what's going on?" He also sounded sleepy, but surprisingly well for his condition.

"You're the only one that I truly trust concerning difficult decisions, so I want to ask you a question that may be crucial to our survival, but I don't want to bias your response, so I won't tell you all of the details."

"Okay, shoot."

"If you were an ambitious scientist in charge of multi-billion dollar cutting edge research that involved an extremely hazardous agent, which, if accidentally released, would devastate huge populations of people, would you ever allow yourself to be taken out of the loop concerning the decision to destroy the agent, if it was suddenly deemed by the military to be too dangerous?"

"No, I wouldn't," said Stephen without hesitation.

"What would you do if they didn't give you any choice?"

"I'd create a backdoor for myself so that I ultimately controlled the decision to destroy the agent or not."

"That's exactly what I thought. I just wanted another scientist whom I trust and respect to confirm it."

"So, now, are you going to tell me what this is all about?"

"Are you sure you want to hear all of this?"

"If it concerns something critical to my children's survival, then the answer is yes."

Spencer spent the better part of an hour explaining everything that he had uncovered concerning the biological agents at Black Diamond. When he had finished, Spencer walked to the cabin and had a brief conversation with Jack Tally. Then he walked back to his seat and reclined it in an effort to finally get a little sleep, but his mind was running in overdrive, so he finally took a sleeping pill to allow him to drift into a nocturnal slumber. However, he would soon find that it would not be a restful sleep, because the same dream that had haunted him at Black Diamond returned with a vengeance.

Like before, it involved the same destruction and turmoil that were cascading out of control, with thousands of voices screaming in agony, and the same fields of charred, mangled bodies. But this time, something else emerged from the fields of destruction that was much more terrifying than any of the other images that were being portrayed in his mind.

Colorado Springs, Colorado: September 17, 8:45 a.m.

Dawn woke up before Mark and walked down to the lobby in the bathrobe and slippers that she found in their suite. She searched the deserted hotel until she found the kitchen and after twenty minutes, she had prepared a continental breakfast for herself and Mark.

When she returned to the room, Mark was just waking up and beamed a big smile at her when he saw the breakfast that she had prepared. "Wow, I must have been really good in bed last night; now you're making me breakfast."

"Actually, you were so pitiful that this is more of a sympathy breakfast."

"Well, that's the last time that I give you seven-hundred-forty-two-million dollars!"

"Aren't we touchy this morning?" she said as she laid the tray of food beside the bed and leaned over to give him a kiss.

He pulled her down on top of him, sliding off her bathrobe at the same time. "You'd be touchy too if I cleaned you out financially and then told you your lovemaking sucked."

"Well, then, I guess I'll just have to give you some more practice at lovemaking before breakfast."

Approximately one and a half hours later, they were dressed and ready to set out on the day's adventure. After gathering up supplies at a local sporting goods store, they began the trek to the top of Pikes Peak, which, at 14,115 feet, is the second highest automobile road in the United States. They first drove to Ute Pass at Cascade and then started up the nineteen-mile Pikes Peak Highway that leads to the summit.

After unloading their supplies, they entered the abandoned visitor center to warm up with some hot chocolate and delicious white chocolate macadamia nut cookies. When they were settled, they found a computer to keep them apprised of the impending cataclysm, so that they would be able to forecast when the event would be visible. They also used a compass to get a bearing on the northwest direction, so they would know which direction to look when the incredible sight was taking place.

When they were both comfortable and warm, Mark said, "You know we're probably going to get a better view of the cataclysmic event than anyone else in the world. We'll be seeing something that probably won't be seen for another sixty- to eighty-million years. It's going to be one hell of a big fireworks display!"

"So, are you telling me that I should feel fortunate to be here?" said Dawn.

"Absolutely!"

"But after we've seen it, we're going to get blasted into a million pieces or fried to crispy critters."

"Well, you can't have everything," replied Mark.

Chapter 6

Hell on Earth

Because there was plenty of fuel at the airport in St. Thomas, Jack Tally chose to leave the air conditioning on in the plane, so that everyone could sleep. He also curled up in one of the comfortable leather chairs to catch a few hours of rest himself.

Michael was the first to awaken, because he felt a painful throbbing in his right side and realized that he had shifted so that the armrest was pressing firmly against his severely bruised chest. At first, he was startled, because he could detect no movement of the plane, but then he realized that the plane had landed when he saw Jack asleep. Then he was confused, because he didn't think it was possible that they had completed the trans-Atlantic flight and had already landed in Switzerland or Austria.

He carefully slid out of the chair, so as not to awaken Cassie, and walked into the cabin to get the best look at their surroundings. What

248

he could see confused him further, so he walked over to Jack and gave him a soft nudge. "What are we doing in St. Thomas?"

Jack stirred for a moment, yawned, and started to talk, but before he said anything, Spencer said, "I think I should answer that, since I'm the one that made the decision to land here."

Spencer had been drifting in and out of twilight sleep for the past two hours but was unable to get any restful deep sleep, because the recurring dream was so disturbing that he found himself constantly thrashing about. His eyes were severely bloodshot, and he had an intense throbbing in his temples that made him wince several times, as if a parasite were trying to tear its way out through the side of his head.

When the pain subsided, he said, "Maybe we should wake up Cassie, so that I can explain this to all of the adults at one time."

Cassie responded, "I'm waking up—just give me a second," as she partially opened her eyes.

After checking on the kids, who were still asleep in the bedroom, and getting a burst of caffeine from the coffee that Jack brewed, everyone sat near the computer console.

Spencer had several graphs with some complicated mathematical formulas that he showed them on the computer before he started his explanation. "First of all, I want everyone to understand that this is all speculation, because we don't know exactly how the catastrophe will unfold, but I did the best I could based on the information I obtained from a lot of different sources. This included data from Black Diamond, the Yellowstone Volcano Observatory, the Long Valley Caldera near Mammoth Mountain, the USGS headquarters in San Francisco, and about twenty different colleagues, both U.S. and international, that I talked to over the past four days.

"I'm going to split this into two different scenarios. First, let's assume that all biological agents at Black Diamond have been completely eradicated…"

Michael interrupted. "You lost me there. I thought we knew that all biological agents had been destroyed by Mark and Dawn."

"I'll address that later, so hear me out on all of this, okay?"

"Okay."

"If all biological agents have been destroyed, then the key to survival in the short term is staying as far away from the Verneshot impactor as possible. Now, the formulas show the probability that the impactor will hit within a hundred-mile radius of each of the locations that are marked on the map. This is based on all known variables that can be used to make such predictions, but there are many unknown variables that we will never be able to take in to account, and that's why this represents nothing more than an educated guess.

"You can see that the highest probability, by far, rests somewhere in the Pacific Ocean. The second highest would be in the region of eastern Russia and Siberia. The third highest in eastern China and so on for another 500 locations spread around the globe. As we go down the list, you can even see contingencies for the impactor coming back down in areas of the U.S.

"In certain ways, if the impactor hits in the ocean, there may be even more devastation and loss of life than if it hits land. Imagine what a 250-mile piece of the Earth's crust would be capable of doing if it hit in eastern China. The devastation would be massive, with a huge crater from the impact, but the blast would be limited to the immediate five- or six-hundred miles around ground zero of the impact site. You see, this isn't like a meteor hit where the meteor is traveling at 30,000 miles per hour; the velocity would be much less than that, so the blast radius would be very limited comparatively.

"Now, let's imagine what would happen with an ocean impact. Regardless of where the huge chunk of rock hits in the ocean, a hundred-foot tsunami would be generated, that would fan out in all directions and travel over 500 miles per hour, ultimately reaching land to form a massive 2,000- to 3,000-foot wave which would cause total destruction of all cities along the west coast of North and South America, as well as the east coast of China and Russia, and the northeast coast of Australia. But the worst hit would be Japan, the Philippines, and Indonesia. Consider the possible loss of life in Japan alone, which could reach up to 125 million people!

"Based on the probability calculations, one of the least likely areas to be hit would be in Central Europe, so that seems like a fairly safe bet, and that's why I initially decided on Switzerland or Austria. But because of the population density, this area would be one of the least desirable places, if DM-19 was unleashed on the world."

Spencer paused to drink some coffee, and then he continued. "Let me give you some scary statistics that I learned about this virus while I was at Black Diamond. Based on the known rate of viral transmission in their studies, if just one person infected with DM-19 hit Europe, the *entire* population of that area, which is 690 million, would be infected in approximately twenty-two days! It would then be inevitable that it would spread to Africa, with 900 million people, and Asia, with a population of 3.9 billion, within four or five months!

"With all of that in mind, I had to decide on which was a bigger threat, DM-19, or the Verneshot impactor. Clearly, our risk of having to deal with DM-19 has been reduced by Mark and Dawn. In fact, I'll go so far as to say that they probably saved our species, because if the entire viral load from Black Diamond was released, from what I learned at the facility, there is almost no way that any humans would have survived the massive pandemic. I didn't tell anyone about this earlier, because I didn't want to demoralize the group or put more pressure on Dawn and Mark.

"But there's one main reason that I believe that not every trace of the virus has been destroyed—it's because of a man named Thomas Pierce. He's the head scientist in charge of research at Black Diamond. You'll have to take my word for the fact that I'm convinced that he left a *backdoor* for himself to stop destruction of certain agents, and his pride and joy was DM-19. It's likely that he only preserved a trace amount of the virus, but that would still be enough to kill billions of people. The only good news is that the human species may have a chance to survive now, whereas we had no prayer of survival before the majority of the virus was destroyed.

"So, here's the bottom line," said Spencer, returning to the map in front of them. "If we assume that Pierce has preserved a trace amount of DM-19, and that even one infected person could wipe out most areas with a high population density, then we need to be on an island a long distance from continental land masses, and the Atlantic is a much safer bet than the Pacific because of the high likelihood of a Verneshot impact in the Pacific and the low likelihood of such an impact in the Atlantic. It doesn't mean that there won't be some risk involved, because if we stay here, and there is an Atlantic impact, then we have no chance of survival. You just have to pick your poison and hope it's the right one."

"So, my Mom and Dad are going to die when the Verneshot blows up?" asked Christopher, who was now standing behind the adults. Everyone turned around to see him standing next to his sister, holding her hand.

Casper, Wyoming: September 17, 4:12 p.m.

As Kate and Stephen watched the news, they quickly realized that further damage was being inflicted on a massive scale by the panic that ensued since the earthquakes had struck with such violent force and since Clinton Wolfe had given his chilling speech at the press conference. Despite the president's warning to avoid panic, a good majority of hospitals throughout the country had experienced a mass exodus of health care workers as they attempted to flee the country, which left many critically ill patients without vital healthcare. Riots and automobile accidents had also claimed an unprecedented number of lives in the past twenty-four hours, as had the rampant violence and cruelty that people inflicted upon one another as they descended into deeper anarchy and chaos.

Most of the earthquakes had suddenly dissipated approximately three hours ago, which the news media interpreted as a possible sign that the worst was over, but Stephen understood that this was, in fact, a particularly ominous sign. He looked over at Kate from his hospital bed and said, "Hey, babe, I think we have just a few hours left."

With that, he reached over and softly grasped Kate's hand and pulled it up to his lips so that he could gently kiss her wedding ring. He had done this on many occasions in the past, including their wedding day, because it symbolized his commitment to her. He didn't tell her that he loved her, because he knew she could see it in his eyes and understood it intuitively.

This beautiful, strong, intelligent woman had given birth to his two precious children, and she now had chosen to die at his side rather than leave him alone to perish when the cataclysm hit. There were no words to express the way that he felt about her as he lay looking up at her face, so he remained quiet for the next few minutes.

"Do you think we should call the kids one more time?" she asked.

"Actually, I'd love to, Kate, but I don't think we should. I can't continue the little white lies, and I don't want to leave my children with the memory of having talked to Mom and Dad just before they died. Let's leave them with the happy memories of our talk with them yesterday."

"I guess you're right. To be honest, I really want to talk to them more for myself. I just want to hear my babies' voices one more time."

Kate's eyes started to well up, so Stephen reached over with his other hand and pulled her to his side. She slid onto the bed and laid her head on his chest. They knew that they had lived a fulfilling life together, but it was impossible not to yearn to see their children's faces one more time.

It was likely that they wouldn't see anyone else before the event occurred, because the hospital had very few employees that had stayed to take care of patients, so they were surprised when they heard the sound of footsteps walking quickly toward Stephen's room. When their curiosity reached a peak, they looked up to see a man turn the corner. It was Michael. He ran to the bedside. "Come on guys. Let's get the hell out of here!"

"What are you doing here?"

"Kate, we don't have time to talk right now. Please, just start walking to the elevators, and I'll be there with Stephen in a minute."

When Kate was leaving the room, Michael removed the IV from Stephen's arm and placed a Band-Aid that he found on the tray table. Then he slid his arms under Stephen and picked him up, with a loud grunt of pain as Stephen's 180-pound body pressed against his plethora of bruises and lacerations.

Stephen shook his head. "I thought you might try to pull something crazy like this."

"Give it a rest, Stephen. You're wasting your breath, because I'm not giving you a choice in this."

While they were walking through the hospital lobby, several healthcare workers gave Michael a strange look, because they noticed that he was carrying a man with a hospital gown, but none of them tried to stop him.

Fifteen minutes later, they reached the empty airport, and Michael laid Stephen on the bed in the rear of the Gulfstream V. He and Kate sat in seats close to the bedroom, so that they could converse with Stephen. Michael explained to them his plan to also rescue Mark and Dawn, and no one raised any objections, despite the fact that they knew they were playing with fire.

According to information on the Internet, the Yellowstone Super Volcano had now erupted, and a huge ash cloud was just beginning to form in northwest Wyoming. Even more disturbing was the fact that there was a very large depression forming between Ogden, Utah and Pocatello, Idaho. From what they could tell, the depression appeared to be rapidly increasing in size and was presently about ninety miles in diameter and about 230 feet deep.

Once they were in the air, no one breathed a sigh of relief, because they all knew that danger was increasing with every second, and they still had one more landing and one more take-off to survive before they were safe. Michael didn't need to tell Jack Tally to push the jet as fast as it would go, because he was acutely aware of their situation.

Michael had been calling Mark on his mobile phone, but once again, his brother wasn't answering his cell phone at a crucial time. They knew he had gone to Colorado Springs with Dawn, based on a voice mail that Mark left on Michael's phone, but they had no idea where to find them in Colorado Springs, and time was rapidly running out. If they couldn't think of a way to locate them within the next 45 minutes, while they flew to Colorado Springs, then they were going to have to leave Mark and Dawn behind.

Pocatello, Idaho: September 17, 4:56 p.m.

Todd Runnels sat on a hillside about four miles outside of Pocatello watching the amazing changes transform the Idaho landscape in dramatic fashion. This first began about an hour ago and was subtle to begin with, but now, there was nothing subtle about what he was seeing.

He chose to stay behind, despite his girlfriend's insistence that he leave with everyone else, in order to distance himself from the impending disaster. Todd had been born and raised in Pocatello and had never ventured out of Bannock County in all of his twenty-six years of life. He considered himself a die-hard local, who was loath to consider venturing very far from his birthplace, despite the chiding and teasing of his friends, especially his girlfriend.

He had no great aspirations in life and was content to spend his time exploring the landscape and wildlife around the city and working as a mechanic in Pocatello, located in southeast Idaho at the western foothills of the Rocky Mountains. He hadn't once visited any of the nearby resorts, including Sun Valley, Jackson Hole or Park City and had never even ventured to Yellowstone or Grand Teton. So, when he started hearing about the earthquakes and the super volcano, he decided to stay in Pocatello, no matter what happened.

Now, as he watched the amazing site unfold before his eyes, he wondered whether his girlfriend had been correct. At first, the only changes that he observed were bouncing treetops, which almost looked ludicrous against the surrounding landscape. From the hill he was sitting on, Todd had a panoramic view of the entire town, as well as an additional thirty to forty miles of Bannock County; he knew every nook and cranny of this entire area like the back of his hand. So, when he started seeing topographical changes, he started feeling like he was being transported to a foreign countryside, with malevolence brewing up from the ground.

The first dramatic change that he witnessed was at the edge of the horizon, which appeared to suddenly expand by another twenty miles in a matter of seconds. After seeing this, his curiosity increased significantly, so that he found himself staring at the horizon without blinking for minutes at a time. The next change was that different clumps of trees in the distance jumped up in the air, only to disappear completely from sight just seconds later. At first, he could see this in only one or two areas, but as time passed and he watched more carefully, he became aware of fifteen to twenty patches of trees that had vanished mysteriously.

Because he was convinced that the changes he was seeing represented an earthquake about thirty or forty miles away, he wasn't concerned about his safety, but when the entire town of Pocatello suddenly collapsed into a hole in the ground, with no buildings visible even from his hillside vantage point, Todd was so startled that he almost fell backwards from the spot where he was sitting. Next, he heard a rumbling sound, followed by something that sounded like a distant muffled explosion, followed by a series of increasingly loud explosive noises that escalated rapidly, and culminating in a tremendous explosive blast that was painful to his ears, even when he held his hands over them.

Moments later, he saw huge sections of large buildings from Pocatello shoot into the air, as if they had booster rockets attached to them. He could also see parts of houses blasting into the air, with furniture and brick walls and timber shooting in all different directions. Most of the flying objects reached a height of at least a thousand feet before gravity pulled them back down to Earth.

This was unlike any earthquake that he had ever heard about—the ground was not trembling or shaking—instead, it was collapsing and then exploding. When he realized that danger was moving rapidly in his direction, he decided to retreat from his position on the hillside and see how far his truck would take him. When he turned around to run to his truck, he could see the enormous ash cloud that now filled the sky in the northeast—evidence of the Yellowstone eruption that was just beginning to gain momentum.

When he reached the truck, he could now feel trembling and shaking of the ground that made it difficult to stand up, but somehow he managed to pull the door open and slide himself inside. He fumbled with the keys and finally turned on the ignition, stomping on the gas pedal at the same time, which caused the truck to lurch forward on the dirt road that led away from the hillside. When he reached the main road, he planned to head north on I-15 toward Idaho Falls—maybe this would be the day that he would finally venture beyond Bannock County.

A few minutes later, he had reached I-15 and was attempting to turn north, when he witnessed one of the mountain peaks off to his right unexpectedly collapse, as thousands of feet of rock abruptly involuted and then exploded with a shower of huge boulders that started raining down upon him. He held his breath, realizing that this might be his last few seconds of life, when one of the smaller boulders landed on the hood of his truck with a horrific crash as it instantly crushed the engine. Seconds later, before he even had a chance to consider his predicament, his truck was launched into the air in a similar fashion to the Pocatello buildings. On the way up, Todd realized that he never would make that trip out of Bannock County, after all.

The Edge of Forever

Great Basin National Park, Nevada
September 17, 4:58 p.m.

Great Basin National Park was one of the favorite locations visited by the Jackson brothers, because of the abundance of wildlife and the virtual lack of other people. Both Hoot and Cal Jackson usually preferred almost complete isolation from the rest of the world and considered themselves the last of a dying breed of true "mountain men." They had spent almost five months living in and exploring Great Basin, with its beautiful lakes and streams, tremendous diversity of wildlife, vast untouched forests—some with groves of ancient bristlecone pines, numerous limestone caves, and the 13,063-foot summit of Wheeler Peak.

Hoot eventually convinced Cal to accompany him on a trip to Ely, seventy miles west of Great Basin, mostly because, after months in the wild, Hoot would always get a little stir crazy until he had his dose of civilization for a few days, and then he couldn't wait to get back to the mountains and forests again.

When the two men walked into Ely, after being disconnected from the rest of the world for several months, they didn't expect to find the town completely deserted, but it was. That their first clue that something was amiss in the world, but when they made it back to Great Basin, they chose not to dwell on the bizarre nature of the abandoned town or the fact that neither one of them had seen another human in the past few days, despite passing through Baker, Nevada on their way back from Ely. They even walked inside the Silver Jack Inn at the center of town in Baker, but they found not a single soul, so they simply returned to the National Park with no further investigation.

On their return to Great Basin, the two men made their way to their favorite spot at the park, which was a hidden cavern that they had stumbled upon in their exploration of the mountainside. The cavern wasn't as beautiful as the limestone Lehman Caves, with its profuse decorations of stalactites, stalagmites, flowstone, and many intriguing, unusual rock formations, but it was relatively large and had no signs of human tampering.

As the Jackson brothers traveled to their secret spot, they started noticing some changes that hadn't been there when they first ventured out of the park two days ago. They found this terribly disturbing, because of their fear of human intervention in this wildlife paradise. Several active mountain streams had curiously dried up and were now simply lined with rocks and plant debris. In addition, some extremely large rock formations on the side of the mountain had shifted or collapsed.

When they arrived at the cavern, to their dismay, the entrance had indeed been altered—half of the arch leading into the cave had broken off and was tilting at an awkward angle, making it more difficult for them to enter the small opening.

But the most startling thing that the two men encountered when they arrived at the opening of the cavern was a strange heat that it was emitting, that they could even detect from hundreds of yards away. As they entered to investigate, they were shocked to find that most of the floor in the largest room of the cavern had been replaced by an enormous bottomless pit that was easily fifty yards across at its center. As they gazed into the gaping hole in the ground, the two men could feel a tremendous upwelling of heat that quickly became painful and caused them to rapidly retreat from the cave.

Minutes later, as the two of them ran down the mountainside, they could hear an explosion coming from the vicinity of the cave, which was now 200 yards behind them. Neither of them had ever seen a volcano eruption, and they were both certain that there was no known volcanic activity in this area, but they had no other explanation for the findings inside the cavern and weren't going to stick around long enough to find out.

Unfortunately, about five minutes later, when they were close to the bottom of the mountain, there was a tremendous explosion, followed by a devastating pyroclastic flow that spilled over from the eruption and traveled down the mountainside at lightning speed with awesome destructive force, instantly incinerating everything in its path, including the two Jackson brothers before they even had a chance to scream.

Long Valley Observatory, California
September 17, 4:59 p.m.

Everyone in the world now knew that Yellowstone was having a super eruption, but the Long Valley Caldera near Mammoth Mountain was also rearing its ugly head, and Patricia Tomlin, one of the scientists with the USGS, understood that the changes at Long Valley were foretelling something much scarier than even a Yellowstone super eruption or a widespread barrage of earthquakes. She couldn't explain why this was happening, but she knew that the magma chamber at Long Valley had rapidly re-accumulated a massive amount of magma in a matter of weeks, and that three eruptive columns had now formed at the caldera rim.

If more columns continued to form, and they coalesced into one huge column, then this would represent the second super eruption in a period of less than one hour in the western portion of the United States. If this were the case, then there would be no question that the country was facing the devastating effects of a continental flood basalt, the likes of which hadn't been seen in tens of millions of years.

Patricia knew that there were lots of crazy theories circulating right now, and she'd heard the report that Spencer Montgomery and Stephen Hanson were involved in a cover-up concerning the disaster, but she knew both of them well enough to realize that this was complete bullshit. She had distanced herself far enough away from the Long Valley Caldera rim that she wouldn't be in immediate danger of pyroclastic flows, but she also knew that the ash-fall in that area would be lethal.

As she watched the columns spew violently upward, filling the atmosphere with an ever-expanding ash cloud, she was glad that the rest of her family, including her parents and two younger teenage sisters were on a Hawaiian vacation. She had talked with all of them earlier today, and they were terribly concerned for her safety with all of the recent earthquakes in the U.S., especially in light of the fact that she was currently in California, which they perceived as the earthquake capitol of the world, although she had tried to educate them otherwise.

She knew that things probably weren't looking good for her as far as survival goes, but at least her family would be safe on an island in the middle of the Pacific, far away from the hell hole that was brewing on the mainland. She looked back in the direction of the caldera rim and decided that it was time to distance herself even further from Long Valley, but as she stared at the ash cloud, she noticed five or six more eruptive columns blast upward and within seconds, a single massive column replaced all others. She thought to herself, *this is going to be a rough day and week for the people of the United States and a rough year for the rest of the world.*

If Patricia had lived to see another day, she would have considered her thought the understatement of the century—or more accurately, the understatement of the last 650,000 centuries.

Grand Teton National Park, Wyoming
September 17, 5:03 p.m.

"I knew I should have left you three years ago when I had a chance, you good for nothing, piece of shit loser!" screamed Dixie Hubbard from the passenger seat of her car, while she glared at her husband Cole. Dixie's twin sister, Patty, sat silently in the back seat with her husband, Cliff, wishing she wasn't there.

The two couples were from Jackson, Wyoming, and when everyone else had evacuated the city yesterday Cole convinced Dixie, Patty, and Cliff that they should stay behind to loot businesses and fill up his trailer with "goodies." He told them this was a once in a lifetime opportunity, because the government didn't even have time to mobilize the National Guard and put the country under martial law. So, when everyone else was fleeing from Wyoming last night, they spent their time getting drunk and celebrating how rich they would be the next day.

After spending most of the morning breaking into office buildings and stores to raid cash registers, they decided to drive north to the Jackson Hole Mountain Resort and Teton Village, so that they could try their luck at some of the million-dollar vacation homes, condos, and lodges that populated the area. Cole loved the idea of stealing from rich assholes, because he'd lived in trailer homes his entire life and had never been able to share in the slice of pie that he thought he deserved.

They were handsomely rewarded at a few of the homes, because some people left behind expensive jewelry, as well as thousands in cash, in their haste to flee the area. But Cole couldn't resist also taking every LCD and plasma big screen TV that they found, because he knew he could sell all of them on the black market later for a substantial amount. When they were finished, they had collected over $40,000 in cash, several hundred thousands in jewelry, and seventeen big screen TV's, all now loaded up in his trailer.

They were so ecstatic about the heist that they had completely forgotten about the threatening disaster and paid very little attention to the huge ash cloud forming over Yellowstone to their immediate north. To celebrate their good fortune, they decided to make a leisurely drive north on Highway 191 to Teton Park Road in order to get a better look at the majestic Teton Mountain Range, including the two principal summits, Grand Teton at 13,770 feet, and Mount Moran at 12,605 feet. Although Cole, Dixie, and her sister had lived in Jackson for many years, they still enjoyed getting an occasional close-up view of the Tetons, which represented one of the most breathtaking sights in the world, with a forty-mile-long mountain front of rock that jets dramatically 7,000 feet into the sky from flat plains in the Jackson Hole Valley.

As they approached a dramatic view of the Tetons, Dixie expressed some concern about the possible impending catastrophe, but Cole would hear none of it. "You're being a typical paranoid, stupid female!" exclaimed Cole with his most condescending tone of voice, as he continued driving north. "I can't believe you actually listen to those rich assholes trying to scare all of us with their doomsday crap. Everyone else can run away, but I'm not falling for their bullshit! We'll leave when I'm good and ready to leave—and not a second earlier!"

He was so adamant that Dixie didn't press him further on this point, until a few minutes later, as they stared at the awesome sight of Grand Teton and Mount Moran, and then watched in horror as the entire forty-mile-long Teton Range suddenly collapsed to the ground in a matter of seconds, as the most massive force in eons was unleashed and shattered the gigantic slabs of granite into trillions of pieces of rock just seconds later.

At first, Cole was so stunned that he just sat there blinking his eyes, thinking that he must be seeing things, but then he decided to minimize what he had just seen by casually commenting, "Well, at least, I'm glad we weren't closer to the mountains when that happened."

That was when Dixie lost it and called him a "piece of shit loser." She continued to glare at him and then said, "You moron! Do you realize the amount of destructive force it would take to do what we just witnessed!?"

He frowned while contemplating her words and was still considering them when the trailer they were pulling was torn off its hitch and flung up in the air forty feet. When it came back down, it landed sideways on the rear roof of his truck instantly crushing the passengers in the back seat into a disgusting heap of flesh and metal.

Cole and Dixie watched the road in front of them rise up 500 feet in the air like a giant serpent ready to strike and seconds later, the aftershock from the collapsed mountain hit the truck and its occupants like a bug colliding with a car windshield traveling at high speed, instantly reducing them to mush.

Provo, Utah: September 17, 5:04 p.m.

Dr. Lane McCollum had thoroughly enjoyed his long tenure as professor of geology at Brigham Young University. For the past twenty-seven years, he had lived in Provo and served as one of the beloved teachers and mentors for thousands of students who came through the university. He had outlived his wife of forty-two years, who passed away three years ago, and presently had no regrets that he could think of, so when he first heard of the amazing, catastrophic, geological events that were predicted to occur, he never even considered leaving Provo.

In fact, if he thought that there was a place that he could travel to that would give him a better view of the action, then he would have made the trip in a heartbeat. But from what he could tell, Provo was a perfect spot to observe the catastrophe, because of its proximity to Salt Lake City, which seemed to be the southern border of the destructive epicenter that was forming in northern Utah, southern Idaho, eastern Nevada, and western Wyoming.

He wasn't sure that he even believed the Verneshot theory, but it was obvious that there was something astronomically massive that was about to happen, and he wouldn't have missed seeing it for the world. So, when he woke up that morning, he was tremendously relieved that the catastrophe hadn't occurred during the night—not because he was afraid of dying—but because he simply wanted to have a chance to see the event unfold in daylight.

That morning, he set out for one of his favorite locations, where he would be perched on a plateau at a great viewing spot in the Wasatch Mountain Range just east of Provo. He wanted to get a full view of the Utah Valley, because he predicted that this would be the point of least resistance for the spreading wave of destruction, if in fact it continued further south.

He waited patiently most of the day, but just when he was starting to fear that nighttime would overtake the landscape before he had a chance to get a glimpse at the awesome event, he was rewarded with a strange sight that was visible in the sky above northern Utah. First, it appeared almost as if a dark cloud had formed almost instantaneously, but this was different from any cloud that he had ever seen, because it was oriented vertically and seemed to extend upward in a linear fashion starting close to the ground, almost like a tornado, but this was much, much larger than a tornado, because he was sure that he was visualizing something that must have been at least a hundred miles away.

Less than a minute later, seven more of these strange, enormous "clouds" began to form, and they rapidly developed a much darker discoloration, which he realized must represent earth, rock, and debris being shot up into the atmosphere at tremendous velocity, because he could see nothing falling back to Earth. Then there was a piercing sound that made him cover his ears in pain. The noise progressively escalated in volume until it culminated in the sound of a huge, thundering distant explosion that rocked the plateau he was standing on, forcing him to kneel down and stabilize himself.

For about twenty seconds, there was an eerie, preternatural silence; that was when he started seeing the earth-shattering spectacle that he had only conceived in his wildest dreams. There was a huge rift forming in the Utah Valley spreading north to south at unbelievable speed, tearing its way right through the center of Provo. At first, he could see what appeared to be a narrow but enlarging crevasse splitting the town almost perfectly in half, with land, houses, and buildings on the east and west side breaking off and falling into the pit. But within eight to ten minutes, the dark abyss had widened by several miles, and the entire town had collapsed into its depths, and it was still rapidly widening. Within another five minutes, the chasm had widened so that it now extended from the Wasatch Mountains to Utah Lake, which was a distance over six miles!

Lane knew that he would probably succumb to the effects of the geological cataclysm, but he had hoped to visualize as much as possible before his demise, so he was very relieved when the chasm seemed to stop widening in the eastward direction, although he could still see the effects of westward expansion, as the chasm started to engulf the eastern shore of Utah Lake, turning it into a dramatic waterfall.

Because he believed that the next major event to visualize would occur due north of Salt Lake City, he trained his eyes on the northern horizon and waited. Moments later, he could see not one but three huge objects blast into the sky in a fiery blaze that he had to shield his eyes from for a few seconds. The smallest of the objects headed toward the east coast at a blistering pace—from this distance, he guessed that this was probably a twenty-mile-wide piece of the Earth's crust that broke off from the bigger sections. The next largest piece, which he guessed was maybe forty miles wide, shot straight up in the air with so much force that it was soon no longer visible. But the largest piece dwarfed the other two objects, easily six to eight times larger than they were, as it shot out in an almost perfect westward direction.

Lane had some idea of the kind of force necessary to launch objects that massive, so after watching the huge Verneshot impactors rapidly fade from view, he simply waited for what he knew would reach him in just a few minutes. He had very mixed emotions about what he had just seen; he was extremely pleased that he'd been blessed with the opportunity to visualize this event, but he was also very worried about man's prospects of surviving this frightening extinction event long term. But then again, he didn't have very long to worry about man's future, so he considered himself lucky for that.

Black Diamond Military Base, Nevada
September 17, 5:09 p.m.

The alarms for a structural breach of the facility initially made Dr. Thomas Pierce believe that the facility was under attack by computer hackers again. He knew about the dramatic barrage of earthquakes that had hit in multiple areas of Nevada and other nearby states, and he knew about the structural challenges that the facility had faced over the last few weeks, but he still was in denial that his impenetrable fortress was in the process of being destroyed. He quickly made two phone calls and confirmed with the engineers at the facility that the breach was, in fact, really happening and that the bottom floor of Black Diamond was already being destroyed.

As the gravity of the situation sunk into his brain, Dr. Pierce realized his mistake and started dashing down to the secure storage unit where he kept the sample of DM-19 that he had salvaged weeks ago. Within five minutes, he had reached the storage unit and entered his access codes, but he could already feel the floor start to give way to the inescapable forces that were pushing up on the facility. He grabbed the metal canister housing the vial of DM-19 from its secure storage cell and tried to calm himself down so that he could think of a solution to the horrendous situation that he had created with his arrogance and pride in his achievement.

He knew that the depths of the facility would likely end up being blasted to the surface by the massive forces at play, so he couldn't rely on the agent being buried under a mile of rock. And he also possessed information that no one else was privy to, concerning certain features of DM-19, and when he thought about it, they had constructed this biological weapon to be far too damn indestructible. It couldn't withstand the Plasma Disintegrator at 10,000 degrees, but it could withstand huge fluctuations in heat or cold and survive outside the host for years.

There was only one way that he knew to limit its spread, using the fact that the agent had a much shorter life span after it had entered the host's body. Also, there was only one way to make sure that the doomsday weapon inside the vial directly infected only one host, instead of hundreds or thousands because of potential spread into the atmosphere before entering a host. Of course, this wouldn't limit host to host spread, but starting with one infected host was better than starting with hundreds or thousands.

Dr. Pierce opened the metal canister and without giving it another thought, he put the vial in his mouth, broke the thin glass with his teeth, and swallowed the broken vial and its contents in one gulp.

Aboard Gulfstream V Corporate Jet
September 17, 5:10 p.m.

Michael had continually called Mark on his cell phone during their flight, because he didn't know what else to do, and as they approached

Colorado Springs, he started to feel panic steadily creeping into his thoughts. For a minute, he stopped compulsively calling Mark and decided to try and clear his mind before his reasoning ability was completely disabled. He took some deep breaths, closed his eyes, and concentrated on relaxing all muscle groups in his body, before he reconsidered their predicament.

It wasn't just Mark and Dawn's lives that were at stake. If Michael pushed this too far, he would also be responsible for Stephen, Kate, and Jack's death. In addition, with him gone, Cassie, Spencer, and the children would have to fend for themselves in the brutal new world that would emerge out of the rubble of their civilization.

When he opened his eyes, he was more relaxed, but Michael still didn't have a clue what they should do in this situation, and they were only minutes away from Colorado Springs. He heard Jack's voice calling out to him from the cockpit, so he walked forward to see what he needed. "What in the name of God is that?" asked Jack.

When Michael entered the cockpit, he could instantly see what Jack was talking about. On their right side, in the northwest direction, Michael could see six or seven enormous clouds that looked like giant tornadoes.

"That is one amazing, scary sight!" Jack said.

The words hit Michael like a sledge hammer—*amazing sight*. He was struck with an epiphany that made everything clear. If he knew his brother, there would be only one place that he could be found at a time like this—watching the most amazing sight in history from the best place possible—Pikes Peak!

Pikes Peak, Colorado: September 17, 5:14 p.m.

Mark and Dawn were certain that they were beginning to see the first traces of the cataclysm, because although they were over 400 miles from the destructive epicenter of the impending disaster, strange dark clouds had been forming in the northwest sky for the past ten minutes. They didn't know what the clouds represented exactly, but they did know that this wasn't a sign of good things to come. Minutes later, even through the walls of the visitor center building, they heard a distant explosion that shook the window panes of the structure.

Mark looked over at Dawn, took her hand in his, and smiled grimly. "Something wicked this way comes."

Dawn seemed to ignore his comment, because she was frowning and staring out of the window toward the north. "What is that?" she asked, as she pointed at an object that was just starting to come into view.

As he stared with curiosity at the object, a look of surprise rapidly transformed his face. "I think that's my plane!"

Both of them looked at each other with bewilderment, and Mark suddenly jumped out of his seat and said, "Oh, shit! My cell phone!"

He ran out the door with Dawn closely on his heels, and they literally leaped into the Hummer, as Mark grabbed his cell phone, flipped it open, and noticed a message indicating that he had 87 missed calls. "Crap! If this gets us all killed, Michael is going to be so pissed at me!"

Just then, Mark's phone rang, and when he answered it, Michael frantically said, "Get your ass down from that mountain RIGHT NOW! Meet us at the Colorado Springs Airport. You have less than thirty minutes!"

Mark did a quick calculation in his head—nineteen miles on Pikes Peak Highway, ten miles from Cascade to Colorado Springs, and another ten miles to the airport. That was almost forty miles in less than thirty minutes—which he could easily do on the highway, but not on a mountain road that had gravel and paved sections, an average grade of seven percent, and hundreds of turns!

As Mark blasted off in the Hummer as fast as he could push it, he threw the phone to Dawn so that he could keep both hands on the wheel at all times, and Dawn switched to speaker phone so that the brothers could talk while Mark drove.

"I don't think I can make it," said Mark. "I have this damn mountain road I'm dealing with."

"Just push it as hard as you can. You know they have an annual car race up to the summit called the *Pikes Peak International Hill Climb* over the steepest part of Pikes Peak Highway. The record is about twelve-and-a-half miles in ten minutes, and that's going uphill."

"I hate to rain on your parade, Bro, but that's also in turbocharged sports cars, not a Hummer!"

"You can make up time when you reach Cascade and get on the freeway. Don't give up on this!"

"Well, I guess there is a positive side to this," said Mark. "The worst thing that can happen is that I drive off the side of the mountain, and Dawn and I die, but that's going to happen anyway if we don't make it down in time, so I really have nothing to lose."

"You always could see the bright side of things," said Michael.

"I'd just like to know if anyone is timing me. I'll bet I set the world record in the 'people who are so stupid they try to race Pikes Peak in a Hummer division.'"

As they prepared for their descent to land, Michael caught a glimpse of the sight that he most feared. He could see the cataclysmic force shoot out three massive pieces of the Earth's crust that formed into monstrous fiery projectiles of doom. He was relieved to see the largest piece shooting westward but horrified when he realized that the smallest piece was shooting southeast, in the direction of the Caribbean! In addition, one of the huge impactors shot straight up in the air, and there was no telling where that massive chunk of rock would land—possibly even somewhere in Colorado!

Michael, who'd kept his cell phone connected to his brother said, "Push it little brother! Push it as hard as you can. The aftershock from seven million atomic bombs is heading your way!"

15 miles from Long Valley, California
September 17, 5:27 p.m.

As she looked up into the sky at the dramatic eruptive column from the Long Valley Super Volcano, something to the north caught Patricia Tomlin's eye. At first, she was confused about what she was looking at, but then she put it all together and realized what she was witnessing, as the 270-mile-wide gargantuan fiery rock blasted its way through the atmosphere toward the Pacific Ocean. She felt her heart sink when she instantly realized the implications of what she was seeing and immediately grabbed her mobile phone to call her family in Hawaii.

When she was finally connected, her father answered the phone and said, "Hi, Patty, we've been watching the news, and we know what's happening. I guess it was a bad time to take a vacation to Hawaii, huh? I want you to know that I love you very much, we all do."

"I love you too, Dad."

Patricia spent the next ten minutes talking with her sisters, father, and mother, as they all said their goodbyes. Then she sat in her car and waited for the inevitable end. She waited for oblivion.

Pikes Peak, Colorado: September 17, 5:33 p.m.

Mark was pushing the Hummer as fast as he dared for every straight section of road and slowing down only for the turns. He could feel his heart beating faster and faster as he pushed the vehicle toward what seemed to be the brink of disaster. He had accepted the fact that he and Dawn were going to die earlier and was relatively calm at that time, but now that there was a tiny glimmer of hope, every muscle in his body was tensed, his head was dripping with sweat despite the cold, and his emotions and anxiety were running in high gear, as were his thought processes.

Although Dawn was hanging on for dear life and her face was white as a sheet, there were no cries or expressions of fear from her during their harrowing descent. Mark tried repeatedly to time the turns, but he invariably hit the brake too early for the first twenty or thirty of them because many of the turns were very difficult to see in advance, and he didn't want to go shooting off the side of the mountain. He knew that they would never make it at this rate, because they had only gone six-and-a-half miles in nine minutes. At this current pace, it would take thirty minutes just to get down from the mountain, and that would leave no time for them to make it to the airport before the devastating blast hit.

That was when everything shifted in Mark's brain, and he was suddenly back in high school hot-rodding with his friends, with a sense of immortality and the total lack of fear that teenagers frequently possess when they're involved in dangerous activities. He re-captured his nonchalant demeanor and looked over at Dawn. "Time to have some fun; if I don't come close to killing us on this mountain with some crazy fuckin' driving, then we're going to die anyway, so hold on tight, and you may want to close your eyes. This is going to get hairy!"

With that, Mark slammed the accelerator down and raced into the next turn after a long straightaway at almost a hundred miles an hour. When he approached the turn, he popped the anti-lock brake hard, and with the car in manual mode, he shifted down to fourth gear, which slowed him down to sixty miles per hour in seconds, and then tried to slide the Hummer through the turn. This took the driver's side tires right up to the edge of the drop-off where they spit dirt out over the side of the mountain before they caught the road again and allowed the car to gain speed on another straight away. The next three or four turns he also negotiated at high speed but then took a turn too quickly and slammed the side of the car into a small tree at the leading edge of the turn, causing sparks to shoot off the driver's door.

After he was bounced back onto the road by the impact, he hit another straightaway hard, and slammed the gas pedal down again so that he could continue at breakneck speed toward the next turn. He realized that if he hit the wrong turn like this, without a tree to act as a guardrail, the end result would not be pretty.

"I think you should see this!" said Jack Tally from the cockpit somewhat frantically, causing Michael to jump up from his seat where he had been talking to Stephen.

They were just beginning the descent into the Colorado Springs Municipal Airport and had a great view of the horizon, because they had just slipped below the clouds. Jack didn't need to tell Michael where to look, because he already knew that death would be coming from the northwest.

"Oh, my God!" Michael exclaimed after scanning the horizon. He could see a rapidly expanding wall of destruction obliterating everything in its path as it fanned out in all directions. "Jack, how long do you think we have before that gets here?"

"I already tried to calculate it. My best guess is that it's traveling at around 800 miles an hour, which would give us about eighteen minutes before it's here. If I'm right, then that means it's traveling faster than the speed of sound, so it will hit us before we even hear it coming!"

Michael ran back to his seat to grab the cell phone, which was still connected to Mark's phone, and said, "Mark, where are you? How much farther do you have to go before you hit the highway?"

"We've gone about twelve miles with seven more to go before we hit Highway 24 in Cascade, but we are getting close to Crystal Reservoir, and the road straightens out after that."

"Push it like you've never pushed before, little brother! You have sixteen minutes to get here, because we need a few minutes to take off!"

"You've got to be shitting me—twenty-seven miles in sixteen minutes!"

Michael didn't respond because there wasn't anything else he could say that would help this impossible situation.

Kate poked her head out of the bedroom, and said, "Is there anything I can help with? I feel like I'm doing nothing."

"Kate, there's a good chance that we all will die trying to save Mark and Dawn. In fact, if I was in Vegas, I'd take odds against us surviving. What do the two of you want to do?"

"Michael, you know the answer to that already."

"I guess I do. I just wanted to make sure we were all on the same page. I didn't want to make the decision about your life for you, especially because of the children."

"If we chose to save ourselves at Mark and Dawn's expense, then I'd never be able to face my children and let them know that we had an opportunity to save their uncle and future aunt and decided instead to leave them to die."

Michael nodded in agreement as the plane approached the runway.

After a few minutes, Mark and Dawn could see Crystal Reservoir in the distance, and the road ahead appeared to be a straight shot, so Mark pushed the Hummer up to 120 miles an hour. He remembered that there was a large bend in the road around Crystal Reservoir, so he knew he would eventually have to slow down, but he wasn't expecting a sharp bend in the road, so when it suddenly appeared, he was caught completely by surprise.

He slammed on the brakes which caused him to lose control of the car and sent the car into a spinout, with a cloud of gravel and dirt flying into the air. He tried to compensate by turning the wheel, but this caused the Hummer to tilt precariously toward the passenger side, and then the car popped five feet in the air after hitting a bump in the road and rolled over sideways on the road twice before falling off the edge of the drop-off.

After they had landed and were taxiing on the runway, Jack once again called for Michael. When he stuck his head into the cockpit, Jack said, "I hate to be the bearer of bad news, but I think I miscalculated the velocity of that wall of destruction that we could see from the air. I think it's probably closer to a thousand miles an hour, which would mean it's going to reach us in about twelve minutes—thirteen at the most. If they're not here in ten minutes, then we're going to have to leave without them. We're also going to be losing cell phone reception very soon because the cell phone towers to the northwest are being knocked down like bowling pins by that wall of doom."

When the Hummer fell off the edge of the drop-off, Mark knew they would survive the fall, because it was only about ten feet at that section of the road, but he also realized that this was the end of the line for Dawn and him. Now, there was no chance that he could get them to the airport before the cataclysmic wall of destruction splattered tiny pieces of them for the next twenty miles. In a way, this was a relief, because the race was over, and the ending was a known entity—a certainty that was descending upon them which confirmed the fact that *all* life eventually ends in some fashion.

During the short fall, the Hummer had rolled one more time because of its momentum and had somehow landed upright, although there was evidence of severe structural damage to the vehicle. He looked over to the passenger side and could see that Dawn was wincing in pain and holding her right hand in an awkward fashion. She waved him off to indicate that she was okay, so he grabbed the cell phone off the floor and called his brother again.

When Michael answered, Mark said, "Hey, Bro, I've got a little bit of bad news. I wrecked the Hummer on the way down from the mountain, and we won't be able to make it for our little rendezvous."

There was total silence on the other end of the phone as Michael let the words sink in, but finally he said, "Mark, are you sure you can't make it here?"

"Definite. The Hummer is pretty banged up, and we still have over five miles just to make it to the highway in Cascade."

Michael was silent for another short while and then said, "Can you drive the Hummer at all?"

"I don't know; I haven't tried yet."

"Then try now."

"But…"

"Just humor me and try."

"I will, if you promise me you'll fly the hell out of here, right now!"

"Agreed."

Mark simply put the Hummer in drive, because it was still running and was surprised to see that it moved forward when he pushed on the accelerator. Despite the screeching of metal and the bumpy ride due to a flattened left rear tire, the car seemed to be driving fine, so he drove forward twenty yards onto a ramp of dirt and gravel that led up to the road.

When he was on the road, he sped up to thirty miles an hour and said, "Okay, Michael, I did what you requested, and the Hummer still runs, just not real fast."

"Mark, listen to me. You have to make it to Highway 24 in eight minutes!"

"If you're planning on landing the plane on the highway then you're insane; you'll end up killing everyone just to save the two of us. There's not enough time."

"Even I'm not crazy enough to have Jack land the plane again. Jack knows this area like the back of his hand, and he said there's an underground bunker just across the highway from Ute Pass Avenue. If you can make it there then you still have a chance."

"But, Michael…"

"Quit arguing with me! We're about to lose cell phone reception, so this is the last time you'll hear from me. Just do what I said now!"

"Oh, shit! Here we go again!" said Mark, as he floored the accelerator and pushed the damaged Hummer to its limit. The screeching increased dramatically as they drove faster and within one mile, the rear tire was driving on its rim. As Mark pushed the car faster, his control of the vehicle decreased significantly, and it started bouncing and lurching forward erratically. With two miles remaining, the left front tire blew, and the entire vehicle tilted dangerously toward the left side, causing him to swerve back and forth on the road to try and maintain some control of the vehicle, although this was rapidly waning. Still he pushed onward, as the Hummer shuffled forward in a helter-skelter fashion.

Dawn had remained relatively quiet the entire time, and as they approached Ute Pass and Highway 24, Mark briefly broke his concentration on the road and looked over at her. Her head was turned away from him, so he didn't notice that something was wrong until he reached over to get her attention and found that she was unresponsive. When he turned her head toward him, he could then see that her eyes were closed, and there was a huge hematoma covering the right side of her forehead.

He pushed the car even faster as panic surged in him, and he repeatedly tried to awaken her to no avail. Because she was occupying his attention and the car was horribly unstable, he almost spun out several times in the last quarter mile before reaching Ute Pass Avenue, but when they were close enough that he could see Highway 24, he realized that the Gulfstream V was sitting in the middle of the highway waiting for them.

As the plane sat on the highway facing southeast, the tension was mounting as each second passed.

"Michael, we're running out of time," said Jack. "I can't outrun this thing."

"Give them just a few more minutes, Jack."

"But Michael..."

"I don't want to hear it, Jack!"

Jack sighed and sat back in his seat, but his heart continued to beat at a blistering pace. He waited for two more minutes and then yelled from the cockpit. "Michael, we have to leave NOW!"

"How long do we have before it's here?" asked Michael.

"I don't know exactly, but it's probably less than two minutes!"

When Jack started firing up the engines, Michael yelled, "They're here! I see them!"

With that, he dashed down the access ramp and waved his arms frantically at Mark, who lurched onto the highway in the battered Hummer, slamming on the brakes so that he stopped ten feet from the plane.

Without a word, Michael pulled the passenger door open and scooped up Dawn in seconds. The driver side door was stuck because of structural damage, so Mark quickly climbed out through the passenger side door and ran to the access ramp, catching a quick glimpse to the northwest, where he could see the wall of death rocketing toward them.

"Oh, my God!" he said, as he ran up the ramp. Jack had already fired up the engines, and when Michael slammed the door after Mark, he tore off as fast as he could push the jet, hoping to lift off and get above the wall of destruction before it caught up with them.

As he looked out one of the side windows, Michael could see the cataclysmic shockwave in the distance, and it seemed to reach into the air at least a thousand feet. As they started to gain a high enough velocity to take off, Michael realized that they weren't going to make it, because the nightmare was catching up to them much too quickly and was way too fast for anything to outrun it on the ground.

He screamed out from his seat, "You have to climb, Jack—NOW!"

The second they were off the ground, Jack gunned the engines as hard as he could and went into a dangerously steep climb, trying to push the jet to its structural limits.

Now, Michael could see that the wall of destruction was less than three miles away, which meant that they had about ten seconds before it hit them, so he started to count down for Jack, "Ten, nine, eight, seven, six, five, four, three, two, one…"

The very top of the shockwave hit the back end of the plane and propelled it to a higher altitude, but the plane remained intact. Michael would have screamed for joy, but he was still terrified at what might happen in the Caribbean if the twenty-mile-wide monstrosity hit too close to St. Thomas. He heard Jack give a shout of triumph from the cockpit, as he confirmed the fact that everything on the plane was still operational.

Kate had walked into the bedroom to check on Stephen, and Mark was still trying to arouse Dawn while she lay reclining in one of the leather seats. Finally, she opened her eyes, and looked at him with a confused look. "Where are we?" she asked.

Mark smiled at her. "We're on my plane. We made it."

She still looked confused, but Mark was relieved that she was responsive, so he leaned over and kissed her on the forehead. She looked up at him, smiled weakly, and closed her eyes again.

"Is she okay?" asked Michael, as he approached their seats.

"I think she just has a concussion," said Mark. "Hey, you lied to me about landing the plane on the highway, and you probably made that crap up about the underground bunker, didn't you?"

"Yep, I didn't have time to argue with you, and I knew that was the only way I could get you to the highway."

"Well, that just sucks that you didn't respect my wishes, Bro."

"So, sue me," Michael replied.

"I can't afford attorneys anymore. I'm broke," said Mark.

"What are you talking about?"

"Oh, it's a long story, but Dawn cleaned me out."

"I heard that, computer boy," said Dawn with her eyes closed.

With that response, Mark knew she was going to be okay, so he leaned back in his seat and relaxed for the long flight. Within minutes, he had closed his eyes and fallen asleep from sheer exhaustion.

Mount Fuji, Japan: September 18, 10:24 p.m.

After the five-hour trek up to the summit of Mount Fuji, Shiraku and Sakura Okuhara were fatigued and somewhat out of breath; but they felt much safer now that they were at a height of 12,388 feet, which was the highest point in Japan. By now, everyone in Japan knew that the 270-mile wide rock of death was heading for a devastating touchdown somewhere in the Pacific, although no one knew exactly where it would hit.

At five o'clock this morning, Shiraku received a telephone call from a friend in the United States, who informed him about the possible Verneshot that might impact in the Pacific, and he made a decision that seemed crazy at the time but now appeared to be brilliant, when he woke up his wife to inform her that they were going to the summit of Mount Fuji. If Japan was hit with the 3,000-foot tsunami traveling at 500 mph that was predicted, there would be very few people who would survive, and the only way to survive was to be higher than the tsunami when it hit. He knew that other people from Tokyo and other areas of Japan probably had the same idea, but it was too late for that now. If they hadn't started out early this morning, before the cataclysm occurred, they would never make it even close to the summit.

Both of them had family in Tokyo and had tried to convince them to come to the summit, but they were confronted with skepticism and disbelief at their insane theory, so they were forced to leave them behind. There was a part of Shiraku that was terrified and deeply saddened with the impending loss of life and devastation that the Japanese people and the other people of the world would endure, but there was also a part of him that was excited at the prospect of seeing one of the most amazing sights in the history of the Earth. He knew that other people would witness the giant tsunami coming toward Japan and other coastal areas of the Pacific, but just about all of those people would not live longer than a matter of minutes and therefore wouldn't be around to talk about this amazing but horrendously catastrophic event. So in a strange way, Shiraku felt that he must be blessed to have received the phone call when he did and to have had the wisdom to act on it.

After they were finished unloading the supplies they had carried to the summit, both of them sat down and watched the serene water in the Pacific, realizing that this was the calm before the storm. The relative tranquility would be disrupted by the strongest force these waters had seen in hundreds of millions of years, long before the dinosaurs even existed.

Shiraku reached over to take Sakura's hand in his as something curious appeared on the horizon to the east. He had been expecting the sight of a hundred-foot wave that would grow to 3,000 feet as it approached shallow water, but he wasn't prepared for what now came into view from the distant horizon. He could now see the monstrous doomsday rock as it blasted through the atmosphere with a fiery trail behind it. Then he watched as it rapidly descending to impact the Pacific about ten miles off the east coast of Japan!

He was so amazed at the sight that he didn't realize what was about to occur until the monster hit the Pacific with unbelievable force and produced a 15,000-foot wave that descended upon the east coast of Japan and towered over Mount Fuji by 2,600 feet.

Shiraku watched as the wave blocked out the sun and converted the mountaintop to darkness and realized that he wasn't blessed after all.

St. Thomas, U.S. Virgin Islands
September 18, 12:54 a.m.

Michael had been unable to sleep on the way back to St. Thomas, because he had no means of getting in touch with Cassie but had found out from overseas news stations that the twenty-mile impactor had hit in the Gulf of Mexico approximately 150 miles off the coast of Galveston Island, producing a tidal wave that grew to 200 feet when it hit coastal areas of the Gulf, as well as the Bahamas and Cuba. By the time it reached the Caribbean, it had decreased in strength so that when it hit the Virgin Islands, the waves were about 130 feet high, which was still very deadly.

The plane reached St. Thomas at about midnight and, although most of the island was dark, they could still tell that large areas had been destroyed, including most of the city of Charlotte Amalie and the entire port area. Hundreds of yachts were scattered along the island beaches after being ripped to shreds by the huge waves.

Although he couldn't relax until he had seen Cassie, Spencer, and the children, in his heart he knew that they were okay, because Spencer had enough knowledge of the possible consequences of the Verneshot that he would have made sure that they were on high ground when the cataclysm was unleashed.

There was a significant amount of debris on the runway at the airport, but Jack was still able to safely land the jet using only the headlights to guide him. He breathed a sigh of relief when he considered the amount of damage they could have sustained from the shockwave hitting the tail; it could have horribly crippled the plane, making it dangerous for them to land. But they were all doing okay and still had a long-range jet at their disposal.

After waiting for forty-five minutes on the runway, the plane was greeted with two Jeep Wranglers, one driven by Spencer and the other by Cassie, with the two kids in the backseat. The two adults had looks of wariness and anxiety on their faces, because although they were pleased that the plane had returned, they had not yet been able to make contact and had no idea how successful the rescue had been.

When the door opened, and Michael emerged with a big smile on his face, Cassie instantly knew that everyone had been saved, and that this was going to be a particularly joyous reunion for the Hanson brothers, but especially for Stephen, Kate, and their two special children.

Michael ran down the stairs and lifted Cassie off the ground with a big hug, and then set her back down, so that he could pick up the children and take them to their parents. By this time, Kate was walking down the stairs with tears streaming down her face, as she looked upon the two faces that she thought she would never see again.

When Michael put the children back down, they ran to their mother, and the three of them held each other tightly, as they all cried tears of joy for several minutes. Then she escorted them up the stairs so that they could see their father, who was still lying in bed.

Michael and Spencer smiled as they watched the touching reunion, but their smiles eventually faded, because they both knew that the battle for survival of the human species had only just begun. So far they had been victorious in their struggle to survive, but they knew something devastating was now brewing in their homeland. Only Spencer had a real inkling of the horror that they would face in the very near future, and even he could not have predicted what would eventually emerge from the fields of devastation and carnage that littered the once great country they used to call the United States of America.

In a way, it was probably good that they didn't know what they would be forced to face—ignorance is bliss. At least for the short while before the ignorance is shattered by a terrifying new reality.

The Edge of Forever

Brink of Extinction

In similar fashion to the first book, *Brink of Extinction* combines realistic science with riveting action and suspense that will leave the reader breathless.

The saga of the Hanson family and friends continues as the group realizes that, although they survived a massive geophysical cataclysm unleashed in the northwestern part of the United States, they must now face something even more devastating. Having found refuge on St. Thomas in the U.S. Virgin Islands, they begin a new adventure: the fight to prevent human extinction from a horror of man's own creation. The tremendous forces of the cataclysm had caused the tragic and apocalyptic release of DM-19, a genetically engineered bio-weapon, from the "impenetrable" underground Black Diamond Military Base in Nevada.

As the plague descends upon them at a frightening pace, a gut-wrenching sequence of events unfolds when they are caught in a race to unravel the mystery behind DM-19. It soon becomes apparent that this group forms the last—and only hope—for human survival. Their courage, intelligence, endurance, and love for each other will soon be tested beyond the boundaries of all human experience.